EARTHW II

DELUGE

BRIAN KEENE

deadite
press

deadite press

DEADITE PRESS
205 NE BRYANT
PORTLAND, OR 97211
www.DEADITEPRESS.com

AN ERASERHEAD PRESS COMPANY
www.ERASERHEADPRESS.com

ISBN: 978-1-62105-084-1

Previously published as The Conqueror Worms

Printed in the USA.

Acknowledgements

For this Deadite Press edition, my sincere thanks and appreciation go to everyone at Deadite Press; Alan M. Clark; Tod Clark, Mark Sylva, and Stephen McDornell; Paul Goblirsch, David Ho, and Leigh Haig; Betty Ann Crawford; J.F. Gonzalez, Geoff Cooper, Mike Oliveri, Michael T. Huyck Jr., John Urbancik, Tom Piccirilli, and Regina Mitchell; and my sons. Thanks also to F. Paul Wilson and William Hope Hodgson for inspiration.

DEADITE PRESS BOOKS BY BRIAN KEENE

Urban Gothic
Jack's Magic Beans
Take The Long Way Home
A Gathering of Crows
Darkness On the Edge of Town
Tequila's Sunrise
Dead Sea
Kill Whitey
Castaways
Ghoul
The Cage
Dark Hollow
Ghost Walk
An Occurrence In Crazy Bear Valley
Entombed
Earthworm Gods
Earthworm Gods II: Deluge
Earthworm Gods: Selected Scenes From the End of the World
The Rising
City of the Dead
The Rising: Selected Scenes From the End of the World
Clickers II (with J. F. Gonzalez)
Clickers III (with J. F. Gonzalez – ebook only)
Clickers vs Zombies (with J. F. Gonzalez)

Author's Note

This book is a direct sequel to my novel *Earthworm Gods.* It is highly recommended that you read that book before beginning this one. It is also recommended that you read *Earthworm Gods: Selected Scenes From the End of the World* either before or after reading this book, since the two share several minor plot points.

This one is for you, my fans and readers.
Thanks for all your support.
It's been fifteen fun years. Here's to the next fifteen.

PART ONE

HIGHER GROUND

ONE

"Why are we stopping?"

"Why?" Kevin pointed through the truck's rain-streaked windshield. "Because there's a worm in the road."

At first, Sarah didn't see it. The downpour severely limited their visibility. But then she spotted a flash of movement amidst the rain—an elongated, gray and white form, glistening with slime and mud. The creature was easily the size of a large dog, but much longer. Its body stretched across the gravel lane, digging furrows in the road. Neither its front nor hind end were visible. The worm seemed oblivious to the idling pick-up truck. Or maybe it just didn't care. Maybe it had already eaten.

"Run it over," she said.

"Are you kidding? Look at the size of that thing. If we hit it, this old truck is liable to—"

"Run it over," Sarah insisted. "We sit here any longer and..."

She didn't finish the sentence. She didn't have to. They both knew what would most likely happen to them if they didn't keep moving.

Gripping the steering wheel, Kevin stomped the accelerator to the floor. The truck's engine sputtered and groaned, and then the old vehicle lurched forward, splashing through puddles. The tires rolled up over the creature, and both of them were jostled around the cab. Sarah's head banged hard against the passenger's window and a seat spring poked Kevin right between his shoulder blades. Old country and bluegrass cassette tapes tumbled out of a compartment under the dashboard and clattered at their feet. The tires spun, losing traction, and for a moment they thought they were stuck. But then the truck shot ahead. The back-end fishtailed, but Kevin regained control before they ran into a ditch.

Sarah glanced in the rearview mirror, and wiped the condensation off the glass. The moisture felt cool on her fingertips.

"Did we kill it?" Kevin asked.

"Sort of."

Sarah shuddered. Their passage had sliced the worm into three pieces. Each segment was still wriggling. Beyond the carcass, she spotted the faint outline of Teddy's house, barely visible through the fog. She couldn't be sure, but it looked like the building was sliding down into the sodden ground.

"We should go back."

Kevin rubbed his whiskered face with one hand. "First you want me to floor it. Now you want to go back."

"They're old, Kevin!"

"And they've both got more balls and guts than you and I put together. There is no doubt in my mind that they can kick that thing's ass. We're gonna do like we promised them. We keep going, and meet up with them at the ranger station when it's all over."

"But what if they—"

"Sarah, listen to me. Teddy and Carl are risking their lives to save ours, just like they did during World War Two. We have to respect their wishes. That's why people called them the greatest generation. They're doing this for us."

Her response was barely a whisper. "I know."

The rain drummed against the roof of the cab.

"They'll be fine," Kevin said. "I feel it in my heart. You'll see."

He was lying. Maybe to make her feel better or maybe just to make himself feel better, but either way, Kevin was lying. Sarah knew it, and she knew that he knew it, too. Before the two of them had fled in Teddy's beaten-up truck, Carl had been lugging around a kerosene heater. He and Teddy intended to turn it into some kind of homemade bomb to use on the Godzilla-sized worm in Teddy's basement. (Crazy old Earl had called the creature Behemoth). The old men's plan was reckless and insane, and if the situation hadn't been so absolutely terrifying, she might have found the idea comical.

"We're leaving them behind. Oh God, Kevin—we're really doing it, aren't we?"

"No. I promise you. If we get to the rendezvous, and they don't arrive, we'll come back for them. Okay?"

She nodded, biting her lip. "Okay."

The windshield wipers beat a steady, monotonous rhythm. The rain kept streaming. The ditches on each side of the road were full of rushing, brown water, and large puddles were forming in the fields.

"This will be flooded pretty soon," Kevin said.

Nodding again, Sarah blinked away tears.

Neither of them spoke again until they'd reached the end of the lane.

"Which way?" Kevin asked.

Sarah searched her memory, recounting Teddy's instructions.

"Hang a right. Keep on going until we run out of road. When that happens, we'll be at Bald Knob. Then we should see the big forest ranger tower."

"And what if we don't?"

"Then we're fucked."

"Jesus, Sarah. Way to stay optimistic."

Kevin drove slowly, hunched over the wheel and staring out into the murk. A scratchy Tammy Wynette tape played on the stereo. Sarah ejected the cassette and tossed it onto the floor with the rest of them. The radio was still on, but no sound came from the speakers. Not even static.

There was only an empty, dead silence.

Sighing again, Sarah turned the radio off.

"It doesn't really matter anyway, Kevin. The truth is, we're probably fucked no matter what we do."

"Yeah," he agreed. "We probably are."

Sarah glanced out the window. "This is the way the world ends. Not with a bang or a whimper, but with a second Great Flood."

The murk deepened as they drove into the deluge.

"I can't see shit." Kevin leaned forward, squinting his eyes and staring through the foggy windshield. His hands gripped the steering wheel tightly, as if they'd been glued onto it. "Is the defroster working?"

Sarah placed her hands over the vents. "It's on. There's air coming out."

"It's not helping."

"Well, how about if I just stop breathing? Then the windows won't get all fogged up."

Sarah winced as she said it. Her tone was sharper than she'd intended it to be. Kevin glanced at her, his expression wounded.

"Sorry," she apologized. "I shouldn't have snapped. I'm just...I hate leaving Teddy and Carl behind like that. It feels like we're abandoning them."

"I know. I know. Let's just focus on the road. Can you wipe the windshield for me?"

Sarah scooted across the seat, lifted her shirttail and wiped the glass in front of him. From the corner of her vision, she saw Kevin sneaking a glance at her chest. She turned to him, frowning.

"Pig. Keep your eyes on the road, not on my tits."

Blushing, he grinned. "Sorry. I couldn't help myself. They were just sort of *there*, you know?"

"They're there all the time, Kevin. I have them twenty-four hours a day, seven days a week. Get used to it."

"Oh, I have."

Sarah's brow creased. She slid back over to the passenger side and shifted uncomfortably.

"Kevin, please tell me you're not getting any ideas? You know I don't like guys."

"I'm not," he assured her. "Believe me. But you can't blame a guy for looking. I mean, no offense, but they *are* nice. And it's been a while since I've seen any others. Since Lori..."

His voice faded. Sarah opened her mouth to speak, but she wasn't sure what to say. How could she console him? Since their departure from Baltimore, Kevin had only mentioned Lori once—when he was sitting in Teddy's kitchen, telling their story. Until then, she hadn't known the depth of his feelings for the girl. Yes, she'd known that they hooked up. Everyone had known, and the group had been happy for them. But Sarah hadn't realized just how distraught Kevin was over Lori's death until he'd recounted it for Teddy and Carl. She reached out and touched his arm. His shirt sleeve was wet and cold. He was trembling. Tears formed in the corners of his eyes and ran down his cheeks. Raindrops continued pummeling the truck, punctuating the silence inside the vehicle.

"Kevin—"

"It's cool." He sniffed, and then turned his head from side to side, cracking his neck. "I'll be fine. I just miss her. Hell, I miss them all."

"Me too. I didn't even like all of them. Nate was a real prick, and Taz and Ducky could be a little hard to take sometimes. But I do miss them. Isn't it weird? Most of us didn't know each other before the rains started. We ended up stranded together on top of that hotel and had to make the best of it, but in a way, they became like family."

"Yeah. I never had much family, even before this started. Jimmy was the closest thing I had to a brother—until Leviathan killed him. Sometimes, when I close my eyes, I can still see his fucking head floating on the water."

"I'm sorry."

"Don't be. You didn't kill him. But you're right. They did feel like a family of sorts. Dysfunctional, maybe, but still a family."

"Well, now *we're* family."

Kevin grinned. "Does that mean you won't flash me your tits anymore?"

"Asshole," Sarah laughed. "Keep it up and I'll—"

Her teeth clamped down on her tongue as the truck suddenly lurched forward. Sarah's hand flew out and grabbed the dashboard. Her forehead smacked into the passenger-side window. She tasted blood in her mouth, and her ears rang. Beside her, Kevin screamed.

TWO

Sarah opened her eyes and glanced around in panic. The world seemed askew—crooked. Then she realized that they were both tilted forward. The front of the truck was pointing downward and the rear was in the air. The engine wasn't running, and the wipers no longer swept back and forth. Whatever it was that had happened, it had been severe enough to knock out the power. She wondered if maybe the battery had been knocked loose?

Kevin groaned, and Sarah turned to him in concern. He was conscious, but there was a small cut on his forehead, and his chest heaved as he gasped for breath.

"You okay?"

He nodded. "Fucking...steering wheel...caught me right... in the chest. No air bags."

"What happened?"

"I don't know. It's like the...road just fell out...from under us."

Sarah tried to peek out the windshield, but it was fogged over again. Instead, she opened her door—

—and gasped.

The road had collapsed in front of them, and the truck had tumbled into a sinkhole. The trench was about five feet deep. Cold rain and wind lashed at her as she appraised their situation. Water churned at the bottom of the hole. Mud rolled off the sides and splashed into the water. She stared closer at the soil, and noticed veins of white mold spreading throughout it. Her breath caught in her throat. She'd seen that white fuzz before. But now, there was a new aspect to it. The dirt around the fungus seemed to be liquefying.

"What the hell?"

"What's wrong," Kevin asked. "Worms?"

"No. It's...I don't know what. It's that weird mold, but it's doing something different. It's turning the dirt into water or something."

"Is that why we crashed?"

She swung the door shut. "I don't know. Maybe. But we're in a sinkhole. The road washed out. Can you move?"

"Yeah. Just knocked the wind out of me. I'll be okay."

"Let's get out of here before the truck sinks down further."

His eyes widened. "How deep is the hole?"

"I don't know. There's water at the bottom. It doesn't feel unstable. The truck's not rocking. But still, we should go."

They rooted through the truck, checking under the seats and in the glove box for anything useful. Sarah found three emergency flares and a hunting knife with a nine-inch blade. The knife was in a leather sheath that said '*Teddy*' on the side. Seeing his name brought a lump to her throat. Behind his vehicle registration and insurance card, she found a small, round can of Skoal.

"Oh my God." She held it up so Kevin could see.

"Shit," he laughed. "That poor guy. He was jonesing for nicotine so bad, and all this time he had a can in the glove box. That's terrible!"

She stuffed the can in her pocket.

Kevin frowned. "You dip tobacco?"

"No. I'm saving it for when we see him again."

"He'll be pissed as shit when he finds out he had one all the time—after everything he went through to get some. Talk about irony."

Kevin rooted around under the seat some more and found a baseball bat, an old blanket, and a fluorescent orange wool hunting cap. He tugged the hat over his head.

"How do I look?"

"Ridiculous," Sarah said. "But I guess it'll keep the rain off."

"Nothing will keep that rain off. I haven't felt dry in months."

Sarah put her hand on the door. "Ready?"

"Let's do it."

They climbed out of the truck, clambered up over the

tilted bed, and crawled out onto the wet ground. They were both careful not to come into contact with the weird mold. The edges of the sinkhole collapsed beneath them, and both had to scramble to keep from tumbling back down. They stood up and rested for a moment, catching their breath. Sarah checked her clothes, looking for signs of the strange white fungus. Then she inspected Kevin, as well.

"What are you doing?" he asked.

"Just making sure we're okay. How's your head and chest?"

"Hurts like a bitch, but I'll be okay. How about you? You cracked your head pretty hard."

"I'm fine."

They set off on foot, giving the widening sinkhole a wide berth. Their boots sank into the muddy ground, and each step they took made a loud sucking noise. The downpour was almost blinding. The wind blew the rain directly into their faces.

Neither Kevin nor Sarah saw the cluster of worms until they were almost right on top of them. The creatures lunged before they could scream. There were four worms writhing together in the mud. Their entwined bodies glistened with slime, and their musky, chlorine-like reek filled the air. The smallest of the creatures was about six feet long. The largest was nearly fifteen feet long and thick as a barrel. There was a bulge in its center—a recently devoured meal. The worm's pale flesh quivered as its dinner squirmed inside of its belly.

The monsters raised their eyeless heads, sensing Kevin and Sarah's presence. Then they collapsed back into the mud and surged forward. They attacked in silence. Sarah darted backward and pulled the hunting knife from her pocket. She fumbled with it, trying to open the blade, but her wet fingers slipped on the metal.

"I got this one," Kevin said.

Holding his ground, Kevin lashed out with the baseball bat, striking the closest worm in the head. Enraged, the creature opened its mouth and made an explosive farting sound. Sarah grimaced. The first time they'd heard the worms make that noise, it had been almost comical, but there was nothing funny about it now.

The worm struck at Kevin's leg, but he danced out of the way. Two more of the creatures slithered forward, trying to flank their prey. Kevin struck the closest worm again, grunting with the effort. The blow split the monster's flesh, and brown, watery blood gushed from the wound. The worm thrashed, hissing in agony.

The large worm heaved itself forward. Mud squelched beneath its tremendous bulk. Sarah continued fumbling with the wet knife while Kevin retreated to her side. Another of the smaller worms wriggled after him. Kevin swung the bat, but the beast dodged the blow and seized the weapon in its mouth, wrenching the bat from Kevin's grip.

"Fuck this." Sarah shoved the knife back in her pocket and pulled out one of the emergency flares instead. Moving quickly, she unscrewed the cap and struck the tip of the flare against it. The flare sputtered to life, emitting a red flame. Sparks burned the tiny hairs on her arm, but she ignored them. She thrust the flare forward, and the worm reared back.

"Come on," she said, stepping in front of Kevin. "Go around the other side of the sinkhole."

The two smaller worms slithered back and forth, hesitant to come near the sputtering flame. The larger creature thrust itself forward, lurking and wallowing on the edge of the sinkhole. Gritting her teeth, Sarah took a step backward. The monster's segmented body tensed, and she knew it was preparing to charge. Before it could, however, the sodden ground collapsed beneath the creature's weight. The worm tumbled into the sinkhole. Water splashed up over the sides of the crater.

Cheering, Sarah swept the flare back and forth in a wide arc, keeping the remaining two worms at bay. She slowly retreated, glancing over her shoulder to make sure she wasn't too close to the edge of the crevice. The worms followed, but slowly.

They're communal, she thought. *We suspected it before, but seeing them close up like this...Somehow, they're communicating with each other.*

When she reached the road, Kevin was waiting for her.

"Got another flare?" he asked.

She nodded, not taking her eyes off their pursuers. "We've got two more. But we need to make them last. No telling how many of these things we'll run into between here and the ranger tower."

"We're still planning to make for that, then?"

"We can't make it back to Teddy's. Not without the truck. The fire tower is closer. It's either that, or stay out here in the open."

"No thanks," Kevin said. "Let's go."

They rounded the other side of the sinkhole. The road stretched ahead of them again, heading into the forest. The downpour prevented them from seeing very far, but it didn't look like there were any more washouts. They'd make better progress on the road than they would in the fields and meadows. Both were muddy, and it would be like running through cement.

Sarah paused, watching the worms. They hovered at the edge of the road, still cautious of the sputtering flame. Sarah reached into her jacket and pulled out another flare. Then she handed it to Kevin.

He frowned. "I thought you said—"

"I'm going to try something different. Just stick that under your jacket. Keep it dry. Don't light it unless I tell you."

"What do you have in mind?"

"Just trust me."

She tossed the flare towards the worms. It landed in the middle of the road. Sarah held her breath, wondering if it would go out, but the flame continued to burn brightly. The worms paused, caught between the flare and the hole.

"That gives us a head start." She grabbed Kevin's arm. "Come on!"

They ran down the road, heading towards the forest. Sarah risked a glance behind them, and was relieved to see that the worms were still trying to negotiate their way around the flare. Then the mist closed in their wake, and the creatures disappeared from sight.

They kept running for another five minutes, until they reached the cover of the trees. Once they were inside the forest, they paused, panting for breath. Sarah noticed that Kevin was wheezing.

"You okay?"

"Yeah," he said. "My chest still hurts. Just need to rest up."

"We can't stay here long. We need to keep moving."

"I know. Just give me a minute to catch my breath."

Sarah studied their surroundings. The rain drummed against the leafy canopy overhead. The sound was surprisingly loud. Many of the trees were leaning to one side, their roots struggling to keep a purchase in the oversaturated ground. Others had collapsed, leaving behind huge holes in the earth that were now filled with water. She spotted white fuzz growing on several tree trunks, concealing the bark. The mold also covered a slab of granite jutting up from the forest floor.

Behind her, Kevin shrieked. Sarah spun around, to see him wiping the back of his hand on his coat. He seemed embarrassed.

"What is it?"

"Nothing. I brushed up against a branch. It tickled my hand and I thought it was...you know, one of them. Scared me."

"Well, you scared me, too. Jesus, Kevin..."

"Sorry." He smiled. "You still love me?"

Grinning, Sarah shook her head. "I'd love you a lot more if you hadn't lost our bat."

"I'll make it up to you."

"How?"

"When we get to the tower, you can have first pick of whatever we find."

"Deal."

They continued on their way. The mist grew thick between the trees, and the road sloped steadily upward. Neither of them spoke. Sarah stretched her neck and shoulder muscles, trying to work out the kinks. Kevin scratched the back of his hand, which had begun to itch.

Neither one of them noticed the fungus growing on the branch he'd touched.

THREE

Henry Garrett knew that he was dreaming.

Lucid dreaming, people called it. He'd seen them talk about it on television, back when the televisions still worked.

The last time he'd had this dream, Henry had floated deep beneath the mountains—not through a subterranean network of tunnels and caves, but through the very ground itself. Ethereal, he'd slipped through rocks and roots and soil. Henry didn't know how far he'd descended. There was no way to tell for sure in a dream. He reckoned it was a long distance. Eventually, he stopped. And there, far below the earth, he'd seen a door open up. As he watched, a worm the size of a school bus had crawled out of it and immediately started to give birth. Slime dripped from its body and coalesced into smaller worms. As Henry gaped, the creatures began to burrow upward, chewing through the planet's core like Japanese beetles through an apple tree. They left slime in their wake.

Henry had woke up screaming.

This time, the dream was different. Oh, there were some similarities, but the location wasn't the same. He wasn't floating down through the ground. Instead, he was sinking to the bottom of the ocean. The other big difference in this dream was that when he saw a similar door opening on the ocean floor, it wasn't a big old worm that came crawling out, but a host of different creatures.

First, dozens of tentacles thrust through the doorway, grasping and wriggling in the current. The tendrils varied in size, but all of them were covered with rows of suckers, and each sucker had a puckered, greedy mouth lined with needle-like teeth.

Schools of silver fish darted through the doorway, swimming around the flailing tentacles. They were about eight inches in length, and reminded Henry of a cross between piranhas and flying fish. Their broad pectoral fins were curved like wings. As he watched, they devoured every living thing in their path. The water turned red.

Next came a group of creatures that looked like a mix of human beings and great white sharks. They had the legs, arms, and partial torso of a person, but the tail, head, dorsal fin and upper body of a shark. Their mouths were the creatures' most striking feature—rows and rows of razor-sharp teeth. Over ten-feet in length, they swam by using both their powerful tails and their lithe legs—propelling themselves through the water with great speed.

There were quivering jellyfish that shot black, corrosive acid through the water. Spiny starfish that glared at him malevolently with human eyes. Blind, aquatic worms that burrowed into whatever they could find and began boring. Beautiful mermaids with long, flowing hair and breasts that made him hard—even in his dream.

One of the mermaids noticed him watching. Smiling, she swam closer. Henry's erection swelled. She opened her mouth and began to sing. He could hear her clearly, even though they were underwater. He strained, trying to make out the words.

And then, the creature that the tentacles were attached to thrust itself from the doorway and emerged onto the ocean floor. Huge clouds of silt and muck were stirred by its entrance. When they cleared, Henry glimpsed the beast.

Just like before, Henry woke up screaming.

He shrieked for a long time, lying there in the loft at the top of Fred Laudermilk's grain silo. Eventually, his gasps became sobs, then moans. His cat, Moxey, rubbed against him, purring. Henry patted her absentmindedly, feeling her ribs beneath the skin. She was losing weight. They both were.

Unable to sleep anymore, Henry sat up in the gloom and listened to the rain. Was it his imagination, or was the rain coming down faster now? The sound of the rain no longer lulled Henry to sleep. Each time he shut his eyes, the weird dreams came back again. Or the pain in his stomach.

Before the flood, Henry used to see commercials on

television, asking folks to send money to help starving kids in Africa. Henry had always felt sorry for the other children, but he didn't think his parents would be helping out. They barely had enough money to feed themselves. If it wasn't for their garden and food stamps, they'd have probably been like those people in Africa. Henry had often tried to imagine what it would be like—being so hungry.

He didn't have to imagine anymore. He knew all too well.

So did Moxey.

During one particularly severe bout of hunger, he'd considered eating her. Then, horrified that he'd even think such a thing, Henry had pulled the cat to his chest, cuddling her while she purred, letting his tears soak her fur.

They had plenty of water. When they'd climbed to the top of the grain silo, Henry had brought along a case of bottled water and a backpack full of provisions. The food was all gone now, even after carefully rationing it, but they still had some water left. He didn't trust drinking the rainwater, and there was no way he was drinking the water surrounding the silo. It was full of *things*.

He had no way to catch fish, and wasn't sure he'd eat them even if he could. The few fish he'd seen looked sickly—a white, mucous-like substance covered their bodies. Some type of waterborne infection, he guessed. Daniel Ortel had caught a catfish like that before evacuating with the National Guard, and when Daniel touched it, the fish's skin sloughed off like pudding. Soon after, Daniel had gotten sick.

He doubted anything was still alive in the water, anyway. It was full of dead folks and animal carcasses, fuel, oil, chemicals, and other debris. It stank, and the lapping waves left a film on the side of the silo.

Stirring, Henry got to his feet and stretched, working out the kinks he'd developed while lying on the wooden platform. In the center of the platform was a large, open pit that led straight down into the silo's depths. It was slowly filling with water. Henry didn't know what he'd do once it breached. At that point, he and Moxey would have to swim.

The pit was surrounded by an iron handrail. Henry leaned

over the railing and spat. It didn't take as long for his saliva to splash down as it had the day before.

"Yep," he muttered. "Still rising."

The sound of his own voice, echoing inside the silo, disturbed him. Henry didn't talk much these days.

Moxey meowed in response.

"I know, girl. I know."

Henry picked up his .17 gauge rifle, uncapped the scope, and decided to see if his luck would be better this time. He was hoping to shoot a bird, or maybe a snake that had been forced from its den by the floodwaters. If they were close enough to the silo, he could grab them before they floated away.

He shuffled over to the small double-doors in the silo's curved wall, and fumbled with the hasp. It was growing rusty, due to all the moisture in the air. His fingers were numb and wrinkled like prunes. Henry couldn't remember the last time he'd felt warm or dry.

He managed to get the hasp unlatched, and then slowly opened the doors. It was impossible to tell what time of day it was—there were no more sunrises or sunsets. The moon and stars and sun were just hazy, gray shapes in the sky, hidden behind the dense cloud cover. Still, Henry's internal alarm clock told him it was evening.

Evenings had always been his favorite time of day. Home from Lewisburg High School, assignments finished, chores completed, he'd sit out on the front porch and stare out at the mountains, wondering what lay beyond them. Renick was Henry's world. He'd only been out of West Virginia a few times, and then, only to go to Virginia Beach with his family. He'd always wanted to see the rest of the world. Feel it under his feet. Marvel at how different it looked from the place he called home. Now, it didn't matter. Henry was pretty sure that all of the world looked the same. One big ocean.

The breeze ruffled his hair, and Henry shivered, clasping his damp jacket closer. He stared out at what was left of Renick. Everything was gone. The only things that remained above the surface were the grain silo and the steeple on the Presbyterian Church. All of the small town's other landmarks—the concrete and steel bridge that had spanned the Greenbrier River, the Ponderosa meeting place, the park, the sub shop, the gas station—were submerged. The mountain remained, jutting far above the waters, but even that was slowly eroding.

He wondered how folks in Punkin' Center were faring. Unlike Renick, which was situated in a valley, Punkin' Center was located halfway up the mountain. Most of the folks there had been evacuated when the National guard came through, but Henry knew that there was at least one person still alive. Old Mr. Garnett. Henry had seen him. He wasn't sure how many days had passed since then. Two weeks, give or take. But he'd seen Mr. Garnett—standing in the road, next to his old pick-up truck, staring down at the remains of Renick. Henry had waved at him, tried to get his attention, but the old man hadn't heard. Or if he had, he'd ignored Henry's cries.

No, Mr. Garnett wasn't like that. He was a nice old-timer, unlike that crazy bastard, Earl Harper. Smart, too. If anyone knew how to survive what was happening, Mr. Garnett would. All Henry had to do was cross the water, climb the mountain, and find him. He stared out across the wide expanse, and then cursed. While he was at it, he might as well wish for a trip to Mars, too. That would be a lot easier than getting to dry land.

The bloated carcass of a dead deer floated by. Something had been chewing on it. He searched the sky for a bird to shoot, but the sky was filled with rain.

Henry's stomach grumbled again. This time, it didn't hurt so much.

He wondered if that was a bad sign.

FOUR

In a normal climate, Kevin and Sarah would have seen the U.S. Forest Service Tower long before they reached it. The ranger station loomed over the forest, jutting up through the treetops on Bald Knob's uppermost peak. With the rain and swirling mist obscuring their vision, they didn't spot the steel structure until they were almost at its base.

The hike to the top of the mountain had been uneventful. Both were grateful for that. Now out of immediate danger, both were experiencing post-adrenaline exhaustion. They shivered in their wet clothes, and their feet hurt. Cold water had soaked through their shoes, and there were blisters on their wrinkled toes and soles of their feet. They walked with a sense of hopeless caution, praying they wouldn't encounter more worms, or another nut like Earl Harper. Luckily, they hadn't. The only danger had been a small mudslide and a falling tree, but they'd managed to steer clear of both. They did notice that more and more of the vegetation was dying—either from lack of direct sunlight, or drowned roots. Many of the tallest trees could no longer keep their purchase in the waterlogged soil, and had simply toppled over.

A concrete platform stood at the base of the ranger station. The tower itself was embedded deep into the mountain's bedrock. Nearby, there was a small utility shed, restrooms, some vending machines, and a fenced-in area that held electrical transformers. They performed a quick, cursory check of the restrooms, making sure there were no surprises waiting inside of them—worms or otherwise. Both stood empty. The door to the utility shed was padlocked, as was the gate leading into the electrical equipment.

Kevin leaned against a soda machine, pressing one of the buttons with his palm.

"The power's out," Sarah reminded him. "That's not going to work."

"I know. Just wishful thinking. Force of habit. I'm really thirsty."

"Me, too. Let's figure out how to get up to the top of that thing, and we'll get settled."

Kevin smacked his lips. Sarah noticed that they seemed paler than normal.

"No," he said. "I mean I'm *really* thirsty. Like, more than normal."

"You're probably dehydrated. You have a headache?"

He nodded.

"That's probably it then," Sarah said. "Come on. We'll get you fixed up."

Swallowing, he nodded again. Sarah watched his Adam's apple bob up and down. It seemed bigger—swollen. Maybe that was just because he'd lost weight over the last few months. They both had.

"How about you?" Kevin asked.

"I'm fine."

"Fine?" Kevin snorted. "Earl punched you in the face—beat the shit out of you. And we've been on the run ever since. Don't tell me you're fine."

Sarah's lip twitched. "I'll manage."

They began circling the base of the tower, splashing through puddles and keeping a careful eye on the surrounding woods. Water streamed off the steel girders overhead, drenching them even more. Kevin sputtered as a particularly forceful stream splashed him. Sarah giggled as he shook his head back and forth.

"What's so funny?"

"You look like a dog," she said. "Shaking yourself like that."

"I feel like a dog. Like I've got fleas or something. I keep itching."

"Maybe you brushed up against some poison ivy on the way here."

"I hope not. I don't think so, though. It's not bad, like

poison ivy is. It's more of a low-grade itch."

"Could be another symptom of dehydration."

"Maybe," Kevin agreed. "It's pretty fucking annoying, whatever it is."

On the far side of the tower, they found a winding staircase leading upward. They began to climb. Sarah took the lead, holding the hunting knife she'd liberated from Teddy's truck at the ready, in case there were any surprises. Her arms felt heavy. Weighted. She was wearing a sweater that had belonged to Teddy's wife, Rose, and the garment seemed to soak up the rain.

Their feet clanged as they plodded upward. They moved carefully, mindful of slipping on the wet metal. Although the stairs had a handrail, there were no other safety measures—just a straight drop to the concrete below. Sarah glanced down once, and immediately, her head swam with vertigo. The sound of the rain seemed to grow louder. Sarah grabbed the rail tight. She felt her butt pucker, and her breath caught in her throat.

"You okay?" Kevin asked.

She nodded. "Just not crazy about this."

"You're afraid of heights? I never noticed. All that time we spent on top of the hotel, and then in the helicopter. I figured you'd be used to it."

"I don't mind heights." Sarah inched herself forward. "But that's a long way down, and I really don't want to have made it this far just to crack my head open on the concrete."

"Good point."

Eventually, after stopping twice to rest, they reached the top of the tower. The door was unlocked, and the hinges squeaked as Sarah opened it. They slipped inside, breathing hard, and glanced around. The room was circular. Instead of walls, it had thick floor-to-ceiling windows all the way around, providing a complete view of the forest below. Sarah supposed that the panorama must have been breathtaking before the rain had started. Now, she could only see a few hundred yards around the base of the tower. Beyond that, the only thing that was visible were treetops jutting through the swirling mist and low-lying clouds.

The open space had been divided into different functional sectors. One portion of the room had two sets of bunk beds. Another area seemed to be the entertainment center, complete with television, DVD player, several different videogame consoles, a stereo, and a bookshelf stuffed with movies, compact discs, and battered paperbacks. A third part of the circular room was equipped with a microwave, two coffee pots, an electric tea kettle, and a small wooden hutch containing mugs, silverware, and plates. Another sector held communications equipment. Scattered throughout the room were boxes and bins, clothing, and other various personal items. Tired as she felt, Sarah realized that she was looking forward to inventorying everything. She'd grown quite comfortable with looting civilization's leftovers, if only for the small comforts that sometimes presented themselves—not to mention essentials like food and water.

She put her hands on her hips and smiled. "Home sweet home."

She was still smiling when Kevin collapsed to the floor.

"Kevin!"

His head smacked against the floor as he crumpled. The sound made Sarah cringe. She ran to him. Her wet shoes squeaked on the linoleum. Kevin was sprawled crookedly, arms and legs akimbo, head tilted, eyes closed. She knelt beside him, calling his name.

"Kevin? Hey, Kevin, wake up!"

His eyes remained shut, but she saw them rolling behind his lids, as if Kevin were dreaming. She checked his breathing, and sighed in relief. It was shallow, but at least he was alive.

What the hell had happened? One moment they'd been talking. The next, he'd collapsed. Had he tripped, and knocked himself out? No, she was fairly certain he was unconscious before he'd struck the floor. He'd been complaining of dehydration—ironic, given their situation. Had that been the cause of this? Was he epileptic or prone to seizures? She didn't know, and the lack of knowledge shocked her. After all they'd been through—surviving Baltimore and the cult on

Cass Mountain near Greenbank and the helicopter crash and all of the events at Teddy's house—she should know Kevin better than she did. They'd gone through a lot together, relied on each other for survival. In some ways, he'd become her best friend. Her partner. And yet, other than the fact that he'd been a video store clerk in Cockeysville, and had been in love with Lori, and that his best friend, Jimmy, was killed by either the Satanists or that squid-thing they'd worshipped, she didn't really know him at all. She knew he could handle a gun, could think quick on his feet and be relied on to step up when shit hit the fan, but what was his medical history? What had he been like growing up? Who were his parents? What were his hobbies?

Sarah ran her hands through her wet hair and debated what to do next. She knew she shouldn't move him, but she couldn't just let him lie on the floor, either. Gingerly, she prodded his arms and legs with her index finger. When Kevin didn't twitch, she ran her hands over his limbs, checking for broken bones. Then she very carefully lifted his head. He moaned, but remained unconscious. She peered into his mouth. There was no blood—he hadn't bitten his tongue or knocked any teeth loose. He seemed uninjured, except for a bright red blotch on the back of his hand. She assumed he must have bruised it when he fell.

Grunting, Sarah got her hands under Kevin's arms, and interlocked her fingers around his chest. Then she dragged him across the room and propped him up in a sitting position against one of the bunk beds. She removed his sodden clothing and found a forest ranger's uniform that looked like it would fit him. After she'd dressed him, Sarah hefted Kevin into the bottom bunk and pulled the blankets up over him. She checked his breathing once more, and then brushed his wet bangs out of his eyes.

"It'll be okay," she whispered. "Just rest for a while."

Sarah changed out of her own wet clothes and put on another ranger's uniform. The pants and shirt were both snug, but their dryness felt luxuriant against her bare skin. She stretched their wet gear out on the floor to dry, and then explored the station. In the entertainment center, she ran her hand over the television, DVD player, stereo, and videogame consoles. Once upon a time, she'd have been overjoyed to discover these things. But not now. How archaic and useless they seemed, with no electricity to run them. She thought of the utility shed and the small power station below, at the base of the tower, and wondered if there was a generator, too. She made a mental note to check later, after she'd had a chance to rest up.

Also among the various home electronics, almost hidden behind a stack of movies on the bookshelf, was a battery-operated radio. Sarah pulled it down and studied it. It was an impressive piece of equipment, offering not just AM and FM bands, but shortwave, emergency, and citizens' band channels, as well. It even had a small television screen built into it. She thumbed the power switch, but nothing happened. Then she popped open the battery compartment and saw why. There were no batteries inside. She wondered briefly why it was stored in this section of the room, rather than with the rest of the communications equipment, and decided that it must either be a back-up or a personal item one of the rangers had left behind. The radios in the communications section were much more sophisticated than this.

She poked around the room some more until she found a drawer full of batteries. She selected six 'D' batteries and put them in the radio. Then, holding her breath, she tried it again. Sarah was rewarded with a burst of static. She jumped at the sudden sound. She hadn't realized how quiet it was inside the tower—just her breathing and the muffled sound of the rain drumming down on the roof. Her pulse throbbed in her throat. Sarah fumbled with the volume knob and turned the radio down to a more tolerable level. Then she experimented with the tuner. She went through the FM dial first, and then the AM dial. Both offered nothing but more static. She switched over to the other channels, but they were silent. Sarah turned it back to the FM dial and sat down, listening to the static. The sound was somehow comforting—new white noise to drown out the rain's familiar white noise. She turned the dial aimlessly, not expecting to hear anything else.

But then she did.

The voice was faint. Male. The speaker had a Boston accent. Sarah leaned forward, straining to hear and wondering if she was imagining the whole thing.

"My name...coming to you...alive...of the Pru Building... downto..."

The radio squawked with feedback. Cursing, Sarah slowly turned the knob, trying to find the signal again.

"...thing I want...Lisa and Alex, I love..."

The voice faded again.

"Damn it!" Sarah leapt to her feet, still holding the radio. She thrust it up over her head, pointing it towards the ceiling.

On his bunk, Kevin moaned.

"Anyway," the voice returned, stronger and clearer now, "here I am. Hope somebody is listening. I always figured that when I died, I'd go out with a fight, getting back up to attack one more time, like Boramir in *Lord of the Rings* or Willem Defoe in *Platoon*. I'm a sucker for those great last stands. But lately, I've been wondering. A friend of mine just told me about the First Principle. Maybe we should talk about that."

Sarah trembled with emotion. She wanted to shout, to tell the broadcaster that she could hear him, that yes, there was somebody else still left alive, somebody else still listening. She didn't realize she was crying until she felt the tears running down her chin.

"Damn," said the man on the radio. "I'm really thirsty."

Kevin moaned again. Sarah lowered the radio and turned to him. He was facing away from her, but she heard him smacking his lips.

"Thirsty," he croaked. "Need water."

She sat the radio down and hurried towards him. "Kevin, there's a man on the radio. I think he might be from Boston or something. The signal is weak, but he—"

Kevin turned towards her. His eyes were rolled up into his head, and all Sarah could see were the whites. Kevin smacked his lips again. When he spoke, his voice was hoarse. He didn't sound like himself.

"*Soft...*"

Sarah paused. "What?"

Kevin's closed his eyes again.

Outside, thunder boomed across the mountaintop. Sarah shivered.

Kevin dreamed.

He was aware that he was dreaming. Not a lucid dream, but a dream all the same. He knew it was a dream because Lori was still alive and they were back in Baltimore, lying together in his bed on the top floor of the half-submerged Marriott hotel. He'd tried to grow an indoor garden in that room, beneath the skylight. In real life, the results had been mixed, but now, in the dream, lush, green plants thrust from the soil, straining towards the ceiling.

He and Lori were both naked. The sheets felt good against his skin. Her warmth enveloped him as they snuggled. She smiled at him, tight-lipped, but did not speak. Her eyes sparkled.

"I miss you," Kevin whispered.

Lori's smile remained, but she still didn't respond.

Kevin reached out to stroke her hair. Surprisingly, it was wet. It looked dry, but his fingers came away damp. Kevin didn't care. His fingertips trailed down her forehead and cheeks. Again, her skin felt wet.

"Are you okay?" he asked.

Lori opened her mouth to respond. Water gushed from between her lips. Kevin watched, not pulling away from her. He wasn't startled. Wasn't afraid. A deep sense of calm settled over him. Lori kissed his cheek and the flow continued. It was as if someone had turned on a garden hose inside of her. The water ran down her chin and between her breasts. Rivulets raced down past her navel, to the slim, trimmed tuft of hair below. It soaked the sheets and splashed across the mattress. Kevin watched, fascinated. The scene was strangely erotic. The wet sheets rose as he stiffened in response.

In addition to the sudden burst of lust, Kevin became aware that he was thirsty. He told Lori, and she winked at him.

Above them, the skylight disappeared. The glass didn't shatter—it just vanished. Rain poured into the room, further soaking them. Lori laughed, and more fluid gushed from her mouth. Lori sat up and rubbed the water into her skin. Her hands lingered on her breasts, squeezing them. Then she grabbed Kevin's hands and drew him to her. He sighed. Her skin felt hot, despite the moisture.

"It's soft," he said. "Soft."

Nodding, Lori grasped his back with one hand. The fingers of her other hand snaked around the back of his head and played with his hair. She pulled him closer, staring at him with those wide, brown eyes. Their lips touched, and the water poured from Lori into Kevin. The sensation was not unpleasant. Kevin closed his eyes and surrendered.

Water pooled on the floor, and ran in under the door from the hallway. Kevin shifted his weight on the mattress and his knee sank into it, splashing water into the air. He looked down, and was surprised to see that the mattress was full of liquid now.

A waterbed, he thought. He didn't say it out loud because to do so would have meant pulling away from Lori, and that was the last thing he wanted to do.

The bed melted beneath them. Kevin and Lori fell into the water, still clinging to each other. Their kiss remained unbroken. They slipped beneath the surface, and it wasn't until Kevin bumped against the table that housed his makeshift garden, that he opened his eyes and broke the embrace. His head broke the surface and he glanced around the hotel room. It was filling quickly. Small waves lapped at the furniture and walls. The couch floated by, and bumped into the door. Kevin stared up at his garden, and was amazed to see that the plants were liquefying.

He stood up. Water streamed from his shoulders and chest. Lori reached for him, but he gently brushed her aside. She floated away, dog-paddling across the room. Kevin strode closer to the garden table, studying the plants intently. As he watched, they broke down completely, reverting back to pure water.

"What the hell?"

The soil in the garden had turned to mud. Before they'd fled Baltimore, Kevin had buried his best friend's head in the garden. He would have buried all of him there, but all that had been left of Jimmy was his head. Now, Jimmy's bare skull poked through the mud. More and more of it was revealed as the mud receded. Kevin stared at the skull. The skull stared back. Then, water began gushing from its empty eye-sockets and from the gap between its yellow teeth.

Kevin realized that he was now treading water. Resisting the urge to hold his breath, he exhaled, and slipped beneath the surface again. He glanced around for Lori, but she was gone. Kevin surged through the water, desperately seeking her. When her arms closed around him from behind, Kevin relaxed. His body went limp in her embrace. He turned to greet her and his hands trailed down her hips.

Then he paused.

Lori's legs were gone, replaced by the lower half of a fish.

He tried to pull away from her, but she clutched him tighter. Lori opened her mouth, revealing fangs. Then her head darted forward.

Gasping, Kevin opened his eyes. At first, he didn't know where he was. He was lying in the darkness on a hard mattress, and somebody had taken his clothes off and dressed him in a forest ranger's uniform. Kevin thought perhaps this was still part of the dream. But then, as his heart-rate returned to normal and his chest stopped heaving, it all came back to him—escaping from Teddy's house, their journey to Bald Knob, the worms, and finally, the forest ranger tower. This last part was disjointed. Dim. He barely remembered arriving, let alone how they'd gotten inside. He glanced around the dim room, trying to get his bearings, and wondered where Sarah was.

The last remnants of the dream faded, and Kevin was suddenly overwhelmed with a deep sense of sadness and loss. It had seemed so real—Lori, her kisses, the feel of her body against his.

His hand began to itch. Kevin scratched it, casually glancing down as he did.

And then he screamed.

***

Sarah started back down the staircase, gripping the cold handrail tightly and moving slowly, mindful of slipping on the wet metal. She'd been hesitant to come outside again so soon after finally getting dry, but Kevin was obviously sicker than she'd thought, and getting the electricity on would only improve their situation. She was fairly certain that the small power station would be beyond her capabilities, but she was hopeful that the utility shed or one of the other shacks might hold a generator.

She reached the bottom and turned on the flashlight that she'd found in a toolbox while exploring upstairs. The batteries were weak. The dim beam did little to dispel the darkness and gloom. The rain fell too thick, and swirling clouds of mist blanketed everything. Sarah started forward, moving slowly, listening for the slightest indication that the worms were present.

The power station was—as she had feared—far too complex for her technical capabilities. Her hopes completely died when she peeked inside the utility shed. It didn't have a generator, but she did note the rest of its contents—a lawn tractor, wagon, cans of gasoline and kerosene, bits of lumber, rolls of fencing, metal posts, and various tools, including several hefty axes, shovels, and pick-axes.

Disappointed, she started back up the stairs. Thunder boomed overhead again, though distant this time. There was no lightning—or if there was, she couldn't see it through the perpetual haze. When the thunder ended, the night seemed to quiet down again. Just the constant drone of the rain, and her plodding footsteps on the stairs. And then, surprisingly, an owl, somewhere in the night. It scared her so badly that she almost dropped the flashlight. Sarah couldn't remember the last time she'd heard an owl. Just the whippoorwills back at Teddy's house.

Steadying herself after the brief fright, Sarah started up the stairs again. And then she heard a scream. She didn't recognize it at first, nor could she tell where it was coming from. It was only when a second scream followed it moments later that Sarah realized it was Kevin.

She ran up the stairs, heedless of the slippery conditions, or the unwanted attention her sudden noise might attract. She burst through the station's door, rain streaming from her clothes, and glanced around the circular room in panic.

Kevin knelt on the floor. In one hand, he clenched a long, metal file; he must have grabbed it from one of the toolboxes. He was using the tool to scrape away the flesh on the back of his other hand. His lips were drawn back in a terrible grimace, and he moaned through clenched teeth. Sweat dripped from his bare skin. Blood welled up from the ruined flesh as he dashed the file back and forth. Kevin looked up and their eyes met in mid-shriek.

"What are you doing?" Sarah ran towards him.

"Get the fuck back," he warned. "Stay over there!"

"Kevin, what is it? What's wrong?"

"It's just like back in Baltimore. Remember? We saw people infected with it?"

"With what? What are you talking about?"

"That white fuzz, Sarah. It's growing on my hand..."

Clenching his teeth, Kevin furiously worked the file back and forth, scraping more skin from his hand. Shreds of flesh peeled away and blood streamed from the wound, running down his wrist and forearm and splattering onto the floor in quarter-sized drops. He didn't scream or wail. The only sound he made was a determined groan.

"Kevin, stop it!"

Shrugging out of her wet sweater and tossing it onto the floor, Sarah ran towards him.

"Get back," he warned. "Just stay over there."

Sarah stopped in her tracks. The file slipped from Kevin's fingers and clattered onto the floor. With his good hand, he gripped the wrist of his wounded hand and squeezed. The skin turned white.

"Look at your hand, Kevin. You're sick. Not thinking straight. You—"

"I know I'm sick. That's the fucking point, Sarah. I've got

that white shit, just like the people back in Baltimore. You remember what happened to them? It grew over their entire bodies—turned them into drones. They ended up going down to the water and taking root."

"But—"

"I'm not going out like that. It's not going to happen to me. Not after everything that's happened. I mean, what's the fucking point? Jimmy is dead. Lori. Salty and Mindy and Juan. Taz and Ducky and all the others. Probably Teddy and Carl, too. But we're still alive, right? That means something. That counts. The world is flooding and there's giant worms and vampire mermaids and weird cults and giant, squid-headed fucks that crawl out of the ocean—and we've survived them all! We're alive. There has to be a point to that. There has to be a reason. It's the end of the god-damned world but we're still alive. I didn't face all that shit just to die from some fucking fungus. That doesn't make any sense."

Tears streamed down Kevin's cheeks. He took a deep breath and shuddered.

"It doesn't make any sense," he repeated. "It just doesn't make sense. Why?"

"I know." Sarah tiptoed towards him and tried to keep her voice calm and soothing. "But you're not going to die. We caught it in time. All we have to do is—"

Sneering, Kevin snatched up the file and waved it at her. "I said to get back, Sarah. I'm not kidding. You get too close, you'll get infected."

She opened her mouth to argue, but then just shook her head. Her shoulders sank in defeat. Deep inside, Sarah knew that he was right. They didn't know for sure how the white fuzz was transmitted, but they both suspected it was through physical contact. She remembered seeing the bruises on his hand when she'd changed him, and tried to remember if she'd actually touched them or not.

"Did you...did you get it all?" She nodded at his bleeding hand.

"I think so. Jesus, it's really starting to fucking hurt. But it doesn't itch anymore. I'm not thirsty. So yeah, I think I got it all."

"We've got to get you bandaged up."

"I'll do it," Kevin moaned. Clearly, the pain was getting stronger. "Find me the stuff and slide it over here. But don't touch me."

"I won't."

"How did I end up in a Forest Ranger's uniform, anyway?"

"I changed you while you were unconscious."

"Fuck! What the hell were you thinking, Sarah?"

"Well, I didn't know then, did I?"

"You're right. I'm sorry. I'm just freaked out, you know?"

Sarah nodded, biting her lip.

"We'll need to disinfect everything in here," Kevin said. "The bed, the floor—everything I've touched. We should burn my clothes and the mattress."

With the initial shock fading, Sarah now felt numb. She searched through the station's storage compartments until she found the first aid supplies. In addition to a bottle of Advil, she grabbed a roll of gauze, some bandages, medical tape, and a bottle of hydrogen peroxide and sat them down near Kevin, making sure they were within reach. She noticed that his entire hand was now red. She opened the Advil and shook out a handful of capsules. She sat those within his reach, as well.

"You won't be able to touch this stuff when I'm done with it," he warned.

"I know. That's why I opened the painkillers for you. There's more peroxide and stuff over there, so we won't have to worry about that."

While Kevin bandaged his wound, ripping the gauze and tape with his teeth, Sarah retrieved the station's cleaning supplies. She found disinfectant cleaner, a mop and bucket, rags, rubber gloves, and a bottle of bleach. She also discovered a pack of disposable respirator masks—the kind people wore when they had the flu or used to avoid hazardous fumes. She took one out of the package and slid it onto her face. The rubber-band strap pulled her wet hair. She winced in pain, and then felt guilty about it. Her discomfort was nothing compared to the agony that Kevin was obviously feeling.

"Where were you, anyway?"

"Outside," Sarah said. The mask muffled her voice. "I wanted to see if I could get the power working."

"Find anything?"

"Nothing useful. I can't figure out the power plant. It's way too advanced for me. There's a little utility shed with a lawnmower and stuff inside. That's about it, though. Nothing else."

"Is there room inside the utility shed?"

Sarah frowned. "Room for what?"

"Room for me."

"What are you talking about?"

Kevin sighed. "Like I said, I'm not itching anymore. I think I caught it in time. But just in case, we need to be careful for the next few days. I can't be around you. If I am still infectious, then you could catch it off anything I touch. And if it's airborne, then I definitely shouldn't be around you."

"If it was airborne, we'd both be dead already. So would everyone else we've met."

Kevin nodded. "You're probably right, but even so, I'd feel better if we limited your exposure. I think you would, too."

"So you're going to...what? Sleep in the shed?"

"Yeah."

"That's ridiculous. It's cold out there. We've got no way to heat the shed. You'll catch pneumonia."

Kevin waved his bandaged hand. Blood seeped through the gauze. "That's the least of my worries."

"What about the worms? They seem to be able to find people."

"I'll lock it from the inside."

Sarah stared, incredulous. "You think that's going to stop them? You saw what happened at Teddy's house."

Kevin paused before replying. When he spoke, his voice was dejected and quiet. "Well, I'm all out of ideas, Sarah. Can you think of an alternative that doesn't endanger you?"

"No..."

Kevin smiled sadly. "There you go. Besides, it will be good to get some uninterrupted sleep. You snore, you know?"

Sarah faked a laugh and then turned away so that Kevin wouldn't see her crying.

Kevin cleaned the blood and skin from the floor, and disinfected the bunk bed and everything else he had touched. He dropped the soiled rags into the bucket, along with his clothes. Then he grabbed Sarah's old clothes that had been drying on the floor, and the goofy-looking hunter's cap he'd taken from Teddy's truck, and dumped them in the bucket, too. Finally, he carried the bucket outside and sat it on the stairs.

"Are there any more uniforms left?"

"Yeah." Sarah tossed him one. "That's probably better than running around outside in your boxers." She tried to keep her tone lighthearted, but she was aware that she sounded anything but.

"After I leave," he said, "you'll want to disinfect this doorknob again."

Sarah nodded.

Kevin pulled the mattress off the bed and dragged it towards the door. He whistled as he worked.

"What's that song?" Sarah asked.

"The Police. I bet you've heard it before. When the world is running down, you make the best of what's still around. It's been stuck in my head."

Sarah turned away again, but this time, not even the rain drumming against the roof was enough to drown out her sobs.

FIVE

Henry awoke with a start, unsure of where he was. He almost toppled over into the water, but his instincts saved him at the last minute, and he grabbed the sides of the door. He glanced around, frantic. His .17 gauge had slipped from his fingers and clattered onto the silo's floor. The noise must have been what woke him up. Henry shook his head. He was lucky it hadn't discharged when it fell. Rubbing his eyes, he picked the weapon up and examined it for damage. The scope was a little wobbly, but otherwise, it seemed unharmed.

He looked around for Moxey, and found her curled up and sleeping on a stack of wet, empty burlap sacks. He ran his hand over her damp fur. He tried to remember the last time either of them had been dry, and couldn't. His heart broke all over again as he felt her ribs sticking out beneath her parchment-thin skin. Moxey had been the proverbial fat cat at one time. She'd had no fixed meal time, and Henry had always made sure there was food in her dish, so that she could eat whenever she wanted. Now, there wasn't much meat on her at all. Just skin and bones and wet fur. Her thighs still had some thickness, like chicken legs, but that was all.

Chicken legs...I could cook her up right here. I've got a cigarette lighter.

Henry's stomach grumbled. His throat burned. He wondered how much meat there actually was on Moxey. If he ate everything—skin, organs, and the rest—that might quiet the pain in his abdomen...

"No!"

Horrified, Henry jerked his hand away from his long-time companion. His cry woke the cat. She looked up at him with adoration, stretched, and then began to purr.

"I'm sorry," he whispered. "I don't know what..."

It had happened again, just like the last time the hunger had been so severe. His thoughts had turned to his cat. He reached out with one timid hand and patted her head. Moxey licked his fingers. Her tongue felt like sandpaper, but he noticed that it was pale, rather than its normal pink hue. Her gums were beginning to recede, revealing black around the bases of her teeth.

"I've got to quit falling asleep on watch. Got to find you some food, soon. Find some for both of us. Because if I don't..."

He wondered if it was too late for her, anyway. Moxey had been drinking less water than normal, and she was lethargic throughout most of the day. Maybe it was crueler to let her starve to death. Maybe the kind thing to do was to put her out of her misery—stop her suffering before it progressed any further. He could do it while she slept. And then, when it was over, he could...

Henry stood up quickly, startling the cat. The plank boards thrummed beneath his boots as he strode back over to the open door. Gripping the rifle in both hands, he stood there with his eyes closed and let the cool breeze blow across his face. He had to stop thinking such terrible thoughts. He could no more eat Moxey than he could eat his parents or friends—had they still been alive. And besides, even if he tried, there was no realistic way to cook her. Sure, he had a cigarette lighter, but all of the combustible material inside the silo was damp, and there was no safe place to build a fire. If there had been, then he and Moxey wouldn't be so cold and wet all the time.

What they needed to do was escape from here—make it to dry land. He eyed the mountainside again, and once more, his thoughts turned to Mr. Garnett. So close and yet so far. Henry shook his head in frustration. If he did find a way to traverse the water, what then? Where would he and Moxey go? Mr. Garnett might indeed still be alive, but reaching his house was an impossibility. Many of the trees were leaning over or had already toppled, their roots unable to find purchase in the mud. From what he could tell, the road looked washed out in places. Even if he were able to find a vehicle and get it running, they wouldn't get far. And going on foot was an even less desirable option. Squinting, Henry spotted something out there, crawling sluggishly back and forth on the hillside, big enough that he could see its shape through the haze. He didn't know what it was, but it certainly wasn't a bear or a deer. At times, he'd seen more than one. Sometimes he thought they might be the worms from his dream, but that was just silly. Still, whatever they were, he had a sense that they were dangerous. There was no way he and the cat could make it past them, especially on foot.

Their options remained the same. Stay here and drown once the water reached the top of the silo. Stay here and starve. Or make it to land and face whatever was out there crawling around.

His stomach growled again. To keep his mind off it, Henry tried to think about something else. Unfortunately, his thoughts turned to his favorite foods, and how much he missed them. Chili dogs and root beer. Cornbread and beans. A giant meatball sub piled high with pickles and tomatoes washed down with a cold ginger ale. His mother's blueberry pie, baked with a recipe passed down from his grandmother and great-grandmother.

Sighing, he sat down again, dangling his feet over the edge. Henry scanned the water, trying to remember where the submerged buildings had been before the flood. It was disconcerting. He'd known this town like the back of his hand, but now that everything was gone, it was hard to get his bearings. His gaze turned to the steeple of the Presbyterian Church, sticking out of the water like a finger pointing skyward. Rain streamed down the white vinyl siding. The bell-tower was hidden in shadow. Henry was just about to glance away when he saw a flash of movement inside.

He sat up straight, peering intently. If it was a bird, and it flew close enough, maybe he could shoot it down and drag it into the silo. He slowly slid the rifle into the crook of his shoulder, eased off the safety, and peered through the scope. He saw it again, a flicker of motion from deep inside the open bell-tower. Too big to be a bird, but the mist prevented him from discerning any more. He adjusted the scope, silently cursing himself for knocking it loose earlier. Then he looked again, and gasped.

There was a figure inside the bell-tower. A human figure. He couldn't make out their features, or if they were a man or a woman, but the shape was definitely humanoid. Someone was alive over there—but how? He and Moxey were barely making it, and they were inside the grain silo. How had somebody survived being exposed to the elements like that? The steeple offered no real shelter—just a roof over their head. No walls or protection from the rain and cold.

"Does it matter how they survived? Jesus, Henry, get your head out of your ass. You're not alone. That's all that matters right now."

Moxey stirred at the sound of his voice. She meowed once, pitifully, and then went back to sleep.

Henry wondered who it could be over there. Reverend Smith, maybe? Or the church caretaker, Mr. Bare? He peered through the scope again, hoping for a better look, but the figure remained hidden. He sat the rifle down beside him and cupped his hands around his mouth.

"Hey," he yelled. "Hey, over there in the church! This is Henry Garrett. Are you okay?"

There was no answer. He tried again, unsuccessfully. Cursing, he picked the rifle up again and fired one shot into the air, trying to get the survivor's attention. Moxey jumped up, startled by the blast, and fled behind a plastic five-gallon bucket of roof tar. When the ringing in his ears stopped, Henry listened for a reply, but there was none forthcoming. He looked through the scope again. They were still there. Maybe they couldn't answer him. Maybe they were hurt, or sick. Maybe the rain and fog were muting his shouts. But even if they couldn't holler back, wouldn't they have heard the gunshot? Wouldn't they have at least waved or signaled him somehow?

Something else occurred to him. If the person in the steeple had managed to stay alive so long under such poor conditions, then they probably had something that he and Moxey didn't have.

Food.

Glancing around the silo, Henry began to formulate a plan. For the first time in weeks, his headache was gone and his stomach didn't hurt. He had hope. He clung to that hope like it was a lifeboat, preventing him from sinking down below the surface.

He paced around inside the grain silo, trying to figure out how to reach the church steeple. Moxey watched him with droopy-lidded eyes, curled up on her burlap sacks and trying to stay warm. Henry's wet boots sloshed with each step. When he coughed, it echoed around the wooden platform. He leaned against the iron handrail, stared down into the flooded depths in the silo's center, and frowned in concentration. Even without the revelation that there was somebody else alive, they needed to get out of here. The water had risen even higher. Just a few more days and it would probably overrun the platform. Then, he and Moxey would have no choice but to leave.

He needed to reach the steeple, find out who was there and what kind of shape they were in. Then he needed to get himself, Moxey, and the mysterious stranger over to the mountainside. Granted, there were probably untold dangers there, as well, but at least they could take shelter on the last bit of dry land.

But how? He couldn't swim across. The water was a toxic stew—full of oil, chemicals, gasoline, dead bodies and debris, not to mention water moccasins and other critters. He didn't have a boat. He'd seen some float by—small bass boats and rubber dinghies—but they'd been too far away to capture.

He took stock of everything they had left—five bottles of water, the rifle, half a box of bullets, a cloth to clean off the rifle's scope, empty food wrappers, a roll of duct tape, a cigarette lighter, a damp cardboard box full of moldering newspapers and magazines, a wet roll of bailing twine, a bucket of roofing tar, the pocketknife with his initials engraved in it that his parents had bought him for his sixteenth birthday, a claw-hammer, two pitchforks, a John Deere ball cap, and a plastic bucket full of rusted nuts and bolts and miscellaneous junk. Nothing he could build a boat out of.

Henry experimented with the floorboards, prying at the heavy planks with the claw hammer, seeing if he could loosen any of them. They stayed firmly in place. The weather had yet to impact the twelve-penny nails holding them down. His attention turned to the small double-doors in the silo's curved wall. The hinges were rusty and weak. Maybe he'd have better luck with them. Henry opened his pocketknife and went to work on the hinges, prying at the screws until they started to work their way loose. Then he yanked them out with the claw hammer and lay the doors down on the floor, one on top of the other, to increase buoyancy. Using most of the duct tape and all of the bailing twine, he lashed them together, forming a crude raft.

"God damn," he said, smiling as he finished. "Wish I'd thought of this before now."

Moxey meowed in agreement.

"Don't you worry none, girl. I'm gonna head over to the church and see what's what. Maybe they'll have some food. Hell, they've *got* to."

Henry decided to leave the rifle behind. It was too valuable to risk dropping it in the water. He'd have to bring it along when they headed for land, but for now, he thought it better to leave the weapon in the silo where it was safe. With the remaining duct tape, he wrapped one of Moxey's burlap bags around the tines of one of the pitchforks, fashioning a makeshift oar. He sat both pitchforks next to the open door—one to navigate with and the other for defense. Cold wind and mist blew through the opening. Henry shivered. He dragged the boat over to the door and dropped it into the water. He held his breath, waiting to see what would happen. It dipped below the surface and then popped up again, floating. He cheered. Startled, Moxey ran to the rear of the silo.

Donning the John Deere cap to keep the rain off his head, Henry slowly clambered out onto the raft and sat cross-legged. Then he grabbed the pitchforks and brought them onboard. The vessel bobbed and swayed, and water surged over the edges. Alarmed, Henry got ready to make a dive back into the silo, but the raft remained above the surface. It wasn't very sturdy, but it would have to suffice.

"Stay here, girl! I'll be right back."

If Moxey heard him, she gave no indication.

Henry pushed off from the side of the silo and floated out onto the open water, buoyed by the slight surf. He was drenched within seconds, from both the relentless rainfall and the small waves lapping over the edges of the craft. His stomach growled. He dipped the makeshift oar into the water and paddled, guiding the raft towards the steeple. Rain beat down on him, but Henry ignored it. He peered through the mist, his full attention focused on his destination. He hoped to spot the figure again, but if they were still there, then they were out of sight. So intent was his concentration, that he didn't look away until he heard Moxey howling behind him.

Henry glanced over his shoulder, hoping that she wasn't considering jumping into the water and coming after him. He was stunned by what he saw. The silo was buried beneath a billowing fogbank. He could just barely see its outline, enveloped in curling white mist.

"Holy shit..."

As he watched, the fog drifted towards him. Henry turned around and paddled faster. By the time he'd reached the church steeple, the mist had caught up to him. Shivering, he pulled alongside the bell tower and cupped his hands over his mouth.

"Hello? Anyone in there? This is Henry Garrett!"

His voice sounded odd, as if the fog were dampening it somehow. Henry rubbed his arms and legs to get his circulation moving. Then he called out again.

"Hey! I know y'all are in there. I saw you. If you're hurt, or can't call out, don't worry. I can help."

He paused, waiting for a response, but none was forthcoming. Somewhere overhead, a bird shrieked. He glanced upward but couldn't see it through the haze.

"I'm coming in," Henry shouted. "Don't shoot me. I just want to help."

Dipping the pitchfork in the water, he got as close to the steeple as he could. Then, moving slowly, Henry grasped the ornate, white railing and pulled himself up into the bell tower. Too late, he wished he'd had the presence of mind to save some of the bailing twine to tie the raft off with. He had no means of anchoring it, and if the vessel drifted away on the current, he'd really be screwed. Realizing that there was nothing he could do about it now, Henry grabbed the second pitchfork that he'd brought along for defense. He really didn't think he'd need it, but just holding it in his hands made him feel safer. More comfortable.

"Hello?"

He peered into the open-air platform beneath the bell. Mist swirled through the space, obscuring his vision. He saw a trace of the wooden door that he new opened into the staircase that led down into the church. That would all be underwater now. If there was somebody here—and he knew there was—they had to be in the center of the platform, concealed in the fog.

Licking his lips, Henry stalked forward. The boards were wet and slippery, so he moved with caution. He shifted the pitchfork in his hands, thrusting it out before him. The wind whistled behind his back. The breeze was picking up, the gust strong enough to shift the ball cap on his head.

"I've been holed up over yonder inside Fred Laudermilk's grain silo. I didn't think there was anyone else left alive. But then I saw you while I was—"

The wind parted the fog for a moment, and Henry caught a glimpse of a figure lying on their back. They reached for him, arms flailing weakly. The mist swirled around them again before he could discern their features.

"Are you okay?" he asked, stepping forward.

"Soft," the figure replied. It's voice sounded like someone gargling mouthwash.

"What?"

"Must become...soft...Henry..."

Another gust of wind parted the haze once more, giving Henry a clear view of the person on the floor. His eyes widened. He tried to speak, but could only stammer. The pitchfork slipped from his hands and clattered onto the floor. Slowly, laboriously, the figure slithered toward him, wriggling like a snake.

Startled, Henry skittered backward until he felt the wet, wooden railing behind him. A strong gust of wind whistled through the steeple, spraying him with mist. His John Deere cap fluttered on his head, and the bell swayed slowly back and forth. Squinting, Henry wiped the rain from his eyes and stared.

The figure made a phlegmatic, rasping noise that reminded Henry of a whoopee cushion. Then it clambered to its feet and shuffled slowly towards him, arms outstretched, fingers grasping at the air.

"Henry..."

"Mr. Burke?"

The shambling form halted, rocking back and forth on the balls of its feet. Its body was almost completely covered with a white fungus similar in appearance to peach fuzz, but thicker. The thing tilted its head, staring at him with sunken, black pinprick eyes. When it spoke again, the fuzz split open, revealing a pale, toothless mouth. Its voice sounded like it was gargling.

"Hello...Henry...soft...Have you...seen...soft...Melissa and...Jaceyn...soft..."

Until that point, Henry hadn't been sure of what he was seeing. The thing in the church steeple was barely human, let alone somebody he recognized. The growth obscured everything—clothing, facial features, anything that would have identified it—everything except for the Masonic ring on its finger. The mold had started to grow over the band, but enough of it was still visible that it caught Henry's eye right away. He'd only known one person in Renick who wore such an item—Mr. Burke, who owned the turkey farm up near Bear Town. Henry had gone to school with his kids, Melissa and Jaceyn. He wondered where they were now, and what had happened to their mother.

Henry stared at the man, wondering what had happened to him. He'd seen this weird growth on other things—birds and fish and the occasional debris that floated by, but never to this extreme. He glanced down at Mr. Burke's feet and saw white, root-like appendages growing out of them.

"*Soft...*"

"Mr. Burke…what happened to you? You're sick."

"Soft..."

"Why do you keep saying that?"

"Soft...Henry...soft..."

"I don't know what that means! What's soft?"

"It's...what you...soft...must become...soft..."

Mr. Burke shuffled forward again, reaching for him. Henry slid along the railing to the left and the figure swerved towards him—but slowly. Even though the platform was slick and treacherous from all the rain, Henry was pretty sure he could outrun the infected man if he had to.

"Everything...soft...will become...soft..."

"Mr. Burke. You're sick. There's something wrong with you. Let me help, okay?"

"Soft...we all...go...soft..."

"I've got medicine back in the silo," Henry lied. "Penicillin. Antibiotics. All kinds of stuff. Let me go back and get it, and I'll help you out. Okay?"

"Soft..."

"Mr. Burke?"

"SOFFFFFFFT..."

He slid closer and Henry darted to the side and then ran behind him, heedless of the wet boards beneath his feet. Mr. Burke stopped and pivoted. Henry ducked down, grabbed the pitchfork and stood back up. He thrust the tines out in front of him and gritted his teeth.

"Stay back! I don't want to hurt you, Mr. Burke, but I will if I have to. I reckon you're infected with something. I don't know what it is, but I don't want it."

Mr. Burke struck at him with one flailing arm. Particles of the disgusting growth flicked from his fingertips and splattered on the floor at Henry's feet. Thunder boomed. Grimacing, Henry jabbed the pitchfork at his opponent.

"Get back…I mean it, now."

"Soft..."

Reluctant to kill his classmates' father, no matter how diseased the man was, Henry turned the tines and tried striking

Mr. Burke on the side of the head. The effect was instantaneous and unexpected. The white figure's head burst open like an overripe melon, turning to grey, sludgy water. The stench was cloying and damp. Musky. Henry's stomach roiled.

"Jesus fucking Christ!"

The headless corpse remained standing. The arms still moved, but they had dropped to its sides now. Water jetted from the stump of its neck and ran down its shoulders and chest. As Henry watched, gaping, the rest of the corpse began to deteriorate. The shoulders melted. The arms fell off and exploded on the platform like water balloons. Henry jumped backward, mindful of not getting any of the foul liquid on him. The chest and abdomen liquefied. Then, with nothing left to anchor them, the legs toppled over and burst. Within seconds, all that was left of Mr. Burke was a wet puddle. Then the rain washed even that away.

Retching, Henry let the pitchfork slip from his numb fingers. Then he ran to the railing and leaned out over it. The John Deere cap slipped from his head and fluttered away on the wind, before falling into the water. Henry watched it go and gagged again. For a moment, he was actually glad that he was starving, and that there was nothing in his stomach to throw up. His throat burned. His stomach cramped. His arms and legs trembled.

He remained there for a long time. When the nausea had passed, he wiped his mouth with the back of his hand and then surveyed the steeple platform. It was empty. He paused, considering the wooden door that opened into a stairway leading down into the church, but decided against it. The building's interior would be flooded by now, and if Mr. Burke had touched that doorknob, then he wanted nothing to do with it. He was relieved to see that the raft was still within reach. The wind and current had kept it bumping against the steeple, rather than floating away.

Retrieving the pitchfork, Henry ran for the raft. There was no food here. No help. And no God, either. Not anymore. The only thing the church had to offer him and Moxey was a death far worse than the one they already faced. Starving to death was certainly more preferable than what had happened to Mr. Burke.

He turned into water, Henry thought as he clambered back aboard the raft. *That's what that white stuff does. It grows on things and turns them into water. What else is it growing on? Is it growing on the silo? Is it down there beneath the waves, turning our shelter into liquid?*

Frowning, he tossed the pitchfork over the side. It had touched Mr. Burke so he no longer considered it safe. He'd have to get rid of his boots and clothes when he got back to the silo, as well. Anything that had touched that platform had to now be considered contaminated.

"What the hell am I gonna wear?"

Then he took a long look around him, surveying the mist and the waves and the endless falling rain. His stomach growled again, reminding Henry that being naked was the least of his problems.

SIX

The ranger station was quiet without Kevin inside. Several times, Sarah considered braving the downpour and going out to the utility shed to check on him. Each time, she decided against it. With the heavy cloud cover blocking out the moon and the stars, and no electric lights, the night was like fresh road tar. If she slipped on the wet stairs or stumbled across a worm in the darkness, Kevin would never be able to hear her, let alone help her. Also, he'd insisted that she stay away from him until he was certain that the fuzz was gone and unable to be passed on to her.

Exhausted as she was, Sarah found herself unable to fall asleep. She lay on one of the bunk beds, tossing and turning and listening to the rain drum against the metal roof. The mattress creaked beneath her. At one point, she heard something scratching in the corner. She bolted upright, gasping, fearing the worst, but it was just a small, gray and brown field mouse. The tiny creature was as frightened as she was. As soon as it saw her, it fled behind one of the bookcases.

"Poor little guy," she muttered. "He's a survivor, just like us."

She lay there restlessly for a few more minutes and then got up again. After lighting some candles and positioning them around the room, Sarah struck a match to a small kerosene lantern that had been hanging on the wall. Then, carrying it with her, she explored her new surroundings again, this time in detail. She picked through the books and magazines with interest, but ignored the movies and video games, since there was no electricity.

Disturbed by the silence, Sarah turned on the battery operated radio again, hoping to hear more from the mysterious broadcaster in Boston, but the airwaves offered nothing but static. She left it on but turned the volume down low. She knew that she shouldn't. Although the ranger station was stocked with plenty of batteries, the supply wasn't unlimited. Sooner or later, they'd run out. Right now, however, she needed something to break the oppressive stillness, even if it was just white noise.

There was food in a hutch next to the microwave and in the cupboards above it—two large cans of coffee, several boxes of tea bags, powdered cream, packets of sugar, canned vegetables and pasta, tins of sardines and tuna, packs of instant oatmeal, bags of beef jerky, candy, instant mashed potato and stuffing mixes, various spices, plenty of bottled water, and more Ramen noodles than she'd ever seen in her life. They wouldn't starve. At least, not right away. Sarah considered making herself something to eat. She needed to keep her strength up. She knew that. But she just wasn't hungry. Not after everything that had happened in the last forty-eight hours. She ran through it all in her mind—the helicopter crash; dinner with Teddy and Carl, during which they'd discussed everything from the White Fuzz to religion; that crazed redneck, Earl Harper, who at the end, had seemed to have shared some sinister, inexplicable bond with the worms; the big worm's attack on the house; her and Kevin's escape to this place; and then Kevin's infection. It was all too much.

Both Sarah and Kevin had seen the White Fuzz in action before. Several survivors in Baltimore had contracted it. The fungus spread quickly, covering a human host in a matter of days. They'd never seen what the final result was, but Sarah didn't imagine it was very pretty. All she knew was that those who were infected with it craved water, and no matter how much they got, it wasn't enough. They wanted more. Which was ironic, considering the state of the world.

Could Kevin have really beat the infection in time? Had scraping the skin from the affected area really killed the fungus? She thought that Kevin believed that it had. But Sarah wasn't so sure.

It occurred to her that she'd run her hand through her hair right before picking Kevin up off the floor. Had she done it since then? She couldn't remember. Yes, she'd done her best to decontaminate herself, but she hadn't washed her hair. Sarah knew that she was being paranoid. Fatigue and shock were wearing her down. But paranoid or not, she decided to be safe. She grabbed a pair of scissors from a drawer and snapped on a pair of rubber gloves. Then she leaned over the trashcan and cut her hair, cropping it as short as possible. It saddened her to do so—her previous girlfriends had always said that her hair was one of Sarah's best features. Shoving the emotion aside, she gritted her teeth and continued, snipping it even shorter. When she was done, Sarah looked down at her locks in stunned silence. Then she dropped the gloves and the scissors into the trash, tied the garbage bag, and sat it out on the steps. She stood in the rain, letting it wash the clippings from her neck and shoulders. Then she came back inside again and dried off.

She didn't look in the mirror. She was afraid to. Not yet. Maybe later. Right now, seeing the damage she'd just done to herself might be the final straw.

And besides, she scolded herself, *it's just hair. It will grow back. And it's not like I'm going to meet anybody way out here. All the pretty girls are at the bottom of the sea.*

Sarah took a deep breath, and forced herself to focus. There were more important things to worry about right now—like Kevin.

As she crossed the room, the static from the radio faded, and then returned, followed by a loud, sharp electronic squeal. When the feedback had dissipated, she heard the familiar Boston accent. Once again, the signal was weak and frequently interrupted with bursts of static.

"...broadcast...distress signal. The Pru...almost eight-hundred feet above Boston, but now...all but the top four floors are submerged beneath the Atlantic. The only other building I...is the John Hancock Tower. Everything else...the Pru's two-hundred foot radio tower..."

Sarah hovered over the radio, listening intently.

"...six of us. Me, O'Neill, Wilson, Mason, Rebecca, and Herndon...maintenance manag...Wilson is from Charleston...speech...government imposed travel restrictions...Lisa and

Alex stayed back in Ohio…might hear this broadcast… journal…"

Sarah tried to concentrate—tried to mine some meaning from the random, disjointed words that cut through the static. She grabbed a pen and tablet from the command desk and jotted down key phrases and things that seemed important.

"…half-man, half-shark…ate Norris…bit…half…plenty of diesel for the generator, so I can broadcast just like a radio station. And with all these radio masts and dishes, anyone with a working radio or telev…should hear it…CB radio… Television signals will only carry in…but the radio signals should hit tower after tower. They could…pretty far, I guess... figure out how to rewire the satellite dishes into the public broadcast system equip…satellites out in space are still operational…transmit even farther…"

Sarah moved to the side, stretching a kink in her neck, and the signal suddenly grew clearer. She remained motionless, hoping the signal would stay.

"I can only transmit, though, so I don't know if anyone out there can hear this or not. If so, hi! How are ya'? Any chance you could send a helicopter or a boat to haul our asses out of here?"

"Only if they come rescue us first," Sarah told the man on the radio.

"Anyway," he said, "I'm pretty tired. Didn't get much sleep, on account of the itching. Think I've got a rash or something. Maybe from all the moisture in the air—like jungle rot or something. Gonna crash for a few hours and then I'll try this again. If there's anyone listening, stay safe. Stay dry. This is Mark in Boston, over and out."

Silence returned, followed by another burst of static. Sarah stood listening to it for a moment. Then she slowly turned off the radio. Mark in Boston was infected with the fuzz. She knew it, but there was no way to tell him. Boston might as well have been the far side of Mars. She thought about going down to tell Kevin about the broadcast, and then remembered that she couldn't.

She returned to the bookshelves and scanned the spines

until she found what she was looking for—several books on first aid and medicine. She pulled them from the shelf, blew the dust off the covers and sat them down on the bunk. She blew out the candles, one by one, until only the lantern and one lone candle were left. Then she returned to her bunk, snuffed out the lantern and read by candlelight.

It was a long time before she could sleep.

Kevin groaned. The painkillers were already beginning to wear off, which surprised him. He'd swallowed more than the recommended dosage—not enough to harm himself, but enough to mute the pain for what should have been several hours. It felt almost as if his body was fighting the drugs' effects—purging the ibuprofen from his system. His bandaged arm felt like it was on fire. The gauze was soaked with blood. Most of it had dried into a brown, flaky crust, but the pain remained.

Gritting his teeth, he turned on the flashlight and shined it around the interior of the utility shed, partly to take his mind off his wound, but also to alleviate his boredom. There wasn't much to see—a lawn tractor, two push mowers, a wagon, several cans of gasoline and kerosene, stacks of miscellaneous lumber, rolls of plastic and metal fencing, a bundle of twine, extension cords, a gas-powered weed whacker, a chainsaw, metal posts, and various tools, including several axes, shovels, hoes, and pick-axes. A spider web dangled in one corner. A mouse trap sat vacant and dusty in another corner, its bait long since stolen or rotted away. The concrete floor was relatively clean, if cold. Kevin was grateful that it wasn't just a gravel floor like so many other utility sheds. The mattress he'd taken from the ranger station was thin and lumpy and not very comfortable. He clicked the flashlight off again and sighed.

"Home sweet home. Top of the world, Ma."

At least it was dry. Maybe too dry, now that he thought about it. Ever since the rain had started, Kevin had gotten used to never being completely dry. There was always moisture in the air. It permeated everything. Dampness and mildew seemed to work their way into every space, no matter how sealed-off or climate-controlled. It had been that way in Baltimore, when he, Sarah and the others had taken refuge on the top floors of the Inner Harbor Marriott, and it had been that way at each of their destinations since then. Getting out of the rain made little difference, since they usually had no dry clothes to put on. Even stripping naked didn't seem to help. If anything, it made the wetness in the air more pervasive.

Now, for the first time in a long time, he felt dry. The sensation should have been pleasant, but instead, it made him uncomfortable. The air seemed thick and dusty. It irritated his nostrils and throat when he breathed. His skin felt shriveled and leathery, and his mouth was parched.

He'd found a few unopened bottles of water inside the shed when he first entered. Already, two of them sat empty. Kevin turned on the flashlight again and rummaged around, finding a third. He unscrewed the cap and drained the plastic bottle in two big gulps.

"Ahhh. That's better."

Smacking his lips, he tossed the empty bottle at the mousetrap, triggering the long-dormant mechanism. The trap snapped, springing into the air and then landing face down on the floor.

Giggling, Kevin turned off the flashlight once more and tried to get comfortable. The mattress poked him. He poked it back. Rain drummed against the shed's roof, steady and rhythmic. The sound wasn't unpleasant. He closed his eyes…

…and then he was thirsty again.

"Goddamn it. What the fuck?"

It occurred to him that despite the amount of water he'd drank in the last hour, he didn't have to piss. That was odd. Usually, when he drank anything, especially beer or water, it ran right through him. When he was a kid, his father had joked on long car trips about how Kevin needed to stop every ten miles or so.

He fumbled in the darkness, not bothering with the flashlight again, found a fourth bottle, and chugged it. The liquid did little to alleviate his thirst, but he forced himself not to drink another. Instead, he lay there and tried to fall asleep.

His thoughts turned to Sarah. He wondered what she was doing up there in the tower, and hoped that she was okay.

Outside, something bumped into the shed hard enough to make the walls rumble. Kevin held his breath. He heard the distinct slithering sound of a heavy body crawling through the mud. He waited, not daring to breathe or move. In the past, some of the worms had displayed the ability to track prey through some kind of sensory ability. Kevin still wasn't sure if it was smell or sight—he'd seen evidence of both despite the fact that the creatures' had no eyes or nose. He considered grabbing one of the axes from the wall, but was afraid that the worm would hear his movement.

Eventually, he heard the creature crawl away into the night. Exhausted, feverish, and in pain, Kevin lay there, listening for it to return, until the sound of the rain lulled him to sleep.

While he slept, something that wasn't blood seeped through the pores of the gauze bandage on his arm and began to grow, sending out small, white, exploratory tendrils.

Henry returned to the grain silo and removed his boots and clothes to avoid the risk of infection. He dropped them into the foul water and then clambered inside the silo. He stood shivering in the doorway. Water dripped from his body and pooled on the floor. He shook himself, spraying droplets through the air.

Moxey was sprawled on her makeshift bed of burlap bags, lying on her back with her paws in the air. Her mouth was slightly open, showing teeth and receding gums. Her ribs were visible beneath her fur. She looked stiff, and at first, Henry was positive that she'd died during his absence. Then her ears twitched. Henry sighed, watching her. Eyes still closed, Moxey shook her paws and twitched her tail. Henry wondered what she was dreaming about. Probably food.

Grunting with exertion, he struggled to pull the raft inside. When it was secure, he walked across the floor to the moldering cardboard box full of wet newspapers and magazines. They smelled musty. He dumped them out and then, carrying the box with him, knelt down next to Moxey. She opened her eyes as he gently scratched her chin.

"How you doing, girl?"

She responded with a weak meow.

"I know. I know. We're getting out of here tomorrow. We can't stay here anymore."

Moxey licked his fingers with her rough tongue.

"But first, I need to borrow some of these sacks."

He picked her up and she whined in protest. Henry lined the bottom of the cardboard box with a few burlap bags and placed Moxey inside it. She turned in a circle, looking at it doubtfully, her claws flexing and prodding. His mother used to call that 'making bread.' After a moment, Moxey lay down and curled up. Henry smiled when she closed her eyes and began to purr.

Using his pocketknife, Henry fashioned a crude kilt and shirt out of the rest of the burlap bags. The shirt was easy. He simply cut holes for his head and arms. The kilt was a little more difficult. He used strips of burlaps as a belt to cinch it around his waist. When he was finished, he got dressed. The sacks were warm from the cat's leftover body heat, but that warmth soon vanished. The rough material grew itchy and irritated his skin.

He strode to the center of the platform. The wooden floorboards were cold under his bare feet. Henry peered over the side, and confirmed that the water was still rising. Within days, the silo would flood.

He lay down next to Moxey and draped one hand over the lip of the box. He scratched her ears and closed his eyes.

"Yep," he promised before falling asleep. "First thing tomorrow, I reckon we'll head for Mr. Garnett's house. I ain't gonna let you starve, or get infected with whatever Mr. Burke had, or drown. I promise. I'll do whatever I have to do to make sure that doesn't happen."

His stomach growled as he snored.

Sarah slept soundly, the first aid book open across her chest. At one point in the night, a particularly loud burst of thunder woke her up, but Sarah forced herself to go back to sleep. She needed to rest—needed to conserve her strength for what she planned on doing tomorrow, if it was necessary.

She thought that it probably would be.

Kevin slept, and dreamed that he and Lori were sitting naked in a huge porcelain bathtub full of warm water. It was the most luxuriant feeling he'd ever experienced. He examined his fingers. They looked like wrinkled, white prunes.

Lori caressed his shoulders. "You're so soft."

"Soft is good," he agreed. "Everything should be soft."

He leaned forward to kiss her, and she turned into water and flowed all over him.

Even as he shuddered in the throes of a powerful orgasm, Kevin did not wake.

The rain continued to fall.

SEVEN

Sarah awoke with a start, groggy and confused. She glanced around the station, not remembering where she was at first. She sat up quickly and the medical book that had been lying open on her chest fell to the floor.

"Oops."

Yawning, Sarah rubbed her eyes and slid out of bed. The floor was cold beneath her bare feet. She reached up to run a hand through her hair and was shocked at first when she didn't feel any. Then she remembered that she'd cut it off the night before, in fear that it might harbor the white fuzz.

She turned on the radio, but Mark from Boston had gone silent again. Even the static seemed muted. She turned it back off to conserve the batteries. Stumbling around the room, Sarah finally settled in the kitchen area. She made a cup of instant coffee and took a sip. It was cold and bitter, and made her long for the hot chicory coffee Teddy had served her and Kevin just a few days ago. She carried the mug over to the large windows and gazed outside. The rain still fell, obscuring anything not immediately on the mountaintop. Mist swirled around the base of the tower and through the surrounding trees. The sky was a gray sheet—the sun nothing more than a pale, hazy disc. She tried to remember what the sun's warmth on her skin had felt like, and was surprised to find that she couldn't.

One thing she didn't see was the worms. They were noticeably absent this morning. Usually, she could spot them—shadowed forms slithering like ghosts through the fog. But not this morning. She wondered where they'd gone. Maybe somewhere else. Some place where the prey was easier to get to.

After she was feeling more awake and alert, she found

a pen and paper and began making a list. Before the rain, Sarah's friends and family had joked about her obsessive list-making. Before she went to bed each night, she'd jotted down a list of things to do the next day. She'd done it since junior high school. The process made her feel better about things—more in control of her life. She'd kept up the practice during their time in Baltimore, but hadn't done it since their escape in the helicopter. She figured now would be a good time to start again.

One-by-one, she listed the items she'd need for what she planned on doing today, should it prove necessary. When she was finished, she made herself another cup of instant coffee and then began a thorough search of the ranger station, checking every compartment, nook, and cranny. Her previous explorations had been done while fatigued and scared. This time, she catalogued every useful item, noting locations and quantities. She also searched for the different things she'd just jotted down on her list. These she sat aside—rubber gloves, a dust mask, rubbing alcohol, waterproof matches, a candle, cotton balls, newspaper, scissors, gauze, rubber tubing, an unopened fifth of Bookers whiskey, kerosene, two coffee mugs, and a small hatchet.

In a previously unexplored drawer, she made a surprising find—a five shot Taurus .357 and a box of bullets. While examining the gun, she was overcome with a burst of seemingly random memories. Teddy handing her a Ruger .22, to which she'd replied, "Anything bigger? As for killing, I don't need a gun." Standing on the roof of the Marriott in Baltimore, taking Juan's M-16 away from him and shooting at the mermaid. Breaking the nose of one of the three cultists that had attacked her.

Despite the fact that her mother had died when she was eight years old, or maybe because of it, Sarah knew how to take care of herself. Her girlfriends had always said that she was tough and smart. And she was. She knew that, deep down inside. But she wasn't feeling so tough right now, and she definitely had doubts as to whether or not she was smart enough to pull this off. Then she thought of Kevin, stepping in front of her to protect her from the Taz, Ducky, and Lashawn meltdown. He'd also saved her from the mermaid, after she succumbed to its song. He'd done these things instinctively, without thought for his own safety. Now, she wanted to do the same for him.

Searching the entire station took a long while, and by the time she was finished, Sarah was exhausted. She rested for a few minutes, turning once again to the first aid book, flipping to the index and searching for entries relating to what she needed. Then she fixed herself something to eat. She wasn't hungry. Far from it—her stomach cramped, threatening to revolt with each bite. She forced herself to keep it all down. She needed her strength. More importantly, for what she was about to do—if indeed she decided to go through with it—she needed a full stomach to soak up the booze.

When she was finished, Sarah took a deep breath. Then she put all of the gear into a garbage bag. She wrapped a towel around the hatchet so that the blade wouldn't poke through the plastic. Then she shrugged into her coat and hat, picked up the pistol, loaded it, and walked outside into the storm.

The descent down the slippery metal stairs seemed to take forever. She gripped the rail tightly with one hand, and clutched the pistol and the garbage bag with the other. She considered sticking the gun in her waistband to keep it dry, but decided against it. Better to have it in hand in case she needed it in a hurry. Plus, she didn't want to risk falling and having the weapon accidentally discharge.

On the way down the stairs, she kept alert for any signs of movement from the surrounding forest, but it was quiet. If the worms were still lurking out there, then they were uncharacteristically still. She wondered again where they'd gone. When she reached the ground, she proceeded with caution, ready to run or shoot at the first sign of an attack—but none was forthcoming. Her pulse pounded. Her ears rang. The rain seemed to fall harder.

Sarah reached the utility shed and after a moment's hesitation, she knocked on the door. "Kevin? You awake in there?"

Inside, something moved.

Sarah held her breath and waited for the door to open.

The sun rose over the flooded countryside, its rays barely able to penetrate the thick cloud cover or swirling mist. Fog swept down the mountain, entwining itself around the forest ranger station. It snaked through the few trees that remained upright, their roots clinging precariously to the soupy mud and fungus-covered rocks. The haze covered the dirt roads from the top of the mountain all the way down to the submerged ruins of Renick, and settled on the remains of Teddy Garnett's home, where it blanketed everything still above ground—the crashed helicopter, the shed, the outhouse, Carl Seaton's truck (which had been flipped over on its side), the cracked and pitted carport, and the jumbled ruins of the house itself.

With the exception of the ever-present rain, there was no sound.

A crow, half-starved and molting, landed on a jagged length of gutter that jutted from the mud like an accusatory finger. The bird tilted its head and scanned the wreckage of the house, looking for something to eat. It squawked when it spied a shattered jar of sunflower seeds. The contents had been scattered among the jumble of crumbling masonry and splintered lumber. The bird swooped down and eagerly pecked at the wet kernels.

Now there were two sounds—the rain, and the sound of the crow's beak as it fed.

Then, there came a third sound—a wet, slithering noise from beneath the ruins. The crow paused, struggling with internal conflict. Alarmed by the unexpected noise, it wanted to flee, but ultimately, its hunger won out. Cautiously, the bird lowered its beak—

—and the wreckage erupted. A pale, elongated shape shot out of the rubble and brushed against the bird's feathers. The touch was fleeting and light, barely glancing across the tip of its wing, but the sudden movement startled the crow. The bird took flight, soaring for the safety of a fallen apple tree. It did not notice the white curds of fungus dripping from its feathers.

The shape stretched further into the open. Fungus rippled and flexed like muscles. It was as thick and long as a man's arm, but it was not a man's arm. It had five finger-like appendages on the end of its hand, but they were not fingers. The arm, hand and fingers were just shadows—ghosts of something they'd once been. Now, they were just *soft*.

The thing struggled and pushed, and the rubble slid out of its way. Everything it touched—each brick, stone and length of wood—sprouted more of the strange white fuzz. Finally, the figure emerged from the ruins and drew itself up to its full height, standing on two fungal legs. It stretched out its arms and turned its featureless face to the sky. Raindrops pelted the places where its eyes and nose had been. All that remained of its eyes were two shadowy smudges. Its nose was non-existent. Its mouth was a gray slash. The creature tried to speak, found that it couldn't remember how, and croaked instead.

The crow, which had been watching from the fallen apple tree, fled in terror. The shape watched the bird fly away. Soon, the bird would be soft. The shape knew that was good. All things must turn soft. That was required. Required by…

…it couldn't remember.

The shape couldn't remember a lot of things. It knew that it had a name once, but it didn't know what that name was. When the shape thought about it, random images surfaced in the fungal growth that had replaced its brain. It remembered the woman hitting it in the head with her pistol. It remembered falling. Becoming one with Behemoth. But that had been interrupted, hadn't it?

What had interrupted that communion?

It recalled being shot several times. In the chest. The shoulder. Other places. But that had happened before it fell. It remembered the worms spilling out of the bullet holes. Their departure had saddened the shape. It liked the worms. They were its friend. It was their priest. The worms crawled inside the shape's head and told it things. Secret things. Things about the maze in the center of the world and the being who lived there—a being who could not be named, because to do so was to invite certain destruction. The worms told the shape about

Leviathan and Behemoth and the Great Deep. The shape shuddered at thoughts of the Great Deep. It wanted to go there. It wanted to plunge into those far-off depths and merge with them forever.

But first, it needed to become soft.

Soft...I want to be soft...Everything should be soft...the bird...the rocks...the trees...the ground...Garnett...

Garnett. The name sparked something in the creature's mind. Garnett. It had been Garnett and his friends that had stopped the shape from becoming one with Behemoth. Garnett. Seaton. The young man. The girl. It couldn't remember their names. Wasn't sure that it had ever known their names. But it remembered their faces and it remembered Teddy Garnett, and in remembering, the shape rediscovered its name. Fungal hands curled into fists.

The shape shouted its name into the sky, and was answered by thunder.

EIGHT

The first thing Henry noticed when he woke up was that he was soaking wet. The second thing he noticed was that he was lying on a slant.

Being wet was relative. He hadn't actually been dry since the rain began. The moisture seeped into everything, permeating buildings and clothes like they were tissue paper. Even if he stayed inside, the pervasive dampness in the air eventually got to him. He was always wet and always chilly, and as a result, he'd developed constant cold-like symptoms. Nothing serious. No fever or rattling in his lungs. But his nose ran a lot and he sneezed quite often. This morning was no different. The only change was that when he'd gone to sleep, his burlap sack kilt had been merely damp. Now it was soaked.

The odd angle he found himself in was more of an immediate cause for concern. He'd gone to sleep with Moxey curled up in the cardboard box next to him. Now she was gone. He propped himself up on one elbow, looking around for her, yawning, and trying to figure out what was going on. His legs tingled as if asleep and his head pounded. When Henry sat up, he realized why.

The grain silo had *moved.*

Sometime in the night, the entire structure had shifted on its base far below. The floor had sloped downward, leaving his legs at a slight angle above his head. Worse, the water filling the center of the silo had sloshed out over the rail and was running across the floor towards the open door, which was now tilted towards the ocean outside. He wondered how he'd managed to sleep through it. They were lucky the entire thing hadn't crashed into the water.

"Shit."

He shook his legs, rubbing them to get the circulation

going again, and waited a few minutes until his headache had subsided. Then he called for Moxey. She came to him, timid and nervous, walking at an angle, her claws gripping the wooden floorboards. She expressed her displeasure at this new turn of events with a weak, mournful howl. Henry pulled her to him and put the cat in his lap. Wet fur came off in his palm as he stroked her back.

"Well, I told you we were getting out of here today. I reckon this just proves it. We can't wait around any longer, girl. We've got to leave now, or else starving will be the least of our worries."

Purring, Moxey raised her head so that he could scratch under her chin.

"I just don't understand how the silo could have shifted like that. I mean, I know the bottom half is underwater, but the foundation should still be strong. It's concrete and steel. Water couldn't weaken it that quick, could it?"

He thought about the strange white fungus. From what he'd seen so far, it slowly liquefied whatever it grew on. Could it have been growing beneath the surface all this time, slowly liquefying the grain silo?

Moxey closed her eyes and snuggled closer. Henry stopped petting her.

"Don't you get too comfortable. Come on. Get up. We can't stay here."

Moxey squeaked as he gently pushed her off his lap. Henry clambered to his feet, struggling to keep his footing on the slippery, treacherous new incline. He felt the floor vibrate through the soles of his feet. Somewhere below the water, the foundation groaned. Debris fell down from the rafters—an old bird's nest, pieces of straw, and a length of rotten, moldering baling twine. Halting, Henry held his breath, expecting the entire structure to crash into the water at any second. Instead, it shuddered once and then stopped.

More brackish water splashed out of the center of the silo and swept across the floor, churning around his ankles. Moxey hissed in alarm. Moving quickly, Henry bent over and plucked her from the stream before she could be swept out the door.

Once more, he was shocked by how weightless she'd become. It was like lifting a stuffed animal, rather than a real cat.

With Moxey under one arm, Henry glanced around at their few belongings. There wasn't much. A few remaining bottles of water, the rifle, half a box of bullets, a cloth to clean off the rifle's scope, empty food wrappers, a cigarette lighter, his pocketknife, and the claw-hammer. Everything else had either been tossed into the water after his encounter with the thing in the church steeple, used to fashion the raft and his new clothes, or was worthless—like the bucket full of rusty nuts and bolts. He was pretty sure that he could fit both himself and Moxey onto the door-raft. He worried about keeping the gun and ammunition dry, but his main concern was how to paddle the raft and keep Moxey safe at the same time. If she remained in his lap, everything would be fine, but if she became frightened or nervous and tried to jump off…

Get real for a minute, he thought. *Even if I do get her to shore, I'm gonna have to carry her through the woods, all the way to Mr. Garnett's house. That'll be tough on her. Tough on me, too. Maybe it would be better to put her out of her misery now. I could do it quick....*

...and then I wouldn't have to try this on an empty stomach...

The silo shook again. This time, Henry felt it slide. He fell to the floor, dropping the cat in the process. His elbows and knees banged against the floorboards, and then he was slipping toward the open door. Henry grasped at the floor, but could find nothing to hold onto. Water gushed over him and tumbled out of the opening. Howling, Moxey scrabbled for purchase with her claws. Then, the silo tilted again, and with a final tremble, stopped shaking. His plunge halted, Henry lay on the floor, gasping breathless prayers.

Getting to his feet, Henry called Moxey to him. After making sure she wasn't injured, he glanced around for the rifle, only to find it missing. Assuming that it had washed out into the ocean with the last surge, he decided not to delay any longer. He grabbed the raft and pushed it through the open doorway. It splashed into the water and floated in place. Henry took the claw hammer and his pocketknife, and decided not to search for any of the rest of their gear. Although the lighter and the bottled water would be good things to have, another delay could cost Moxey and he their lives. Too late, he realized that he had nothing to paddle with. Frantically casting about, he noticed that one of the planks in the floor had come loose. The twelve-penny nail holding it in place had popped out, probably during one of the tremors, since they'd all been secure the day before. Using the hammer, he pried the floorboard loose. Then he slid down onto the raft. Moxey fought and struggled, and for a moment, Henry thought she might bite through his hand. But then she settled down. She trembled against him, and she wasn't purring, but neither was she trying to get away. If anything, she seemed resigned to her fate.

After making sure the cat was settled, Henry started to row. His nose wrinkled at the stench wafting from the toxic water—a nauseating mix of oil, gasoline, and chemicals. He saw a few dead bodies floating and bobbing, and many more partial corpses—severed arms or legs, an ear, and something that was either a scalp or a wig. He stayed alert for water moccasins or other snakes, but saw nothing. It was hard for him to gauge how far away the shoreline was, because of the thick mist enveloping the mountainside. Henry peered through the fog, catching glimpses of fallen trees and boulders. With his attention so focused on what lay ahead of them, he didn't notice the disturbance behind them until it was too late.

There was a tremendous splash from the rear of the craft. Water splattered them both. Moxey hissed and spat. Her claws sunk into Henry's thigh. Her attention was focused behind them. Henry pulled the makeshift oar from the water and glanced over his shoulder. A black, wheelbarrow-sized dorsal fin glided toward the raft.

Henry had time to think, *There aren't any sharks in the Greenbrier River...*

Then the creature leapt from the water and he saw that it wasn't a shark at all. It was something much worse. The thing was over ten feet long. Henry guessed that it must have weighed several hundred pounds. It was an impossibility—

half-man and half-shark. The creature's neck, arms and legs were those of a human being, but it had the head, upper body, dorsal fin, and tail of a Great White shark.

When Henry was little, his parents had let him watch *Jaws* with them once. The movie had given him nightmares for weeks after. As he watched the man-shark soar through the air, a crazy thought went through his mind.

We're gonna need a bigger raft...

The beast must have misjudged its leap, because it soared over the raft and splashed into the water on the other side. Plumes of water smashed down on Henry and Moxey, almost pressing them flat. The cat yowled and struggled, but Henry managed to keep a firm grip on her with one hand. With his other hand, he drew in the wooden plank that had served as his makeshift oar and opened his pocketknife. The weapon seemed absurdly small, and did nothing to boost his confidence or make him feel better. If anything, it merely increased his despair.

The massive dorsal fin emerged from the water again and cleaved the water as it slowly glided towards them. The pocketknife shook in Henry's trembling hand as he watched the creature approach. He had no idea how far away they still were from shore. The fog was too thick. The beast drew closer, nudging corpses, tires, and other flotsam out of the way. It began circling the raft, almost as if it were toying with them. Henry watched it pass beneath the surface—a long, gray shadow. He noticed that the thing was using both its tail and its arms and legs to propel it through the water.

It circled again and again. With each concentric pass, it narrowed the space between them. Moxey hissed and spat, her wet fur sticking up like someone had stuck her tail into an electrical socket.

Henry thought back to High School. Specifically, Mr. Young's biology class. They'd studied sharks, hadn't they? It was hard to remember, because Henry had spent more time sneaking glimpses at Jean Pearcy's boobs and playing Jewel Quest II on his cell phone than he had paying attention to the curriculum. What did he know about sharks? They had extra-sensitive hearing, right? Something about an organ called the lateral line? Yes, he remembered that now. Sharks could detect sounds and vibrations from hundreds of feet away. Their sense of smell was extra-sensitive, as well. They could smell a drop of blood for miles.

The shark completed another circle. It was close enough now that Henry could have struck it with the plank.

What else, goddamn it? Think!

Their eyes were a weak spot. So was the snout. If you hit a shark in the snout, it was supposed to hurt them. Sort of like kicking a man in the balls. That wouldn't kill them, but it would make them think twice about eating you. If he remembered correctly, you could kill a shark by stopping it from swimming. If a shark stopped swimming, it died. Henry didn't know if that rule applied to man-sharks, as well—and even if it did, this one didn't look inclined to stop anytime soon.

As if reading his thoughts, the monster's bullet-shaped head emerged from the water, stretching towards him on a thick, human neck. The man-shark regarded Henry and Moxey with black, soulless eyes. Then it opened its mouth, revealing rows of razor sharp teeth. Henry was sure that the creature was grinning.

Then it attacked, leaping once more from the foul water and grasping at the edge of the raft with its hands. The powerful jaws snapped shut, then opened again in anticipation of the weakened morsels aboard the raft. Foam and drool dripped from the corners of the creature's mouth. It pulled itself onto the silo door, and the craft tilted dangerously to one side. Henry and Moxey slid towards the open jaws. The stench wafting from the shark's mouth was revolting. It made Henry's eyes burn. He was reminded of the slaughterhouse at the nearby turkey farm.

Not nearby, you dummy. It's underwater now, like everything else. Focus on not getting eaten.

Henry slashed at the beast with his pocketknife. The blade barely grazed the creature's flesh. Moxey dug her claws into Henry's thighs and held tight. Screaming, Henry dropped the pocketknife and grabbed the claw hammer. The shark pressed down harder on the raft, trying to capsize the vessel with its weight. Henry and Moxey slid within inches of the mouth. Still shrieking, Henry swung the hammer and hit the man-shark directly under the nose. It uttered a deep, booming cry. Its breath was like a hot, foul wind. The thing released its hold on the raft. Then, roaring, it bumped the craft with its head. The raft shuddered and groaned, threatening to come apart. The floorboard that Henry had been using as an oar slipped into the water and floated out of reach. His pocketknife plunked into the depths. Henry leaned forward and struck again, this time, using the claw end of the hammer. The dull blades bit deep into the monstrosity's bulging, black eye. Pink and gray pulp squirted into the water. Blood flowed from the wound. Henry swung a third time, knocking several of the half-dollar sized teeth from the creature's mouth.

The great tail thrashed, slapping at the water, and the man-shark dove, vanishing beneath the raft. Henry held his breath and gripped Moxey tight, expecting at any moment for the creature to emerge from beneath them and smash the silo door to bits. But it didn't. Instead, the water's surface fell calm again. The waves died down. Silence returned. Moxey lay stiff and sodden in his lap, her claws still embedded in his thighs. Henry became aware once more of the rain, falling incessantly, providing background music to everything that had just occurred.

Minutes passed. Henry glanced behind them, but could no longer see the grain silo. He couldn't see much of anything. The entire landscape was enshrouded in mist. Then the raft came to a sudden, jarring halt. Henry shouted again, believing that they'd run into the shark. But then he realized that they'd run aground of something—the top of an oak tree. Its upper branches barely jutted from the water. The raft had snagged on them. He snapped one off and used it to push off from the tree and then paddle. The branch wasn't very effective, but it was better than nothing. Moxey began to relax. Henry focused on remaining alert.

They bumped over a few more trees and scraped across the

roof of a barn. Then, a few minutes later, Henry noticed that the water was getting shallow. The trees and other obstructions stuck up further. The fog parted and Henry shouted with relief when he spied dry land—although dry wasn't really accurate. More like muddy land. At this point, however, Henry didn't care.

The mountaintop rose out of the water. The raft bumped into a large rock clinging precariously to the earth behind it. After glimpsing the graffiti that had been spray-painted on the rock, Henry recognized it as the boulder that had overlooked Lil' Devil's Hole—a small cave located halfway up the mountain. Could the water really be so deep that the cavern was now at sea level? It seemed impossible.

He noticed that the strange white fungus was growing on the rock. He carefully climbed off the raft, holding Moxey tightly and making sure that neither of them came into contact with the malevolent growth. When his bare feet sank into the mud, Henry collapsed to his knees and cried tears of joy. He stroked Moxey and sobbed, shuddering as the delayed shock of everything they'd been through began to take its toll on him. He wasn't sure how long he remained there, but eventually, he felt Moxey pushing against him with her head. He glanced down. The cat was pacing back and forth. She seemed impatient.

"We made it girl. We're safe. All we have to do now is make it to Mr. Garnett's house. Then it will all be okay."

He picked up the cat and the hammer, stood, and then plodded forward. The mud squelched and sucked at him with every step. The slope was slippery. His footing treacherous. But Henry didn't mind. As far as he was concerned, it was much better than what lay behind them.

NINE

Sarah knocked a second time before the door opened.

"Good morning, sunshine."

It took Sarah a moment to respond. Kevin stood in the doorway, smiling at her, seemingly rested and refreshed. His hair was messed up and a piece of lint dangled from the stubble on his face, but otherwise, he seemed fine. Sarah took a tentative step toward him, but Kevin held up his hand.

"No, don't."

"But you look better."

Kevin's smile faded. "Looks can be deceiving. I thought I was…*soft*…better, but it grew overnight."

He stepped out of the shadows and Sarah gasped. Kevin's entire forearm was overgrown with white fuzz. The fungus ran from his elbow all the way down to his fingertips, covering his flesh like a sleeve and glove. As she watched, he raised his arm and stretched it out into the rain. As the water beat against it, he closed his eyes and sighed.

"It likes that," he said. "The fuzz. It likes the water. That feels…*soft*…good."

Sarah tried to speak, but she couldn't find the breath around the lump in her throat. She felt dizzy. Her pulse throbbed in her temples. She bit her lip until the sensation passed. She was distraught over his situation, but also disturbed by how complacent Kevin had seemingly become, rather than freaking out like he had before.

"Where'd you find the gun?"

"Upstairs," Sarah whispered.

"That's good. I heard some worms slithering around outside last night, but they don't seem to be around now. Did you see any?"

Sarah wiped raindrops and tears from her eyes and shook

her head.

"Maybe they're gone." Kevin stepped back into the doorway of the utility shed. "What's in the bag?"

"Booze. I found an unopened bottle of Bookers. I thought maybe we could have a few drinks."

He arched an eyebrow. "Kind of…*soft*…early in the morning for that, isn't it?"

Sarah shrugged. "Who pays attention to what time it is anymore? And besides, we could use a little celebration."

"What are we celebrating? That I'm infected with this… *soft*…shit? That all our friends are dead?"

"We don't know for sure. Teddy and Carl could still be alive."

"Do you really believe that, Sarah?"

She paused. "No. I guess I don't. But we're still alive, right? Like you said, there has to be a reason. We can't have gone through all of this for no reason at all. Let's drink to that, if nothing else."

"We can't share a bottle. I don't want you catching this shit from me."

"It's okay. I brought two coffee mugs. As long as the bottle doesn't touch your mug when we refill it, everything will be okay. And I brought rubber gloves and a dust mask, too. I can wear those, if it will make you feel better."

"Kind of hard to drink through a dust mask, but yeah, put the gloves on. It can't hurt. Better…*soft*…safe than sorry."

"Why do you keep saying that?" Sarah asked. "Soft. What does it mean?"

"I don't know," Kevin admitted. "It's the stuff. I think soft is what it wants to be. It wants to turn soft. I don't know how to explain it better than that. I just keep hearing it inside my head. It doesn't like hard things. It likes…*soft*…"

"I don't understand."

"Neither do I. But never mind. Let's have a drink. Who knows? Maybe alcohol will kill it."

Sarah bent over, opened the garbage bag and rummaged through it. She pulled out the whiskey, mugs, and gloves. After pulling the gloves on, she placed a coffee mug within

Kevin's reach. Then she sat down and faced the open door. Her butt and legs sank into the mud.

"I'd invite you in," Kevin said, "but that's probably not safe."

"It's okay. I'll sit here. As long as you can keep an eye out, in case one of the worms tries to sneak up behind me or something."

"I've always got your back."

"I know." The words caught in Sarah's throat. "We've been through a lot together, haven't we?"

"Yeah, we have."

Kevin was quiet for a moment. Then he observed, "You cut your hair."

"Yeah. Last night."

Sarah unscrewed the bottle of Bookers and poured some into each of their mugs. Her hands shook as she dispensed the whiskey. The bottle tapped against the rims of the mugs.

"You okay?" Kevin asked.

"I'm fine. Just feeling a little emotional. Thinking about the past."

Kevin reached for the mug with his good hand. He raised it into the air.

"To Teddy and Carl. Let's hope they're in a better place now. Someplace dry."

Sarah picked up her mug and echoed the toast. "To Teddy and Carl."

Kevin tilted his head back and drained the mug. While his attention was diverted, Sarah quickly dumped the contents of her mug onto the ground. Her original plan had been to fill her stomach with food, to soak up the booze, so that Kevin would get drunk quicker than she did. But as long as he was distracted, she figured she'd try it this way. The less booze she had in her system, the better. The rain washed the whiskey away before Kevin was finished. He smacked his lips and put the mug back down on the ground.

"Damn, that's good stuff."

"Yeah," Sarah agreed. "It is."

"How about another?"

"Coming right up."

Sarah glanced at the garbage bag, and saw the outline of the hatchet through the thin plastic. She poured two more shots, and tried not to sob. She was careful not to let the bottle touch the rim of Kevin's mug. When she was finished, Kevin raised his mug again.

"Can we toast Lori this time?"

Sarah nodded. "Sure. I'd like that."

"Okay. To Lori. I miss you, baby. So much has happened since then, and I don't think I've really had time to process it all. I still can't believe that you're gone. Maybe I'll see you soon."

While he drank, Sarah dumped her whiskey again.

"You don't have to keep doing that," Kevin said.

Startled, Sarah dropped the coffee mug. It fell into the mud with a squelching sound. Dirty water splattered her already wet clothes.

"W-what?"

"You don't have to fake it. I'm not…*soft*…stupid, Sarah. I saw what you just did. And I saw the other…*soft*…stuff inside the garbage bag when you opened it—the medical supplies and the kerosene and…" His voice dropped to a whisper. "And the hatchet."

"How did you…?"

"The bag looked a little too…*soft*…heavy and bulky for just a bottle of whiskey and some coffee mugs."

Sarah picked up her coffee mug and wiped the mud off it. When she looked at Kevin again, he was grinning at her. It was a sad, haunted expression, and when he spoke again, his voice echoed of resignation.

"I know what you're up to, Sarah. I know what you're planning."

"Kevin, I don't—"

"You're going to get me drunk, knock me out, and then amputate my arm. Right?"

She paused, unsure of what to say next. How did he really know what she was planning? Was Kevin merely guessing? And if he had indeed guessed her intentions, why was he reacting so calmly? If the situation had been reversed, Sarah knew that she'd be fighting and screaming.

"Give me another refill," Kevin said. "Hell, if you're not going to drink any, just pass me the entire bottle."

Without a word, Sarah leaned close to the doorway and sat the whiskey bottle down in front of him. She caught a faint whiff of mildew—not from the shed, but from Kevin himself. He smelled musty and damp, like clothing that had been left in a flooded basement. After she leaned back, Kevin picked up the bottle with his fungus-covered hand and tipped it to his mouth. He drank long and deep, gasping and grimacing when he'd finished. The liquor glistened on his lips.

"God, that feels good. It's all...*soft*...warm in my belly, you know? I'm kind of surprised, though."

"About what?"

"I figured the fuzz wouldn't like alcohol. Figured I'd pay for drinking that. It can do that—reward and punish. It wants water. The more water it gets, the quicker it can liquefy me."

Sarah gasped. "*Liquefy* you?"

"Yeah."

"But, we saw dozens of infected people back in Baltimore, and Teddy said that he'd seen a deer with it, as well. None of them liquefied."

"How do we know? We weren't there to see their ends, were we? Every time somebody infected rowed up alongside the Marriott, Juan, Mike, Lee and the others sent them away so that the rest of us wouldn't get it."

"But how do you know that's what the fuzz is doing to you?"

"Maybe that's what it means by soft." Kevin shook his head. "I can't explain it. I just know. Maybe it's some kind of weird symbiosis. Maybe me and the fungus share a consciousness now. It certainly feels that way, at least. This shit isn't just mold. It's intelligent. It has thoughts of its own."

"Maybe that's just some sort of hallucinogenic side-effect."

"I don't think so. Trust me. You're not inside my head. But the white fuzz is. All I know is that it wants to liquefy me, and it needs water to finish the job. Water helps it break my body down chemically. Food halts that effect. I tried eating a little last night, and it made me so sick, I thought I'd die right here on the floor of the shed. When I don't do what it wants, the fuzz hurts me. It's like little jolts of electricity in each of my nerve endings. Only thing that makes it stop is if I go stand out in the rain, or drink some water. This shit itches, too. It's taking everything I can do right now not to scratch myself until I fucking bleed. Every time I try to scratch, the fungus releases something into my bloodstream. I don't know what. Maybe a sedative or something, because it makes me sleepy. Anyway, bottoms up!"

He winked at her, and then took another long swig from the bottle.

"Kevin, are you *Kevin* right now?"

Kevin snorted, spraying whiskey from his mouth. Sarah flinched, inching away so that the droplets wouldn't splatter on her. Then she looked him in the eye.

"What are you talking about, Sarah? I'm still me. Just a little uglier is all. Good thing Lori can't see me now, huh?"

"Your speech has changed," Sarah said, trying to keep her tone calm. "Your Baltimore accent is gone, and for the last few minutes, you haven't said 'soft'. You were saying it so much before that you sounded like a broken record."

Kevin took another sip and shrugged. "I don't know. Maybe I'm more in control again. Maybe the alcohol makes it go dormant or something. If so, that's bad news for my liver, because I'll be the biggest fucking alcoholic left on the planet."

Sarah did not laugh with him. Instead, she blinked back tears and stared at the mud between them. When Kevin noticed her silence, he followed her gaze to their feet. Both of them paused.

While they'd been talking, the white fuzz growing on Kevin's arm had sent a pale, tendril-like root from his wrist to the floor, and then out through the open doorway. The appendage was no thicker than an electrical extension cord. The tip had burrowed into the sodden ground. Tiny feelers, as fine as Sarah's hair, had sprouted from the root and were slowly inching their way toward her. Sarah watched them with a strange sense of calm. They reminded her of the worms. She tightened her grip on the pistol.

"Jesus fucking Christ!" Kevin reached out with his free hand, grabbed the root just below his elbow, and pulled. It stretched, but held fast. Gritting his teeth, he tugged harder, ripping the tendril away. Patches of his skin and hair came with it. Kevin threw back his head and screamed. He dropped the dismembered growth into the mud. Blood poured from his wound, but Sarah noticed that it was thin and watery.

"Oh fuck," Kevin wailed. "Oh fuck me running, that fucking hurts!"

Sarah stood up, clutching the pistol in one hand. "Hang on. I've got gauze in the bag."

"Gauze? What good is gauze, Sarah? A fucking bandage isn't going to do shit."

Sarah glanced down at the tendril. The feelers had stopped moving. It lay there in the mud, lifeless—or waiting. Slowly, she took a few steps backward and relaxed her grip on the handgun. She switched the weapon to her other hand and flexed her fingers. Her hand had cramped. In the doorway, Kevin gasped and thrashed, obviously in pain.

"Did you know it was trying to do that?" she asked.

"No. Hell, no! I told you, it's got a mind of its own." He paused, covered his mouth and coughed. When he took his hand away, his palm and lips were crimson.

"You're spitting up blood."

"I don't think the fuzz likes whiskey very much. Oh, fuck this hurts!"

Sarah's heart broke at the pain in her friend's voice. With one hand, she brushed rain and tears from her eyes.

"You've got to do it," Kevin pleaded. "I'm gonna chug this fucking bottle, and lets hope like hell that it knocks me out. If it doesn't, then do it anyway."

"Kevin—"

"Promise me, Sarah."

She stared at him.

"Promise me…*soft*!"

Slowly, Sarah nodded. "Okay, I promise."

"You got a belt or something to tie me…*soft*…off with so I don't bleed to death? Because that would be a real bitch if you cut off the fuzz and then I died anyway."

She nodded again. "I brought everything—disinfectant, a tourniquet, a way to cauterize it. I read up on it in the medical book the forest rangers had up there."

"Damn, you did think of everything. Ah, fuck—it's like knives in my gut. And in my…*soft*…head. Okay. Jesus, I'm scared now. I wonder what it will be like, when I wake up?"

Sarah looked away, pretending to search the tree line for any lurking worms. She bit her lip so hard that it bled. If Kevin noticed, he gave no indication.

"Maybe it won't be so bad," he said. "Having one arm. At least I'll still be…*soft*…alive, right? That's more than you can say for ninety-eight percent of the rest of the world's population. Okay, let's do this before I chicken out, or before the fuzz tries to stop us."

"Okay," Sara agreed. "And Kevin?"

"What?"

"I'm sorry."

"Don't be…*soft*…sorry. It has to be done. Just promise me you'll do it quick. I don't know what I'll do if I wake up… *soft*…and you're still hacking at my arm."

He brought the bottle to his lips and began to chug. Whiskey dribbled down his chin.

And that was when Sarah raised the pistol and squeezed the trigger. The first round shattered the bottle and most of Kevin's jaw. Fragments of glass and teeth flew through the air. The second shot hit Kevin in the left eye, knocking him backward. He toppled to the floor, his upper half hidden in the utility shed's shadowy interior.

Sarah snapped the pistol around and placed the still smoking barrel against her head. It singed the skin around her temple. The smell of cordite was strong. Her ears rang. Trembling, she stroked the trigger. Then she dropped the gun, collapsed to her knees in the mud, and shrieked at the sky. Above her, the thunder answered.

The rain fell harder.

TEN

Moxey was growing restless. She squirmed in Henry's arms, stretching her legs and pressing her claws against his chest and biceps. She hadn't actually clawed him—at least, not yet, but she was clearly unhappy with being carried as he slogged through the mud.

"I can't put you down, girl. You're weak. You ain't had nothing to eat for God knows how long. And look around us. You don't want to walk in this shit, anyway."

The cat squeaked feebly in response—lacking the strength to even meow properly. But she lay still again and snuggled up against him. A moment later, Henry felt her start purring. He lowered his chin against her wet fur and rested it there as they walked. The hammer dangled from the strips of burlap holding his makeshift kilt together. He'd placed it there so that he could hold onto Moxey with both hands. The handle banged against his thigh with every step.

Henry couldn't stop shivering. The rain beat down on them relentlessly. Wisps of fog hung thick in the air. Between the two, it was hard to see more than a few feet in any direction—but Henry was glad for that, because what he saw terrified him in ways that fungus zombies and half-human sharks hadn't.

Everything he'd known was gone, and what remained was no longer recognizable. After stumbling around for a while, he'd managed to find the winding, one-lane road that led from Renick and the valley up the mountain to Punkin' Center. Much of the blacktop was concealed beneath a thick layer of mud, rocks and other debris. Before the rains, one side of the road had been bordered by pastures and cornfields and soybean fields. Those were gone now. The steady downpour had eroded the vegetation and the topsoil, exposing the layer of clay that ran deep beneath the ground. The clay was like quicksand. Uprooted trees and huge chunks of gray rock jutted from it in places. The rest of it looked like rust-colored soup. The few shacks and houses that had dotted this portion of the mountain were also gone. The other side of the road had once been a steep drop straight down the forested mountainside, with only a steel guardrail to act as a buffer. When he'd been younger, Henry used to get dizzy every time he looked over the side. Now, the chasm was flooded. Brown water rushed past far below, pushing trees, cars, dead cattle, and other flotsam in its wake. The mountainside itself had been stripped bare of trees. All of them had fallen over—their roots unable to retain a purchase in the sodden ground.

In addition to the widespread destruction, Henry noticed something odd. Threading across the landscape were a series of trenches and furrows, as if a group of large gophers had been tunneling through the mountain. The smallest mound was the size of a dog. The biggest was larger than a school bus, and had collapsed inward, filling with water. Henry didn't know what they were or what could have made them. He hoped that he wouldn't have to find out.

Maybe it's those giant worms I saw in my dreams.

A week ago, he would have scoffed at this thought, but he had dreamed about the half-man, half-shark, too, and now he knew that they were real. Why couldn't the worms be real, as well?

The white fuzz was ever-present—growing on fallen trees, rocks, and even in the mud itself. He chose his steps with care, not wanting to come into accidental contact with it. Henry wondered how fast the fungus grew, and how long it would take for it to cover the entire mountainside. Worse, what would happen once it did? Could an entire mountain turn into water, the way Mr. Burke had? How was such a thing possible?

At one point, the wind picked up for a few minutes and the fog cleared. He glanced back down into the valley. All that remained above the floodwaters were the Presbyterian Church steeple and Fred Laudermilk's grain silo. Both structures jutted upward like the fingers of a drowning man.

Henry shivered, thinking about what had happened in both. He half expected the silo to collapse into the water while he watched, but it didn't. Then the breeze died down and the mist descended again, swallowing his view. Henry turned around and continued up the mountain. Mud squished between his toes. Rocks jabbed at his bare feet.

The road began to level out as they approached Punkin Center. Surprisingly, many of the tiny town's buildings were still standing. Carl Seaton's combination post office and feed store had collapsed into a sinkhole, and two of the seven houses along the road had fallen down, but the barns and other houses remained upright—albeit in bad shape. Many were missing roofs, or had collapsed walls. Two of the houses were slowly sinking into the ground. He saw evidence of the white mold growing on all of them. Most of the trees, while still upright, tilted dangerously to one side. Henry steered clear of them. The last thing he or Moxey needed was to be trapped beneath a falling tree.

Henry re-adjusted Moxey, putting her in the crook of one arm, and then cupped his hand around his mouth.

"Hello? Anybody here? Hello?"

There was no answer, save the steady drumming of the rain. He hadn't really expected one, even as he hoped he'd hear one anyway. The National Guard had evacuated everybody in Punkin Center when they evacuated Renick and Frankford.

Except for Mr. Garnett, he thought. *Teddy is still here. I saw him. All we've gotta do is make it to his place. Then everything will be okay.*

He considered going into one of the houses that was still standing upright. Most of the people in these parts had gardens during the summer and canned their produce for use during the winter months. Surely, one of the basements or storm cellars would have food in them. At the very least, he could find some dry clothes to wear—something other than the wet burlap he was currently wearing. And a better weapon, too—something other than the claw hammer. But then he eyed the sickly pale growth covering the homes' exteriors, and decided against exploring them further. Getting food or clothing wouldn't do him much good if he ended up infected. He could wait until he made it to Mr. Garnett's place.

His stomach grumbled as another jolt of pain rumbled through it. Gritting his teeth, Henry hugged Moxey tight and walked on—unaware that he was being followed.

His pursuers waited until Henry rounded the bend. Then they crept forward, following his trail. One of them had once been a deer. Another had been a red fox. Another a dog. Three of them had once been human, including Tammy Lapp, who'd gone to school with Henry. Now, they were something else. All of them were infected. The white fuzz covered them from head to toe. Soon they would be soft. All of them had been attracted by Henry's shouts. They'd resisted the urge to attack, choosing instead to follow him in the hopes that he was part of a larger group. If so, then that group would become soft, as well.

They encountered more of their kind as they followed their prey. The newcomers fell in step, joining the fray. They moved slowly, careful not to become *too* soft. They wanted to. They ached for it—craved the moment when they could just fall apart and melt. Soon. But not quite yet. The worms, having done their part, were gone from the planet. Now it was their turn, and there was still much to do.

When he reached the narrow, gravel lane leading to Teddy Garnett's home, Henry paused to catch his breath. They had traveled by foot for a long time, and he was exhausted. He'd had to negotiate his way around fallen trees, vast pools of water, and numerous mudslides, all while grappling to keep his hold on the cat. His bare feet were raw and nicked from all of the debris he'd stepped on during his trek up the mountainside. Luckily, the thick mud acted as a salve, stopping all the cuts from bleeding. His wet burlap kilt clung to his skinny frame. The coarse material made his skin itch. He held Moxey in the crook of one arm and scratched with his free hand. Each time he did, he glanced down, paranoid that he'd find a weird critter crawling on him or that white fungus, rather than just a red, irritated spot from the burlap.

Moxey clung to him, her claws pricking his skin. She shivered constantly, and hadn't made any sound since they'd entered Punkin' Center. He stroked her wet fur and tried to console her.

"It's gonna be okay, girl. We're almost there. Then we'll find you something to eat."

He wondered what they'd do if Mr. Garnett's house was covered with the fungus, the way the buildings in Punkin' Center had been. The only other options were crazy Earl Harper's shack, or the Forest Ranger station up on Bald Knob. The latter was probably deserted, and the former was a place he'd rather avoid at all costs. Earl Harper was mean as a copperhead snake, and Henry was scared of him. He had to believe that Mr. Garnett was okay. After all, he'd appeared fine when Henry had spotted him across the water.

Readjusting his hold on Moxey, Henry started down the lane. Gravel poked his feet with each step. He stepped over broad ruts that had been formed by the water. The ditches on each side of the road were full of rushing, brown water, and the fields were flooded. In another day or two, the lane would be flooded, too. He peered ahead, looking for any sign that Mr. Garnett was home, but thick, swirling fog concealed the house.

About halfway down the lane, Henry came to a sudden stop. There was something lying in the middle of the road. Three pieces of what looked like raw meat, each about the size of a beagle. Henry approached them cautiously, and gagged at the unexpected stench—a nauseating mix of decomposition, ammonia, and fish. After a closer examination, Henry realized what they were—severed sections of a monstrous worm. The frayed ends of the rubbery segments had clear tire treads embedded in the pale flesh.

"Holy cow…"

Water pooled around the corpse, and the all-too-familiar white mold floated atop the puddles like mutant lily pads. The root-like strands seemed to be emanating from the dead worm's body. Henry made a wide berth around them, and continued on his way. The mist parted as he neared the end of the lane, and when it did, Henry gasped.

Mr. Garnett's house was destroyed. All that remained was rubble—burned and splintered wooden beams, broken concrete blocks, and scorched bricks. Henry tried to fathom what had happened. It looked like there had been an explosion of some kind—certainly a fire, at the very least. But the ruins also looked sunken, as if a great pit had opened beneath part of the structure and tried to swallow it up. It was almost as if the piles of debris were jutting up from a pool of quicksand. The surrounding yard was flooded, and the few sections of ground that remained above the water were riddled with more of the strange tunnels he'd seen earlier. The only part of the house that had escaped the destruction was the carport.

Henry stumbled toward the ruins, slipped in the mud, and almost fell. He struggled to keep his balance, accidentally dropping Moxey in the process. She yowled her displeasure, and then darted towards the rubble, hissing and spitting.

"Moxey, get back here!"

Henry chased after her as fast as he could, ignoring the pain in his feet. Moxey scrambled up a mound of collapsed masonry and perched atop the arm of a couch that was sticking out of the center of the pile. She licked herself and pointedly ignored him. Henry reached her, out of breath, and started to scold the cat for running away. His words were halted by a sound from deeper within the ruins. Something shifted, sending bricks and lumber and roofing tiles sliding to the ground.

"H-hello? Is somebody there?"

More debris was pushed aside. Henry peered into the swirling fog and saw a figure crawling from the wreckage.

"Mr. Garnett? Is that you?"

The figure spoke. Its voice was a coarse whisper. *"Who... is...it?"*

"It's me...Henry Garrett. Are you okay? Are you hurt?"

The shadowy form rose to its full height. Henry was relieved to see that they were human. For a moment, he'd almost been convinced that it was another man-shark.

"Are you hurt?" he asked again. "Moxey and I came

looking for you. You remember her, don't you? My cat? We've been holed up at the top of Fred Laudermilk's old grain silo. We saw you come down the mountain but we couldn't get to you."

"Sssssssss...."

"Mr. Garnett?"

The figure shuffled toward him. Moxey arched her back and hissed.

"Teddy?"

"No...not Garnett...soft...you little...shit bag..."

"Earl Harper," Henry tried to disguise the sudden tremble in his voice. He hated the sound. "What the hell is wrong with you?"

Then the thing that had been Earl Harper emerged from the ruins and Henry saw for himself what was wrong with him. Arms outstretched, the thing lumbered forward. Henry was surprised at its speed. Before he could act, the creature seized Moxey from her perch amongst the debris and lifted her into the air. Weakened, she howled and scratched, but her efforts to defend herself did not deter her attacker. Moxey's claws ripped through the pale fungus. Water dribbled from the cuts.

"Put her down, you fucker!"

Earl laughed. Even as Henry charged him, his root-like fingers bored into Moxey, burrowing through fur and skin. Blood welled from the wounds. The cat's howls reached a frenzied, frantic pitch. Earl flexed his arms and ripped Moxey in half. Henry screamed as parts of her splashed into the mud. The puddles turned red. Earl tossed the halves aside and beckoned Henry forward.

"That'ssss...right. Come get...soft...some."

Henry skidded to a stop. He was nearly overwhelmed with rage. His ears burned, his lips felt thick and swollen, and his pulse pounded behind his temples and in his throat. But his survival instinct overrode his anger. The creature wanted him to charge—wanted him within arm's reach. Only then could it infect him, just like Mr. Burke had tried to do. That was why Earl had killed Moxey.

"Come…on…," it urged with a phlegmatic gurgle. *"Here…kitty kitty…kitty…"*

Henry shook his head and backed away, trying very hard to resist the morbid compulsion to glance down at Moxey's body. Some part of him was convinced that she was still alive—that if he could just get to her, he could scoop her up and put her back together again and make her good as new. He opened his mouth to breathe and heard someone screaming. After a moment, he realized that it was him.

Earl clambered over a mound of broken masonry and reached for him. Henry retreated, more through instinct than any conscious act. It was hard to focus on anything other than Moxey. He couldn't get the image of what had just happened to her out of his head. He stumbled backward, almost tripping over the scorched and cracked remains of a microwave oven. Laughing, the creature pursued him.

Henry glanced around the wreckage, searching for a weapon. A photo of Mr. and Mrs. Garnett stared up at him. The glass in the frame had shattered and raindrops pelted the photograph. Soon, the rain would wash them away. Henry paused, intent on rescuing Teddy before that happened.

What the heck is wrong with me? It's just a photograph! Moxey…I should rescue Moxey instead.

The world stopped. The rain ceased. Earl fell silent. The only sound was Henry's heartbeat. He took a deep breath, flexed his fingers, curled them into fists…

…and then the world came rushing back again. The rain was cold on his skin. Earl's mocking laughter turned into a howl. Henry spun around, alarmed. The creature was only inches away from him. Ducking, he scrambled away as Earl grasped at him. The mold-covered fingers clawed the air, instead of Henry's arm.

"Basssstard…"

"You killed my cat, you asshole!"

"No…your…cat is now…soft…"

Henry jumped over a pile of splintered wooden beams. His bare feet squelched in the mud. Something sharp punctured his heel, but he barely noticed. Gritting his teeth, he picked up a length of pipe and faced his opponent. Before he could swing, however, he saw more of the creatures stumbling out of the mist. Most of them were human. He'd known them in the past, before the rain had come. He was surprised to see Tammy Lapp among them. Henry had a crush on her when they were in middle school. She'd been beautiful once, but that beauty was now lost beneath the white fuzz growing on her cheeks. The fungus had already engulfed the rest of her body, bulging out from beneath the tattered remains of her clothing. In addition to the infected humans, there were other creatures that the fungus had taken over—a deer, a fox, several dogs, and even a few cows.

"My Lord," Henry whispered. "Oh my Lord."

"Henry," Tammy rasped. *"Don't...fight...it's so nice..."*

Earl crept closer. He stepped on the picture of Teddy and his wife, leaving a moldy footprint on the photograph. Over the creature's shoulder, Henry spotted Moxey's remains.

"I'm sorry, girl. I'm so sorry."

Then he flung the pipe at Earl, turned around, and fled into the mist. Blinded by tears, he heard the monsters give chase. Spurred on, Henry wiped his eyes and ran faster. Starved, thirsty, wet, nearly naked, and bleeding from dozens of cuts and scratches, he felt like stopping—just kneeling there in the mud and allowing them to catch him. After all, Tammy had said it was nice, hadn't she? And maybe it was. At the very least, he could be with Moxey again. All he had to do was stop running. Then Earl made a hooting cry and Henry shuddered. No. No way would he allow himself to become one of those things. He could avenge Moxey by living long enough to fight them on his own terms.

Determined to do just that, Henry fled toward Bald Knob and the forest ranger tower.

ELEVEN

Kevin was dead but the rain kept falling. Sarah hated the rain's indifference. She hated how it remained steady and constant even as the rest of the world fell apart around her. She loathed the feel of it on her body and her scalp. She cringed when she felt it in her lungs as she breathed or tasted it on her tongue when she spoke.

Sarah stood in front of the ranger station's huge window, looking outside but not really seeing. She felt drunk, even though she wasn't. Her ears and eyes burned, and her vision was blurry. She swayed back and forth, unable to keep her balance. She'd had the presence of mind to strip out of her wet clothing, but lacked the strength or desire to put on something dry. Naked, she shivered. When she raised a hand and touched the window, she noticed that her hand was trembling—but not from the cold.

"I like you, Mr. Window. We've got a lot in common, you and me."

The window didn't answer, but she hadn't really expected it to. Sarah giggled. The sound was very small inside the large circular room. Using her index finger, she drew a smiley face on the glass. She frowned, remembering Carl Seaton doing the same thing in Teddy Garnett's kitchen just a few days ago. Sighing, Sarah drew a bullet hole in the smiley face's forehead. Then, as an afterthought, she drew several squiggly lines around it—worms with cheerful expressions. Choking off another round of laughter, Sarah stepped back and admired her handiwork.

The glass was fogged. So was her brain.

The glass was damp with rain. Her cheeks were damp with tears.

The glass was strong and unbroken. She was…she didn't know what she was anymore, but she certainly wasn't unbroken.

People who were whole and complete and balanced and unbroken didn't leave friends behind—especially when those friends were kindly, gentle old men under attack from giant, carnivorous worms. People who were whole and unbroken didn't shoot their only remaining friend in the head, either. Nor did they try to burn the friend's remains, or set fire to the utility shed where the friend's remains lay, or get pissed off and scream at the sky when the rain kept putting the fires out.

What had happened to her? Who was this new Sarah and where had she come from? Had she always been this way, or was this simply a reaction to everything she'd been through over the last few months?

Until now, Sarah had only felt guilty over one thing in life. When she was younger, she'd kissed Erin Godfrey in the high school auditorium. They'd both had bit parts in the Senior musical—*Annie Get Your Gun*. They'd been backstage. The lights were out and no one was around. One thing had led to another, and they kissed. It was the first time Sarah had ever kissed a girl, and the experience was scary and exciting and right. For the first time in her life, she'd felt like she belonged. Felt safe. Then a bunch of jocks who'd been drinking behind an unused bit of scenery leftover from the school play had laughed and taunted them—calling them dykes and lesbians and shouting out crude suggestions of what they should do next. Terrified, Sarah had fled, leaving Erin to stand there alone. Tears in her eyes, she'd run out into the parking lot, hopped in her car, and driven out to the lake, where she spent the night curled up in her backseat, her stomach a ball of dread.

For the rest of the school year, whenever she was asked about it, Sarah had denied that the kiss was reciprocal. She insisted that she'd been minding her own business and that Erin had forced herself on her, and that she'd then pushed her away. She avoided Erin in the halls. And when Erin's hurt and reproachful eyes got to be too much, Sarah changed classes just to get away. She'd always felt guilty about that. Years later, she'd even tried to track Erin down and apologize to her. But Erin didn't want to be found. Sarah had always held out hope that they'd meet again at their high school reunion, and she'd be able to make things right. In the fantasy, they'd kiss again, but this time there would be no fear or shame.

Except that there would never be a high school reunion. There would be no reunions of any kind. Not with Erin. Not with any of her other girlfriends. Not with her family or friends. Not with Teddy and Carl. And now, not with Kevin.

She hadn't intended to kill him. That hadn't been her plan. Sarah had been sure that she could amputate the infected limb and cauterize the wound before the white fuzz spread any farther. But when she'd spoken to Kevin, looked him in the eyes and heard his voice—and saw the fungus moving on its own—instinct had taken over.

Instinct.

It was instinct that had kept her alive so far. Instinct that had allowed her to survive the slide from civil unrest into total anarchy that had accompanied the early flooding. It was instinct that had led her to the Marriott hotel—one of the highest points in Baltimore. It was instinct that had allowed her to survive Leviathan's attack of the building, and to escape in the raft with Kevin and Salty. Instinct had kept her sane when they were captured by the cultists in Greenbank, and had allowed her to escape once more. Instinct had helped her survive the helicopter crash, attacks from both Earl and Behemoth, and the long trek from Teddy's home to here. Now it had helped her survive again, and all she'd had to do was murder her friend. She was alive, and all it had cost her was death.

"I'm alone now," she whispered. "It's just you and me, Mr. Window. Just you and me and the little mouse I saw running around in here earlier. And sooner or later, I'll probably have to kill him too, because although there's a lot of food in this tower, it can't last forever, right?"

She stared at the window. Her condensation doodle was already fading as the glass fogged again.

"No. Nothing lasts forever. Except me. I can't seem to fucking die, even though I want to. I couldn't even shoot myself. I wanted to, Mr. Window. As soon as I pulled the trigger on Kevin, I wanted nothing more than to pull it on myself. But I couldn't. Something inside of me just wouldn't let me do it. And now I'm alone."

Exhausted, Sarah crossed the floor and sagged into one of the chairs. She eyed the forest ranger uniforms, all clean and dry and neatly folded. She considered putting one on, but then decided not to bother. Maybe she'd catch pneumonia and die from that, since she couldn't seem to kill herself any other way. And besides, it wasn't like there was anyone else to see her in the nude.

"All alone," she repeated. "All alone."

Sarah leaned back in the chair, closed her eyes, and began humming The Church's 'Under the Milky Way Tonight'. In year's past, the song had always brought her peace.

And that was when she heard footsteps pounding up the metal staircase outside. They stopped in front of the door. There was a brief pause, and then something thumped against the door. The knob rattled again, more forcefully this time. Sarah jumped out of the chair and dropped into a crouch. She glanced around, searching for the gun, unable to remember where she'd put it. The door shook in its frame.

Did I lock it? I must have. Otherwise, whoever...whatever is out there wouldn't be having so much trouble opening—

The door crashed open and a figure lunged into the room. Shrieking, Sarah scrambled backward and ducked behind the chair. The figure answered her scream with one of its own. Sarah peeked up over the top of the chair. The bedraggled intruder was a young man—maybe seventeen or eighteen years old. He was dressed in some kind of makeshift burlap kilt. His arms and legs were covered with mud and blood, and there were dark circles under his eyes. The boy's cheekbones were sunken and his scalp showed through his wet hair. His skin was too pale, his arms and legs too thin. She could see his ribs sticking out beneath the soaked burlap. If he was infected with the fuzz, she couldn't see it.

Spotting her, the intruder held his arms out. Water dripped from his fingertips and elbows. He let out a strangled, sobbing cry and said something that sounded like "Moxey."

Sarah spied the pistol laying on top of the communication

equipment to her left. Taking a deep breath, she darted out from behind the chair and grabbed it. The boy stumbled backward toward the door. Holding the weapon in both hands, Sarah pointed it at his chest and spread her feet apart shoulder-width.

"Freeze! You take one more step and I'll blow your fucking lungs out the back of your chest."

Eyes wide, he thrust his hands higher. "Don't shoot. Please. The bastard killed my Moxey."

"Who are you? What do you want?"

"My name's…" The boy paused, blinking. Then his mouth fell open. "You…you're naked!"

"So are you, sunshine. Now what the hell are you doing here?"

He stared at her breasts for a moment, and then his gaze traveled down to her crotch. The boy sighed. Then his attention focused on her breasts again. Suddenly self-conscious, Sarah relaxed her shooter's stance and brought her legs together. Then she waggled the pistol.

"Those are my tits. Not my ears or eyes. I'm up here, asshole. If you need to gawk at something, look at my gun."

He jerked his head up and stared into her eyes. His Adam's apple bobbed up and down.

"You're bleeding," Sarah said. "Are you okay? Did the worms attack you or something?"

"Worms?" He frowned. "No, the only worm I saw was a dead one. Biggest damn worm I've ever seen. I wouldn't want to come across a live one. They'd make good bait down in the river, though. A person could catch Old One-Eye with one of them."

By his accent and his reference to the same fishing hole legend that Teddy had once mentioned, Sarah made the youth for a local. But who was he? Teddy and Carl had seemed convinced that everyone else in the area was either dead or evacuated by the National Guard—except for Earl Harper, of course. But even Earl was dead now. Sarah studied the intruder closely. He was unarmed, and clearly in bad shape. Weakened, distraught, and just as scared as she was. Crazy? Perhaps. But he didn't seem threatening. She didn't lower the gun, but when she spoke again, her voice was softer.

"Look, kid. You barged in here and scared the hell out of me. Why don't we start over. Who are you?"

"My name's Henry Garrett."

"Nice to meet you, Henry. My name is Sarah. Where did you come from?"

"Me and Moxey were living in the top of Mr. Laudermilk's grain silo."

Sarah shook her head. "I don't know where that is. I'm not from around here."

"I didn't think you were. Never seen you around before. And you ain't got an accent. How did you end up here?"

"It's a long story. Why don't you finish telling me yours first?"

"We were in the silo. It's in Renick, down yonder at the bottom of the mountain. We had to leave. We were starving, and there were…things. So we left. I carried Moxey once we made it to land."

"Is Moxey your girlfriend?"

"No. She's my…was my…cat." His voice choked and his eyes welled up. "She was so weak. Like I said, we were hungry. I knew that Mr. Garnett was alive, so we—"

"Mr. Garnett? You mean Teddy?"

Henry flinched. "Yeah. You know him?"

Sarah nodded, and the boy continued.

"We made it to his house. I cut the hell out of my feet on the way there."

"Did you find Teddy? Is he okay?"

"No." Henry's expression darkened. "The whole place was in ruins. Looked like something smashed it flat. An explosion, maybe?"

Sarah lowered the gun, and sagged backward, leaning against the radio equipment.

"I didn't see his body," Henry said. "Reckon he could have escaped. Mr. Garnett was a tough old bird."

"Yeah. Yeah, he was." She wiped her nose with the back of her hand. "So how did you end up here? And where's your cat?"

"Earl got her."

"Earl? You don't mean Earl Harper? Don't tell me that crazy son of a bitch is still alive."

"I'm afraid so," Henry said. "You know him, too?"

"We've met. He hurt your cat?"

"He…killed her. And he's not right anymore. Not that he was ever right to begin with. But he's changed. He's not the same. There's something wrong with him. It might sound crazy, but he's got this white fungus growing all over him. I ran away after he…after Moxey, but I'm worried that he might be following me here. That's why I was trying to get inside—so I could hide."

Sarah stood up. "He's coming here?"

"Maybe," Henry said. "And I'll tell you something else. He's not alone. There's a whole bunch of people out there who have the same stuff growing on them. Animals, too."

"And they're all heading this way?"

"Yeah." Henry shrugged. "I reckon they will be."

"Shit…"

"They move pretty slow. I reckon it will be a while before they arrive. You got any ideas on what to do when they get here?"

Sarah sighed. "We'll see."

The first thing they did was get dressed. After he'd cleaned himself up, Sarah gave Henry the last clean pair of the spare forest ranger uniforms. The outfit hung loose over his emaciated frame. While Henry looked at himself in the mirror, Sarah turned away, stifling a grin. A few months ago, she would have found the sight horrible rather than darkly comical, but a lot had changed since then, including her.

Using the first aid kit, Sarah tended to Henry's cuts and bruises as best she could. Judging by his reaction, she guessed that the youth missed his mother. She didn't ask him what had happened to his family. She didn't have to. In this world, it was a safe bet that they were now worm food. Or mermaid food. Or worse.

Henry talked while he ate. Clearly ravenous, he wolfed the food down with both hands, shoveling it into his mouth and speaking between bites in short, clipped sentences. He told her of his harrowing journey from Renick to Teddy's house, and what had happened when he arrived there. His expression darkened when he talked about the death of his cat, but the mood passed as he turned his attention back to the meal. Henry punctuated his story with grunts and groans of pleasure as he ate. His lips kept smacking together. Sarah wasn't sure if the teen was even aware that he was doing it.

As she watched and listened, Sarah considered her new companion. Despite his age and physical condition, Henry was obviously tough. Assuming his story was true—and she had no reason to believe otherwise—then he'd been through as much shit as she had, and appeared to be holding up just as well. Strong and resilient—he reminded her of Kevin. Her stomach lurched, and for a moment, Sarah thought she might vomit. The memory of shooting him played through her head like a film. Biting her lip, Sarah wiped a single tear from her eye and focused on Henry again. If he noticed her emotional reaction, he didn't mention it. She smiled and nodded at him, encouraging him to continue. He did, reciting a bestiary that rivaled her own, complete with a half-human, half-shark monstrosity.

"You weren't kidding," she said after a lull in the conversation. "You really were hungry. I don't think I've seen anybody eat like that since before the rain started."

Henry leaned back from the table and grinned. His ears turned red. "Sorry. I don't know how long it's been. We had water, but the food was all gone."

"Well, I'd recommend that you take it easy for a while. You don't want to overdo it."

"Are you worried we'll run out of food?"

Sarah shrugged. "Not so much that. It's just, if you haven't eaten in that long, your stomach has probably shrunken. You'll mess your system up if you gorge right away."

"I reckon you're right." He glanced down at the table, regret clearly showing on his face. "Maybe that wouldn't be so bad, though."

"What do you mean?"

"I don't know. Everybody I knew is gone. Without Moxey or my family or friends, what's the point of going on? Maybe I'd be better off eating myself to death."

Sarah sighed. "Know what I was doing before you showed up?"

Henry shook his head.

"I was contemplating suicide. You're not the only person that lost someone today, kid. I'm sorry about your cat. I really am. But I lost somebody, too."

"I saw a body outside," Henry said. "Lying in that utility shed at the base of the tower. The door was open. Was that your friend?"

Sarah nodded.

"What happened to him?"

"He…he was infected with the same stuff that infected Earl and the others."

"I thought that might be it. That stuff is all over him. I only saw skin from the neck up. Looked like he'd been shot in the head. Who killed him?"

"I did."

"Oh…"

They sat in awkward silence for a few moments. Then Henry cleared his throat.

"If it makes you feel any better, when I ran by him, it looked like he was starting to melt."

"Melt?"

"Yeah. He was turning liquid. His legs were mostly gone, already, and his chest had sort of collapsed."

"That's what the fuzz seems to do," Sarah agreed. "We need to find out more about it. There's a guy on the radio, broadcasting from Boston. He's got one hell of a strong signal. He was talking about the fuzz earlier. Maybe we'll listen later. See if we can learn anything that might help us."

"No offense, but maybe we shouldn't stick around here. Like I said, Earl and the others are probably following me."

"Where else are we going to go? I'm open to suggestions. You probably know the area better than me. Is there another safe spot?"

Henry frowned. "No. Not above water, at least."

Sarah stood up and walked to the window. Clasping her hands behind her back, she stared out into the deluge.

"Pretty soon, Henry, this place isn't going to be above water, either."

"So what do we do?"

"I don't know," Sarah admitted. The words tasted bitter in her mouth. "I don't know. We should get this place secure, of course. If Earl does show up, there's no sense in making things easy for him. We can barricade the door. Maybe booby-trap the stairs outside."

"And then? What do we do after that?"

"I guess we just wait to see what happens next. We don't really seem to have any other choices—except for suicide. You really want to kill yourself?"

Henry paused before answering. When he responded to her question, his voice was barely a whisper.

"No, I don't reckon I'm ready to yet."

"Neither am I. Not yet. Not until it's the only option we have left."

"That might be sooner than you think."

Sarah didn't reply. She stood, staring out the window and listening to the rain beat against the glass. Each drop was like a falling hammer.

PART TWO

DEEPER WATERS

TWELVE

Before Gail could react, the school of fish had stripped most of the skin from Hansen's face. He swatted at them with both hands, as if they were bees, rather than flying fish, and a moment later, his fingers had been reduced to raw, bloody stumps of bone and cartilage.

Gail screamed, stumbling backward across the boat's slippery deck. Attracted by her cry, Hansen turned in her direction. His eyes were gone, and when he opened his lipless mouth to plead for help, the fish took his tongue in quick, savage bites. Then they started in on his gums. They hovered around his head, mercifully obscuring it from sight again. The sound of their wings was audible over the waves and the steady drumming of the rain and even the shrieks of the other people on deck, all of whom, like Gail, were trying to flee, rather than helping the dying man.

Like we've got anywhere to flee to, Gail thought, running for the hatch. *We're surrounded by water. Where would we go if we* could *escape?*

She reached the hatch and slid to a halt. Morgan stood in the opening, watching as the fish went to work on Hansen's torso. His expression was one of dreadful fascination. Gail didn't know the man well—they'd found him clinging to some debris in the waters over Cleveland—but she was willing to bet Morgan had been the type to slow down on the highway and gawk at car wrecks.

"Morgan, move."

If he heard her, he gave no indication. His eyes remained fixed on Hansen's demise. He licked his lips slowly. Hansen's blood pooled on the deck, mixing with the rainwater.

"Morgan!" Gail placed her palm against his chest and pushed. His flannel shirt was wet. He didn't budge.

McCann and Riffle ran up behind her, panting for breath.

"Jesus Christ, Morgan," McCann shouted, "get the fuck out of the way!"

Blinking, Morgan turned to him. "W-what? Oh…yeah."

He stepped aside slowly. Gail, McCann and Riffle shoved past him. The two men clambered down the ladder, heading below, while Gail positioned herself at the hatch, shouting at the others on deck to hurry. They needed no encouragement. With a speed that belied imagination, Hansen's corpse had been reduced to nothing more than bones and some scraps of wet clothing, and now the flying fish were darting after new prey. Raindrops rolled off their silver scales. One by one, Lynn, Caterina, Paris and Mylon ran toward the open hatch, hands held uselessly over their heads in a futile effort to protect themselves.

Mylon slipped on the wet deck and almost went down. The fish darted toward him, but he scrambled to his feet and limped on. As he flung himself through the opening, Gail shoved the door, slamming the hatch closed. Only then was she aware that Morgan was standing beside her. He finally seemed to come out of his trance, at least long enough to push the lever on the inside of the door. The tumblers clanked into place, sealing them inside.

Gail leaned against the bulkhead and began to tremble. Her hands and feet felt jittery. Her stomach turned.

Booted footsteps pounded up the ladder. Novak appeared, a lit cigar chomped securely between his teeth. In his hands was the makeshift flamethrower he'd fashioned from two propane bottles and assorted spare parts. McCann was right behind him, his face ashen.

"What are we fighting today?" Novak asked. "Not those fucking shark men again, I hope? I've had enough of those things for a while."

"No." Gail shook her head. "This is something new. They're like silver piranha, but with wings."

Novak nodded, seeming to take this in stride. "Everybody make it?"

"All accounted for except Hansen."

"Any chance he's still alive?"

She swallowed. "I doubt it. If he is, then we have to…"

Novak raised the flamethrower and nodded at the hatch. "Open it up, and shut it as soon as I'm outside."

"But you—"

"Just do it, Gail."

His tone wasn't stern or argumentative, nor did he act as if he was giving an order. If anything, Novak just sounded tired.

Gail did as he asked. Novak stepped forward as the tumblers clanked again, and said, "Get the fuck out of the way, Morgan."

He puffed the cigar until the tip glowed orange. Then he touched it to the flamethrower's nozzle. Gail opened the door and Novak stepped outside, his pace slow and measured. He stood with his feet at shoulder-width apart, raised the flamethrower, and unleashed its contents on the fish, all of which were soaring toward him. He swept the weapon back and forth, engulfing them all in a fiery arc. The creatures fell to the deck, flopping and thrashing as they burned. Novak hit them with another burst and they lay still. Then he stepped over their smoldering bodies and trained the flamethrower on Hansen's grisly remains. When he was finished, Novak turned off the flamethrower and strolled back to the door. He smiled at Gail, McCann and Morgan.

"Thought I told you to shut the hatch behind me?"

"I- I'm sorry," Gail stammered. "I just…"

His grin grew wider. "You couldn't resist the smell of fried fish, right?"

McCann frowned. "How can you joke around after that?"

"It's not so bad." Novak shrugged. "Everybody's alive, right?"

"Everyone except Hansen," Gail reminded him.

"Well, that's okay. Nobody liked him much anyway."

The cigar jiggled as he laughed. A moment later, Gail and McCann laughed too. Morgan stared at the three of them and then joined in.

"It could have been worse," Novak said as he stepped inside. "Much worse. And if things keep going the way they have been, it probably will be soon enough."

They went back down the ladder. Gail felt the tension drain from her body as they rejoined the rest of the crew. She preferred being below decks rather than topside—not because of the protection the ship's steel bulkheads offered, but because when she was inside, she couldn't hear the incessant sound of the rain.

They gathered in the galley. When they were all assembled, the small space soon stank of body odor and bad breath. They'd run out of toiletries weeks ago. Normally, Gail's senses were dulled to the smell, but with everyone in a group like this, the stench became overpowering. Caterina cleared her throat, and Mylon cracked his knuckles, but no one spoke. The silence was disconcerting.

Gail glanced around at the group and saw the same expressions mirrored on each of their faces—exhaustion and a grim sense of hopelessness. She felt the same things. How much longer could they go on like this—traveling aimlessly, scrounging for increasingly dwindling supplies of food and fuel, and picking up the occasional survivor stranded amidst the flotsam of the civilized world? Indeed, could they even handle more castaways onboard? As Novak had explained to Gail when they'd first rescued her, the multi-hulled super catamaran was one-hundred and twenty five feet in length. While the large vessel looked imposing from the outside, the interior was actually cramped. Living space was limited, especially given the size of the group, and finding a quiet place to be alone was almost impossible.

Novak, McCann and Riffle had been among the original crew. There had been two other crew members, but both had been killed before Gail came aboard. In addition to Gail, there was Lynn, Caterina, Paris, Mylon, Morgan, Tatiana, Ben, and Warren. It was funny to think that only hours before, Hansen had also been a part of this group. Now he'd joined the ranks of those they'd lost.

There had been many more castaways at one point. Howard had suffered a massive heart attack. His death had been the only one from natural causes. Dickinson had been killed by a human-shark hybrid. Diane became infected by the white fuzz and had been immediately set adrift with enough food and water to last her seven days. She hadn't been the only one to go into the water, either. Lieberman had jumped overboard one night, lured by the siren song of a vampiric mermaid.

The worst death, in Gail's opinion, had been Andre's. He'd bravely jumped into the ocean to retrieve a floating crate of produce after their efforts to snag it with poles, hooks and fishing rods had proven unsuccessful. Andre was a strong swimmer, and he'd reached the wooden crate and dragged it back to the boat without incident. It wasn't until he was below deck and drying off that they noticed the leech on his thigh—a squat, bloated thing, the length of an index finger and the width of a quarter. Its skin was the color of liver. Novak had safely removed it and then they'd put antiseptic over the pinhole-sized bite. Everyone had assumed he'd be fine.

Andre began complaining of a stomachache a few hours later.

Two nights after that, he was dead, eaten from the inside out by a horde of tiny leeches. The creature had impregnated him with thousands of her young. Andre had remained alive through the entire grisly process, even as the spawn wriggled from his mouth, nose, ears, and anus.

Shuddering at the memory, Gail studied the group again. Everyone was present, except for Riffle, who she assumed must be on the bridge, piloting the ship. She wondered what Novak was waiting for.

As if reading her mind, the makeshift captain cleared his throat. Immediately, all eyes turned to him.

"I guess you all know that Hansen's dead."

Some nodded. A few shrugged or looked away. Nobody spoke.

"Riffle's piloting. I told him if that guy from Boston comes back on the radio, he's supposed to patch it through the intercom immediately. Meanwhile, we've got some things to discuss."

"Like what?" Mylon asked.

"Well," Novak continued, "I'm afraid I've got some bad news."

Lynn flipped her blonde bangs from her face. "What kind of bad news?"

"The kind where, once I've told you what it is, you guys will have to decide if we want to continue on, or if we'd be better off forming some kind of suicide pact and just ending it all now."

Gail felt the boat rock beneath her feet as it encountered what must have been a particularly large swell. She wondered if she'd ever grow totally comfortable with being at sea—not that she'd have a choice anymore. At least the seasickness had passed after a few days. Now, the only time she got nauseous was during a bad storm, or if she drank a lot of fluids without eating first.

For a moment, nobody spoke. They all sat staring at Novak. Mylon cracked his knuckles again. Then Warren snickered, and everybody glanced in his direction. The young man smiled at them, clearly nervous with the sudden attention, and then shrugged.

"What's with all the drama, Novak?"

"No drama." Novak's voice was low and steady. He stared at Warren without blinking. His expression was grim. "We're in a world of shit, and things are about to get worse."

"How so?" Ben asked.

Sighing, Novak leaned back against the bulkhead and raised one hand, counting off on his fingers. "One, we're almost out of fuel. Both of our engines are in good shape, which is sort of surprising, given all the debris in the water. McCann's been doing a good job of keeping the intakes free of junk and making sure the engines are running."

McCann nodded from his position by the hatch.

"It also doesn't hurt that we've been sticking to a relatively slow speed," Novak continued. "But even so, we're running low on fuel. Only reason we've been able to conserve it is because in addition to our two engines, we've got a pump-jet engine hybrid. I know that doesn't mean shit to the rest of you. This was an experimental super catamaran. We were supposed to be researching various methods of propulsion and fuel reduction." He paused, took a puff of his cigar, and blew a smoke ring in the air. Then he continued. "Well, we've reduced the fucking fuel consumption, all right. We've got maybe enough gas to run for another four or five days. Then we'll be drifting."

"Is that so bad?" Tatiana asked. "I mean, it's not like we've been coming across any dry land anyway. Drifting is better than drowning."

"Sure it is," Novak replied, "but there are a few things to consider. If we get attacked again—and let's face it people, we *will* get attacked again—we're going to have a hard time outrunning whatever it is if we have no fuel. Drifting might work if we're dealing with something like those little fish that killed Hansen today, but we'll be shit out of luck if something big shows up—like one of those sea serpents we saw a few weeks back. The other problem is our location. If the GPS is right, we're over the middle of Kentucky right now. I was hoping we'd find some dry land—mountaintops or whatever. But we're not. As hard as it is to imagine, the waters are still rising. Either that, or the world is melting."

Morgan snorted in derision. "Don't be ridiculous, Captain."

"I'm not," Novak said, "and I've told you before, Morgan. Don't call me Captain. Anyway, my point is this. There's not a lot of stuff above the waterline anymore, but there's a whole bunch of shit beneath us. Buildings and treetops and hills—hitting those is like hitting a reef. We've been luckier than most. Because of our multi-hull design, we've been able to ride above a lot of it. But sooner or later, we're going to hit something and it's going to bash a big fucking hole in our side. And then we'll be screwed. I've been trying to avoid the cities since Cleveland. Figured if I got us out here over the country, we'd have less debris. Now, I'm not so sure. I've talked it over with McCann and Riffle. Our plan is to head for the Atlantic—or the place where the Atlantic used to be. Shit, the whole world's the Atlantic Ocean now. But I want to get us out over the original ocean, where we won't have to worry about running aground."

"Do we have enough gas to get there?" Mylon asked.

"Not without drifting. That's problem one. Problem number two is that our chances of scavenging anything useful are probably lessened out on the open sea. Granted, we've been seeing less stuff as time goes by, but we've still been able to snag stuff from the debris. There will be less chance of that in the real ocean. Which brings me to problem number three."

Caterina groaned. "You mean there's more?"

Novak nodded. "Fuel's not the only thing we're running low on. Beginning immediately, we're going to have to start rationing our food and water. Riffle says if we keep eating the way we have been, we'll run out in the next two weeks."

Mylon frowned. "But what about all the stuff we found a few days ago? Those crates of food?"

"Most of it was already spoiled. Some of it had that white fuzz shit growing on it. I had Riffle toss it back over the side."

Several of them stirred restlessly. After a moment, Gail asked what everyone else was thinking.

"He didn't come in contact with the fungus did he?"

"No. He's fine. You don't have to worry about that. But the fact remains, we're running low. We've got rainwater to drink, of course, although I personally think we ought to stop drinking that unless we absolutely have to."

"Why?" Paris asked.

"Well, keep in mind, I'm no scientist—but what if that white shit is in the rain? What if that's how it's spreading?"

Ben sighed. "Then we'd be pretty much screwed."

Nodding, Novak took another puff on his cigar, which was now burned down to a stub. Then he took it out of his mouth and snuffed it out, grinding it on the tabletop until it was extinguished.

"That was my last one."

He didn't seem to be speaking to them. His eyes remained focused on the floor. Gail thought his voice sounded sad.

"So," Novak said, looking back up at them again, "to recap—we're almost out of gas and food, and tomorrow's forecast calls for rain. The only thing we're not low on is ammunition. So we need to decide if we want to keep going and take our chances in the Atlantic, or if we want to explore a more *final* option."

"You can't be serious," Morgan scoffed. "You're talking about a suicide pact?"

"I've never been more serious in my life."

"So," Ben said, "do we like, take a vote or something? A show of hands?"

Novak shrugged. "I don't know. Whatever you guys prefer. I don't think we should decide right now, though. My point was to apprise you of our situation—make sure you understood just what we're facing. Personally, I think we should take our time. Mull it over. Talk about it amongst yourselves."

"I agree," Warren said. "I mean, we've got time. We don't have to decide right this second."

Paris nodded. "It's not like we're going to die tonight."

"Tell that to Hansen," Mylon muttered in his thick southern accent.

"Which reminds me," Novak said, "we've still got to divvy up his stuff. Anybody want to volunteer to help McCann inventory it?"

Gail raised her hand. She'd done it before, when Andre had died after being infected with leeches. The act itself was morbid and sad—separating and listing the belongings of a dead shipmate—but it made her feel useful. Also, she didn't trust some of the other survivors to be honest with their tally. After Lieberman had been lured over the side by a mermaid, Paris and Riffle had been assigned to inventory his personal belongings. Gail suspected—but had no proof—that they'd kept four packs of Juicy Fruit gum that Lieberman had hidden beneath his pillow. Gail had known about the gum because he'd shared a stick with her. The day after his death, she'd seen both Paris and Riffle chewing gum. When she stood close enough to talk to them, she'd noticed the unmistakable smell of Juicy Fruit.

"Thanks, Gail," Novak said. "Same rules as always. Anything like food, batteries, toiletries or medicine should go in the communal pile. Anything else—clothes, books, shit like that—gets divided up among whoever wants it."

Morgan sniffed. "Why bother?"

"What do you mean?"

"I mean, why bother sorting through Hansen's effects? Fighting over the Advil or toilet paper he may have left behind seems pointless given the fact that you're suggesting we decide whether or not we want to enter into a suicide pact."

"Suit yourself." Novak turned away, effectively dismissing him. "If you don't want his stuff, that just leaves more for everyone else."

"I call dibs on dry socks," Tatiana said. "If he's got any."

"Nothing's dry anymore," Lynn said.

"If they are," Caterina replied, "then you'll have to fight me for them. His underwear, too. Mine's soaked."

Warren nudged Ben in the ribs and both men smirked at the unintentionally lewd comment. Caterina seemed oblivious to their reaction. Gail felt a momentary flash of anger. Was this what they'd been reduced to—arguing over a dead man's personal belongings just minutes after his death? Maybe Novak was right. Maybe they should think about killing themselves now. Maybe the human race would be better off extinct.

Shaking her head, Gail stood up and walked over to McCann, who was nursing a cold mug of instant coffee. "You ready?"

"Sure. Might as well get it over with." He drained his mug and grimaced. "God, that tastes like shit. I'd kill for a Starbucks right now. I always hated those places before. Thought their coffee was overpriced and tasted like something had died in my cup. Now, I'd love to come across one. Remember how they used to be on every corner?"

"They still are," Gail replied. "All you have to do is dive straight down to the bottom of the ocean."

"No thanks." McCann frowned. "Hell, Gail. You're getting as cynical as Novak. He's a bad influence on you."

"Fuck you," Novak said, grinning. "And hey, if Hansen has any cigars stowed away, I call dibs. Unless anybody else wants to split them with me?"

Lynn laughed. "You're the only one who smokes them. And besides, if Hansen did have any, they probably wouldn't be dry, either. Just like his socks."

"How did you manage to keep yours dry, anyway?" Warren asked Novak.

"You kidding?" Novak's grin grew broader. "This is perfect cigar weather! I haven't had to fuck with the humidifier in my humidor once since the rain started."

Warren opened his mouth to respond, but a sudden squawk from the boat's intercom made him stop. McCann and Gail paused at the hatch. Everyone in the galley looked up at the speaker mounted to the bulkhead.

"Hey, folks." Riffle's voice was muffled by static. "That dude in Boston is back on the air. I'm patching him through now."

The group fell silent, and listened. They all recognized the voice. No matter how faint or distorted, it was always the same guy—Mark from Boston, the world's last disc jockey, broadcasting from atop the Prudential Building in beautiful, flooded downtown Boston. According to Novak, they'd first picked up his transmissions while sailing overtop Illinois. The man had rigged up his own pirate radio station. He'd described it in one of his previous broadcasts. Gail hadn't understood most of the technical specifics, but apparently, the roof of the building was equipped with an array of radio masts and satellite dishes that allowed Mark to transmit to anyone in the world who still had a working radio, CB or television set. He'd also recently routed one of the dishes into the public broadcast system equipment, so that he could broadcast even further.

The only drawback, according to him, was that he couldn't receive communications. He could only transmit, and had no way of knowing for sure if anyone could hear him. To Gail, that was the most frustrating part. She wished there was some way to reach him, some method of letting him know that he wasn't alone, and that there were survivors out here aware of his plight.

"I always figured that if I was going to bite the big one," Mark said, "I'd go out with a fight, like Willem Defoe in *Platoon*. I'm a sucker for those great last stands. But now, I don't know. I doubt it will happen like that. This shit is… *soft*…spreading."

"He's got the fuzz," Mylon said. "Poor bastard's infected with that white shit."

Gail, Paris and Lynn all hushed him, and the group turned their attention back to the overhead speakers.

"Anyway," Mark continued, "this is day two of my broadcast and nobody has shown up to rescue us yet. My name's Mark Sylva. If anybody is listening, we're on top of the Prudential Building in Boston. We're sick. Boston is underwater, except for us and another building. I keep thinking about my wife and son in Ohio. I just hope things are better there."

"They're not," Novak muttered.

"Everybody's acting weird, and we're all so…*soft*… lethargic and thirsty. It seems strange, being so thirsty with all the water outside. I hope help comes soon. Otherwise, I think some bad shit is about to go down."

McCann nudged Gail with his elbow. "You ready?"

She shrugged, then nodded. "Let's get it over with."

The two of them left the galley and shut the hatch behind them. Then they walked down the passageway towards the berthing area. Mark in Boston's voice followed them, echoing out of each overhead speaker.

"The rash is getting worse," he said. "I think I know what it is now. I don't want to admit it to myself, but yeah, what the hell else could it be? I think we're all…*soft*…infected."

"Mylon's right," McCann said. "Sounds like the poor bastard is infected with the fungus."

"We need to learn more about it," Gail said. "Find out how it spreads. How to avoid infection. We know that you can get it by touching something that's already infected, but there has to be more to it than that."

"Yeah, but how are we going to find out? That's a job for scientists in a lab somewhere—not a bunch of castaways on a boat. I mean, what kind of research team would we make, Gail? Mylon was a bus driver. Warren sold cars. Lynn worked for a health insurance company. Me and Riffle and Novak—all we know is this boat. I don't know about any of the others, but none of them strike me as the scientist type. We're just spitting in the wind, here."

"You sound like you're ready to give up. How about it, McCann? Do you agree with what Novak said in there? Do you think we should just…" She choked, unable to finish the sentence.

"Quit while we're ahead? I don't know. I don't think I'd have the balls to kill myself, and I don't think I could kill any of you, unless you were dying and in pain, or trying to attack me or one of the others. Except for Morgan, maybe. Him I could kill."

He kept his expression serious for a moment, and then a toothy, mischievous grin slowly took its place.

Gail laughed. "Yeah, me too."

"So what were you, before all of this?"

"Divorced," Gail said. "No kids. I was a social worker. At night, I came home to my dog, a little Yorkie named Terrance."

"And what happened to him?"

"We're here," Gail said, side-stepping the question.

They knelt by Hansen's rack and opened his footlocker. They went through the items cautiously, double-checking for any sign of white fungus, but found none. There wasn't much inside the footlocker. Some spare but damp clothes. A cell phone with a dead battery. Half a bottle of flax-seed oil capsules. A key ring in the shape of an apple which said 'I ♥ NY' with car and house keys dangling from it. And a black leather wallet. While McCann sorted through the items, Gail opened the wallet. It too was damp, and a faint musty smell rose from inside. She found a few mildewed snapshots—Hansen with two smiling children, obviously his, and a wedding photo of a much younger version of Hansen posing with his wife. Gail frowned, trying to remember if the man had ever mentioned his family, or what had happened to them.

"Did Hansen have a wedding ring?" she asked.

"I don't know. I never noticed. Why?"

"No reason. Just curious as to who he was."

"Why? He's gone, now. It's not like we can carve this stuff on his tombstone."

"Maybe not, but all the more reason we should know about each other, don't you think? Somebody should remember us after we're gone, don't you think? A part of us should live on, even if it's just somebody honoring the little things in our lives."

"What about the soul?"

"Do you believe in a soul, McCann?"

"No. I mean, not anymore. I used to believe in God and Heaven and the immortality of the human soul, but I pretty much stopped believing around the time it started raining."

Gail stared at the picture of Hansen and his kids and whispered, "Who were you, Hansen? What was the story of your life?"

"Does it matter?" McCann asked.

She closed the wallet and tossed it back into the footlocker. "No, I guess it doesn't. Not anymore. Nothing really matters anymore."

"Thirsty," Mark's voice echoed through the static. "Think I'll lie down for a bit. I'm exhausted, and this cot is so... *soft*..."

THIRTEEN

Gail slept through the night, lulled by the rocking of the boat. She did not dream. She hadn't dreamed in weeks, or if she had, she didn't remember them. Given their close quarters, she assumed that Caterina, Paris, Lynn or Tatiana would have told her if she'd cried out in the night or talked in her sleep, but they'd never mentioned it.

When she woke the next morning, Gail sat up and stretched, slowly working out the aches and kinks that the thin mattress had given her. She longed for her bed back home, now underwater, and then her thoughts turned to other things from her past that were now submerged. Determined not to fall into a mood, she climbed out of her rack and got dressed.

Breakfast was a multivitamin, crackers, canned pears and sardines in olive oil. She'd hated sardines before the rain, and still did, but she ate them anyway, using the crackers to mop up the oily bits left on her plate. She sat in the galley with McCann, Ben, Caterina and Warren, all of whom, like her, were eating their meager breakfast before beginning their turn at watch. None of them spoke much, other than sporadic small talk. Ben read his newspaper, as he did every day. It was mildewed and wrinkled and torn, and much of the ink had smudged from the constant humidity. The headlines spoke of things that no longer mattered—wars and the economy and which Hollywood starlet was entering rehab. Gail had often considered asking Ben why he re-read it every day, but she suspected that she already knew the answer. It was a ritual; it provided him with a sense of normalcy in an otherwise fucked up world.

One-by-one, they finished eating and headed topside, stopping only long enough to put on their rain gear. Gail pulled a heavy, bright-yellow rubber slicker over her head and then grabbed a matching rubber rain hat. She wished the boat had some boots or waders that would fit her. Her feet invariably ended up getting wet on each shift. Each of them also selected a weapon for the day. Warren and Ben had handguns. Caterina was armed with a long spear fashioned from a tent pole. Gail had a machete. They also had two pair of binoculars. Gail took one pair. Ben took the other.

Gail followed the others up the ladder and walked through the hatch. The mist immediately hit her face. It was windy this morning, and the rain whipped across the deck. She glanced out over the rails and saw that much of the ocean was hidden beneath deep, swirling fog. Lynn, Paris, Morgan and Mylon filed past them, nodding in greeting before heading below deck to dry off and sleep.

Gail, Caterina, Warren and Ben each took a position along the rails. Gail and Warren went forward. Ben and Caterina went aft. McCann headed up to the bridge to relieve Riffle, who had been on duty all night. Once they were in position, they began another long, weary, miserable day of scanning the water, looking for any salvage, survivors or threats. Gail stared out into the haze and shivered.

They were three hours into their shift, and the fog had mostly burned off, when Warren shouted a warning. He hadn't been talkative this morning, and had brooded silently on his side of the vessel, leaving Gail to her own thoughts. She'd been staring up at the muted silver sun and trying to remember what its rays had felt like on her skin before the rain started, when he yelled. She turned toward him, instantly alert.

"Give me the binoculars!"

She crossed the slippery deck and handed them to him. Warren brought them to his eyes, looked starboard, and then handed them to her.

"There," he said, pointing. "Do you see it?"

Gail squinted, adjusting the binoculars until the object became clear. On the horizon was a massive, grayish-black shape. From this distance, she couldn't tell for sure what it was—perhaps a hillside or a mountaintop? The formation was roughly forty square feet in size, and utterly devoid of buildings, trees or grass. The surface looked firm and smooth. It was also slightly bulbous and had what appeared to be a small dome in its center.

"What is it?" Gail asked.

"An island?" Warren took the binoculars back from her. "Or maybe the top of a water tower or a grain silo or something. I'm not sure. Looks pretty sturdy. The waves aren't topping it. Maybe we should check it out."

They hollered for the others and all four of them regrouped on the bridge, and Warren and Gail reported what they'd seen. Novak was present, as well. He'd brought a thermos of instant coffee for those on watch.

"Was just getting ready to hand it out," he said, yawning. "But screw it. Go ahead and help yourselves now, while I take a look."

Using the bridge's binoculars, he peered out over the ocean, studying the land mass. He was quiet for a long time. Gail and the others sipped the hot coffee and waited in silence. After a few minutes, Novak lowered the binoculars and turned to McCann.

"Take us in," he ordered, "but go slow. Can't tell if there's any debris around it or not, but I don't want to take any chances. If we bottom out on something, that little island is gonna be our final resting place."

"We're going to land?" Ben asked.

"Sure," Novak answered. "Might as well investigate. Can't tell much from here, but there could be useful stuff we can scavenge. And I think we could all do with standing on dry land, even if only for a little while."

"Except that it's not exactly dry," Gail said.

Novak frowned. "Beggars can't be fucking choosers. Let's go have a look."

McCann gripped the controls tightly as he piloted them toward the formation. Gail noticed that his complexion had paled. Sweat and rainwater ran down his forehead and face. His knuckles were white, his arms stiff.

He's scared, she thought. *And so am I.*

At Novak's request, Warren went below decks to wake up

some of the others and form a landing party. Ben and Caterina returned to their lookout positions. Deciding it best to let McCann focus on the task at hand, Gail glanced around the bridge and found herself alone. Novak had walked back out on the deck and was standing at the rail, studying the island intently through the binoculars. The boat rocked over a sudden, particularly strong swell, nearly knocking all of them off their feet, but Novak didn't seem to notice. His attention remained focused on the mysterious mass. Clutching her coffee, which was now lukewarm, Gail inched her way across the slippery deck and tapped his shoulder.

"Anything different?"

He shrugged, lowering the binoculars, and turned to face her. "Nothing. Can't figure out what it is. I don't think it's metal or wood. Guess we'll know soon enough. Here. Have a look."

He handed her the binoculars and held her coffee while Gail peered at the structure. She squinted, straining to make out any details, but the lenses were fogged and mist and rain swirled around the mass. She handed them back to Novak and accepted her coffee in return.

"Are you sure about this?"

Novak shrugged again. "No. But it's like I said last night—we're running low on fuel, food and clean water, not to mention other things. If there's anything to be scavenged off this island, then it's worth the risk, if only because we won't be fishing it out of the ocean like usual."

"But if there's danger—the shark-men or maybe more of those flying fish, is it worth it?"

"If we worry about that, then we might as well all check out now. Quick death getting eaten by one of those fucking monsters or a slow death by starvation. Not much of a choice, is it?"

"No, it's not."

"Sounds to me like you've made up your mind about our conversation from last night."

Gail flinched, blinking rainwater from her eyes. "I'm not saying that. I'm just scared. Something doesn't feel right."

"Nothing's felt right for a while, Gail. It starts raining at the same time, all over the world, and doesn't stop. Everything floods. Then the monsters come—giant worms and fungus creatures and fish with scales like razors and all kinds of other bullshit…none of that is right. Chances are this place won't be either. But it's not like we're going ashore unarmed. If we can find supplies—if we can find *anything*—then it's worth the risk."

They fell silent, watching as the boat slowly approached the mysterious mass. Even as they drew closer, their visibility didn't improve. The smooth grayish-black surface lacked any topography—there were no buildings or vegetation. The small dome in the center didn't appear to be man-made, but a natural formation.

"Know what I keep thinking of?"

Gail shook her head. "What?"

"The serpent mound in Ohio. Ever hear of that? The Indians built it a long time ago. This giant fucking hill that looked like a snake when you stared down at it from above. People lived around it for years and didn't realize that it was man-made, or what it was supposed to resemble. They didn't figure it out until the airplane was invented. There's all kinds of similar mounds in this part of the country—barrows and burial sites. I mean, most of them are probably underwater by now, but what if that thing is one of them?"

Before Gail could respond, Warren pounded up the ladder and emerged on deck. With him were Riffle, Ben, Mylon, Tatiana, Lynn and Morgan. All of them appeared tired but alert. While the others yawned and stretched and flinched at the rain, Tatiana was fresh-faced—the benefits of sleeping through the night without a watch shift. Only Morgan seemed angered by being woken. His expression was dour and impatient. When Novak nodded at him, he sneered.

"What's this all about, Captain?"

"I've told you before, don't call me that. I'm about as much of a Captain as you are."

"And yet you're in charge."

"You want to volunteer, Morgan? Cause if you've got any

better ideas, I'm all fucking ears."

"I think you're doing a commendable job."

Gail noticed Novak's shoulders stiffen, but he ignored the sarcasm.

"What this is about," he said, turning back to the ocean, "is that land mass over there. At least, we're pretty sure it's a land mass. Might be some type of man-made structure—a water tower or something similar. In any case, we're gonna find out. That's why I had Warren wake everybody up. I know that most of you just went to bed three hours ago, but I need all hands on this. Riffle, I want you to take over piloting for McCann. He's more awake than you are, so I want him out there with me. Go slow as we approach. I don't want us bottoming out. The rest of you come with me. Each of you gets one weapon. Half of you are going to stay behind to defend the ship. The other half are going ashore with me and McCann."

Morgan's gaze went from the island to Novak. "And if we refuse?"

"Shit, Morgan. I'm not twisting your arm. If you don't want to go, you don't have to. That just means if there's anything of value over there—like food, for instance—you don't fucking get any of it. Fair enough?"

Novak turned and winked at Gail. Then he strode past the sulking man and headed for the weapons locker. Grinning, Warren and the others followed him. Morgan trailed along a few steps behind. When Gail turned to glance at him, his face was twisted into a hateful, loathing grimace.

Well, she thought, looking forward again, *this should certainly be fun...*

"I've got an idea," Gail said to Novak as they lined up at the lifeboat.

He blinked rain from his eyes and nodded, indicating that he was listening.

"If there is stuff on the island that we can salvage," Gail continued, "then maybe we should leave some room in the boat, so we can bring it back? Which means taking less people ashore."

Sighing, Novak pulled off his rain hat, ran a hand through his hair, and then plopped the hat back on again. He shook his head. His smile was rueful.

"You're right," he said. "What the hell was I thinking?"

McCann shrugged. "It's cool, boss. You're tired. We're all tired. Nobody's bringing their A-game anymore, you know."

"Yeah, but still…this is just common sense."

Morgan raised his hand. "I'll be glad to stay behind."

"I'm sure you would." Novak glared at him. The silence between them lasted a full thirty seconds before Morgan finally turned away.

Warren sneezed.

"Go on back to your rack," Novak told Morgan. "If you're skipping out on this then you're pulling double watch tonight so that someone else can get caught up on their sleep."

"I'll do no such thing."

"Fine." Novak turned to McCann. "Go get Riffle. Then I want the two of you to throw Mr. Morgan over the side."

Morgan sputtered. "What? Now just wait a goddamn minute!"

"I'm kidding, you asshole." Novak grinned, but it was a humorless expression. He stared at the man a moment longer, as if daring him to respond, and then turned back to the others. "Okay. Gail brings up a good point, so let's split this up. Who wants to volunteer to go ashore?"

Warren and Lynn raised their hands. Morgan glanced down at the deck.

"Mylon?" Novak said. "Tatiana? Paris? How about you guys?"

"I'd be okay with pulling a double tonight." Paris spoke so softly that they had to strain to hear her over the rain and the waves. "I could use some more sleep this morning."

Tatiana nodded in agreement. "I know that's right."

"Doesn't matter much to me," Mylon said. "I'll do whatever you think is best, Novak."

"Okay, then. Me, McCann, Gail, Warren and Lynn will go ashore. That leaves enough room in the lifeboat to carry back supplies—unless we hit the mother-load, in which case, we'll just make a couple trips. You guys stow those weapons again, and then get some frigging sleep."

"Sounds good." Mylon's tone was relieved.

As they walked away, Morgan muttered something about being woken up. Gail noticed Novak stiffen and bite his lip, but he said nothing.

"Would you have really thrown him overboard?" she asked.

"I don't know." Novak climbed into the lifeboat. "I just don't know anymore. The kind of man I used to be? Of course not. But sometimes it feels like that man was part of another life."

FOURTEEN

Gail was tense during the short journey from the ship to the mysterious island. She assumed that the others were, as well, because nobody spoke. The only sounds were the waves, the oars creaking as Warren and McCann rowed, and the ever-present patter of the rain. Novak sat at the bow, leaning forward and watching the formation intently. Lynn and Gail watched either side of the lifeboat, alert for any signs of trouble.

Despite their fears, the crossing was uneventful. Debris churned by, floating on the surf, but none of it was salvageable. They encountered an eight-foot-long aluminum bass boat with the name 'Goffee' emblazoned on the side with the type of block letter stickers usually used for mailboxes or front doors. Gail wondered if 'Goffee' was the name of the boat's owner or the boat itself. Warren prodded the capsized craft with one oar. It spun slowly, and they recoiled. One side was covered with white mold.

"You didn't get it on the oar, did you?" McCann asked.

Warren shook his head. "No, we're okay."

They fell silent again. It occurred to Gail that she hadn't heard any seagulls or other birds. Normally, they were as ever-present as the rain, but now they were noticeably absent. She frowned, trying to remember when she'd actually last seen one. A few days ago? A week? She didn't know.

The mist grew thicker as they approached the formation. It swirled around them in thick, chilly clouds. Gail glanced behind them and was alarmed to see that the ship was no longer visible. What if they got lost out here? What would they do then? Would Novak's suicide solution become more palatable after a few days of drifting aimlessly in the lifeboat? Suddenly, she toppled forward in her seat as the lifeboat came to a jarring halt against the island.

"Easy," Novak hollered. "What the hell, McCann? You trying to bottom us out?"

"I can't see shit out here. This fog's like cream of mushroom soup."

"You've got to be more careful."

McCann nodded, and then laid the oar across the bench. "Look on the bright side, boss. We're here. Let's check it out."

"Ladies first." Grinning, Novak made a sweeping gesture with his hand.

"I don't think so," Gail said, returning the gesture. "You should have the honor."

"Yeah," Lynn agreed. "After all, you're leading this expedition. It's only right you go first."

Nodding, Novak stepped forward and onto the island. The boat rocked slightly. Gail went next, followed by Warren and then Lynn. McCann went last. He stood next to the boat with a rope in his hand.

"Don't see anywhere to tie off, boss."

"Is the current strong enough that you won't be able to hold it?"

McCann shook his head.

"Standby then," Novak said. "I think we'll be alright. Just make sure you keep a good grip on that line. You let that boat float away, and we'll eat you first."

He tried to sound lighthearted and joking, but Gail noticed the edge in his voice. Novak was nervous. So was she.

They spread out and began slowly exploring the formation. The ferocity of the rain and the swirling mists hampered their visibility, and even now, standing atop the mass, Gail still couldn't tell for sure what it was. The gray surface was hard like stone, but smooth and unmarred by cracks or fissures. Raindrops bounced and splattered against it, and pooled at their feet. As they'd seen from the ship, there were no buildings, trees or grass. Other than the strange hill in the middle, the island was utterly featureless. It was also larger than it had appeared to be from the ship. Gail knelt and placed her palm against the surface. It was warm and slick.

"What do you think, guys?" Warren asked. His voice

sounded distorted in the fog.

Novak sighed. "I think we wasted a fucking trip. There's nothing here."

"Maybe we should try that hill?" Lynn motioned with her makeshift spear. "There could be something behind it, or maybe inside of it."

"Might as well," Novak agreed. "We've come this far."

They shuffled forward, weapons held at the ready, but without conviction. Gail was about to stand up and join them, when the ground trembled slightly. She felt the vibration run through her palm and up her arm. She glanced up to see if any of the others had noticed, but their attention was focused on the hill.

From the shore, McCann called, "The waves are starting to get stronger."

Novak turned around. "What do you mean?"

"I mean it's picking up all of the sudden."

Gail frowned. Could it be an earthquake? She grabbed her pistol and stood up. Novak was still facing her and McCann. Lynn and Warren were approaching the hill.

"There's something here," Lynn said.

They all looked to where she was pointing, and as they did, the hill opened up, looked at them with one giant, baleful black eye, and then blinked. The island shuddered beneath their feet. Screaming, Warren scampered backward. Gail was torn between running toward him and fleeing for the boat.

McCann gasped. "Holy shit!"

The eye opened again. Lynn, prodded by fear or panic, jabbed her spear forward, thrusting it into the orb.

"Don't," Novak shouted. "Let's just—"

The island shivered, and then surged upward, knocking Gail, Warren and Novak off their feet. The handgun slipped from Gail's grasp and slid away from her. She realized that it was plunging toward the water, and that she was suddenly clinging to a slippery slope. She scrabbled for a grip on the smooth surface, but her fingertips couldn't find a purchase. Warren zipped past her, following the pistol's trajectory.

And then the island roared.

***

"Do you see anything?"

Yawning, Mylon shook his head. He lowered the binoculars and pointed at the lenses. "Can't see shit through these things. They're all fogged over. Got anything dry I can wipe them with?"

Riffle laughed. "You're kidding, right? I can't remember the last time I had something dry."

"I dream about it sometimes. It's funny. Before the rain started, I used to dream about other stuff. Food, mostly. And sex. But these days, I just dream about being dry. And warm."

Nodding, Riffle peered through the haze, trying to catch a glimpse of Novak and the others. The mist had grown thicker since their departure, and the rain fell harder. The island was still visible, but the small boat had disappeared from sight. He felt uneasy. Granted, he usually felt that way all day long in this new world, but now the feeling was amplified.

"I hope they're okay."

"Yeah," Mylon said, raising the binoculars again. "I hope so, too. I reckon they will be. Novak's a tough son of a bitch."

Riffle grinned. "That he is. I remember when I first met him, he—"

A scream cut him off. Mylon sat the binoculars down and both men ran out onto the deck. They skidded to a halt. Paris knelt by the rail. Morgan stood overtop of her. He clutched a pistol in one hand and Paris's hair in the other. He yanked her head back, forcing her to cry out again. Ben stood next to them, armed with a rifle. He appeared anxious and sick, almost as if he were going to vomit.

"What the fuck?" Riffle yelled.

"I'm sorry," Paris sobbed. "They didn't give me a—"

"Shut up." Morgan pulled her hair again, and then pointed the handgun at her head.

"Where did you get those guns?" Riffle asked, staring at them in disbelief.

"Your boss man is slipping," Morgan said. "Seriously, he's not well. He woke us all up, and wanted half of us to go to the island and the other half to guard the ship. Then, a few minutes later, he tells those of us staying behind to go back to sleep again. Not a very rational thing."

"That still doesn't explain what you're doing with that gun."

"Novak told us to stow them again and then sailed off to Fantasy Island—after threatening to toss me over the side. I guess I forgot to lock my gun again. Oops."

"What the hell is wrong with you, Morgan?" Mylon took a step toward him. "What is this?"

"It's a mutiny. And if you come any closer, I'm going to decorate the deck with this girl's brains."

The rain fell on them all. Paris sobbed. Riffle and Mylon froze, their hands in the air. Ben's eyes darted from the two of them to Morgan and then back again. The rifle shook in his hands.

"Okay," Riffle said, his voice low. "Look…you guys don't need to do this. Ben, come on, dude. This isn't you."

"I don't want to die," Ben said. "Novak's gone crazy, Riffle. All that talk about suicide pacts? He needs to step down."

"And you're gonna put Morgan in charge instead?" Mylon's tone was incredulous. "Listen to yourself, man!"

Morgan released Paris and prodded her with his foot. "Get over there with the others."

Still sobbing, Paris crawled across the slippery deck. Riffle reached out a hand and helped her to her feet. She clung to him, shivering.

"Now," Morgan said. "We need to figure out where everyone stands. Tatiana and Caterina are below, sound asleep. It's just us. Believe it or not, we're doing this for your own good. It's like Ben just said, Novak isn't fit for command of this vessel. All we want to do is relieve him of duty. The question is, where do you stand on that?"

"You know where McCann and I stand on that, you son of a bitch."

Morgan nodded. "I expected as much. Both of you are loyal to a fault. How about you, Mylon? Want to join the winning team?"

"I'd rather chug gasoline and then piss on a campfire. I ain't throwing in with you."

"Suit yourself."

"Morgan," Riffle said. "Think about this. If you kill me and McCann and Novak, who's going to pilot the boat? You need us."

"I've already considered that. Ben has had experience and I've been watching. Studying. I think we'll manage. And besides, who said anything about killing you? We're not savages."

"Well," Mylon said, "you're gonna have to kill me, cause there's no way I'm putting up with this happy horseshit."

He snorted and then spat at Morgan's feet. Morgan twitched, and Ben trembled harder.

"Then I guess there's nothing more to say."

Morgan raised the pistol, extended his arm, and pointed the weapon at Mylon's head. He stepped closer, until the barrel was only inches from Mylon's face. Then he motioned with the gun.

"Get over there by the rail. Ben, you keep the others covered."

Mylon swallowed. "N-now wait…"

"No? I thought you were ready to die?"

"I…"

"That's what I figured. It's one thing to talk about it in the galley. It's another to actually face it head on. Get out of here, Mylon. You too, Paris. Go below. Dry off. Wake the others if you must. Tell them there's been a change in management."

Riffle grabbed Paris by the arm. "Don't. He'll shoot you soon as your backs are turned."

"I'll do no such thing," Morgan said, sounding offended. "How many times do I have to say it?"

Paris wiped her eyes. "You'll really let us live?"

Morgan nodded. "Now go."

Mylon and Paris hurried past them. Mylon glanced over his shoulder once and mouthed an apology to Riffle. Then they went below.

"So what now?" Riffle asked.

"Get on over by the rail."

"I knew it. You're gonna kill me after all. Fucking lying bastard."

Morgan sighed. "No, Riffle. I'm not going to shoot you. I'm going to give you a chance. The same chance your boss offered me."

Riffle's eyes went wide. "W-what?"

"You're going overboard. You can take your chances in the water. If I were you, I'd swim for the island. You wanted to stand beside your shipmates. I'm sure they'll welcome you."

"You're crazy if you think I'm jumping."

"You jump or I *will* shoot you. If you think I'm kidding, just try me."

Riffle stared at them both. Ben refused to meet his gaze, and turned away. Morgan returned the glare, and what Riffle saw in his eyes convinced him. Mouthing the Lord's Prayer, he stepped over to the rail and fought to keep the panic out of his voice.

"You'll pay for this, Morgan."

"Not today I won't. Now jump."

Shaking, Riffle climbed over the side. The water churned below him. The waves suddenly seemed louder. His hands clutched the cold, wet rail. He dangled there, heart pounding in his ears. Salt spray stung his eyes.

"Let go," Morgan said.

"I—I can't…"

"Then let me help you."

Morgan spun the pistol around and smashed the butt against Riffle's fingers. Screaming, Riffle plummeted into the ocean and sank beneath the waves.

Moments later, Riffle came up screaming. He sucked air as a wave smashed into his face, filling his mouth and nose with seawater. He choked, tasting chemicals and salt. The foul mixture felt slick on his skin. His nostrils and eyes burned. A second wave forced him below the surface again. He kept his eyes closed, too terrified to risk glimpsing what might be swimming around beneath him. When he came up again, the ship's motor thrummed.

"Morgan," he shouted. "Get back here, you son of a bitch!"

There was no response from the ship. The deck remained deserted. He spotted two silhouettes on the bridge—probably Ben and Morgan. Bobbing on the waves, he could only watch helplessly as the engine grew louder and the vessel pulled away, slowly at first, but then picking up speed as the motor throttled higher.

"Morgan…"

Thunder boomed overhead. Sputtering, Riffle treaded water and tried to get his bearings. He glanced around, searching frantically for the mysterious island, but it was gone. Mist and rain swirled around him, hampering his vision. He pushed his wet bangs from his eyes and squinted, searching for the lifeboat, or some other sign of Novak and the others, but all he saw was a grayish-white haze.

"Oh, hell."

Whimpering, Riffle began to tremble. He kicked harder, struggling to stay above the waves. His breath came in short, labored gasps. Another wave slammed into him from behind, plunging him beneath the water. When he surfaced again, he was not alone.

A black stalk-like object was sticking out of the water about ten feet away from him. It was as thick as his forearm and covered in sleek, fine hair. Muscles rippled beneath the flesh. The tendril bent in the middle and leaned toward him. The tip held a single hooded eye. It stared at him without blinking.

Four more tentacles thrust up from below, surrounding him. Each was like the first—just an eyeball and an appendage. They had no mouths or nostrils. Not even a discernable head. One by one, they bent in his direction and studied him. Panicked, Riffle swam to the right, hoping to dart between two of the tentacles. They swayed quickly, matching his movements. He darted to the left and the creatures did the same.

Fuck it, he thought. *They don't have mouths or arms. What are they going to do? Stare me to death?*

He slapped the water. "Go on. Get out of here."

The tentacles straightened up again, stretching to their full height. Riffle stared up at them, blinking as raindrops splattered against his face. The sea churned around him and suddenly, he was no longer treading water—he was standing on something solid. He looked down and saw a huge oval shadow beneath him. The five tentacles were attached to it. As he watched, the black object opened beneath his feet, revealing a wide, crescent-shaped mouth full of teeth. He slipped inside, up to his waist and the mouth slammed shut. Impassive, the eyestalks watched his death-throes as the water turned red.

FIFTEEN

Gail plunged into the ocean. She had a momentary sensation of striking something with her feet. Then the waves closed over her head. She opened her eyes and glanced around. The water was dark and murky and she could only see a few feet in any direction. Warren thrashed beneath her, his arms and legs flailing weakly. She reached down, grabbed a handful of his hair, and tugged him upward. He extended his arm and she grasped his hand. Together, they kicked for the surface, and emerged, gasping and choking. They clung to each other and treaded water. There was no sign of the others.

Gail spat seawater. “Are you okay?”

Warren nodded. “You kicked my head when you came down.”

“I’m sorry.”

“It’s okay. I’m okay. Where are the others? Where’s the…?”

She noticed that he couldn’t bring himself to call it an island. Not now. Islands didn’t have eyeballs. They didn’t move when you stabbed them.

The surf was stronger than it had been. The sea churned around them, almost tearing them apart. They clung tighter to each other, legs kicking together.

“Hope I don’t need a breath mint,” Warren said.

Gail laughed, but then it turned into a sob.

“It’ll be okay, Gail. All we need to do is find the lifeboat. If we can’t find that, we’ll swim back to the ship.”

“How? We can’t see anything out here? The ship could be gone and we wouldn’t even know it.”

“They wouldn’t leave us. Riffle would make sure…oh shit.”

Warren’s mouth hung open. He stared up over her shoulder. Gail noticed that it had gotten darker outside, as if a great shadow had fallen over them. Slowly, she turned her head and looked. Then her sobs turned to screams.

Later, when they talked about it, Gail would have trouble accurately describing what she'd seen. Despite the creature's massive bulk, much of its body was concealed by the fog, rain and surf. She had a sense of a cross between a dinosaur and a whale, but the anatomy was all wrong, as were its colors and markings. Its hide looked like earth, rather than flesh. The thing's lower half was beneath the water but its upper bulk towered far above the waves, looming over them like a skyscraper. Mist swirled around it and raindrops bounced off its body. When it roared, the fog momentarily parted before congealing again.

Warren began muttering the Lord's Prayer. Gail simply stared, too terrified to speak or even breathe. Then the shadow deepened as the monster loomed closer.

"Hang on," Warren shouted. "It's getting ready to dive. Hang on to me and don't let go! We've got to—"

The rest of his words were lost as the beast slammed into the water and sank beneath the surface, kicking up huge waves in its thunderous wake. A twenty-foot swell slammed into them, tossing them about like corks. For one moment, they rode the crest together. Then, the surge forced both of them below and pried them apart. Gail opened her mouth to scream. Water rushed down her throat. She turned and spun, not knowing which way was up or down. All she could see was bubbles. She reached for Warren, but he was gone.

When Gail's head broke the surface a second time, Warren was nowhere to be seen. She tried to shout for him, but she couldn't. She'd swallowed too much water, and her throat felt raw. Her lungs ached, desperate for air. She inhaled and then choked. A spasm rocked through her. Barely staying afloat, she clutched her stomach and vomited seawater. She squeezed her eyes shut and gasped. When she opened them again, it was just in time to see a massive wave bearing down on her. Before Gail could move, the wall of water slammed into her, forcing her beneath the surface again.

She opened her eyes underwater, glancing around

frantically, but all she saw was churning foam and bubbles. She kicked upward, emerged, and gasped for more air. Her stomach cramped again, but thankfully, she did not puke. The rain hammered her scalp. Each drop felt like a hailstone.

"Warren? WAAAAARRREEENNNN!"

Thunder answered her. Gail raised her head and stared into the sky. The gray haze flickered momentarily blue, lit by unseen lightening. The mist grew thicker, seeming to cling to her. Shivering, Gail rubbed her arms and bobbed on the surf.

"Warren? Lynn? Anyone?"

"Gail!"

The voice was faint, almost obscured by the roar of the waves and the driving rain. Gail cocked her head and listened closely. The call came again.

"Gail! Gail, over here!"

"Novak? Where are you? I can't see you."

"Keep shouting. I'll find you."

She did. The mist had a strange, dampening effect on sound. Novak still sounded far away when the bow of the lifeboat suddenly emerged from the fog less than eight feet from where she floated. Sobbing and shivering, Gail swam toward it. Her arms and legs felt heavy, and for one panicked moment, she didn't think she'd reach him, and that Novak would drift right on by. Then she was clawing at the sides of the craft. His powerful hands closed around her wrists. His skin was cold. He pulled her up into the boat and deposited her on one of the benches.

"Are you okay?"

Gail nodded. Her teeth chattered uncontrollably. She noticed McCann lying beneath one of the benches. His eyes were closed. He didn't move.

"Is he…?"

"He's alive," Novak said. "Just unconscious. But his pulse is strong and his breathing's steady. Something knocked him out. He was floating face down in the water. I fished him out. Lucky for us both I managed to snag the boat before it drifted away."

"But how?"

"I don't know. I was dog-paddling, looking around for the rest of you, and it came drifting toward me on a wave. Damn thing almost ran me down. Have you seen or heard the others?"

"Warren…he…we were together and then a wave pushed us under."

Novak cupped his hands over his mouth and shouted for Warren and Lynn. He repeated the process several times but there was no answer.

"The ship's gone," Gail said. "There was a break in the fog, and we saw—they left us here."

"Bullshit. Riffle wouldn't do that."

"I'm telling you, it's gone! What are we going to do, Novak?"

He stared at the ocean, and then suddenly leaned forward and pointed over the starboard side. "Look, it's Warren."

Gail turned to see. Sure enough, Warren floated by on the crest of a wave. His body was limp.

"I'll get him."

Before she could react, Novak leaped into the ocean and quickly swam toward the unconscious man. Gail gripped the sides of the lifeboat, watching carefully, urging him on. With a few powerful strokes, Novak reached Warren and flipped him over. Then he screamed.

Warren's head was gone.

"Get in the boat," Gail yelled. "Novak, get back here, Whatever did it might still be out there."

He waved her off and began tugging at Warren's corpse.

"We've got to find his head," Novak called. "If we can find his head, he'll be okay."

"Novak, you're in shock! Goddamn it, McCann and I need you alive if we're going to make it out of this. Now come back here. Please?"

He turned toward her and when Gail saw the haunted expression in his eyes, her heart broke all over again. She had to strain to hear him over the rain and surf.

"You're right. Need to get my shit straight."

He released Warren's body and gave it a gentle push. The

headless corpse floated away, spinning slightly as the current caught it. Novak swam toward the lifeboat. A sleek, black fin appeared behind him.

"Swim," Gail yelled, waving her hands. "Oh my God, Novak—fucking swim!"

The shark fin sliced across the surface, drawing closer to him. Novak raised his head and stared at her. Seawater dripped from his chin.

"What's wrong?"

"Don't turn around. Just swim. Hurry!"

Novak turned around. "Oh, shit."

"I said not to look!"

Eyes wide, he plunged toward the boat with broad, powerful strokes. He kicked his legs. The water churned behind him. The fin closed the distance between them. Novak glanced over his shoulder, saw its proximity, and screamed.

Gail watched from the side of the boat, leaning so far forward that the craft tilted dangerously under her weight. She'd never felt more helpless than she did at that moment. She had always scoffed at the idea of events occurring in slow-motion, but that's what was happening now. Each heartbeat, each breath, seemed to last an eternity. For an instant, her senses were hyper-accentuated. The rain drumming against the boat sounded like gunshots. The waves roared like freight trains. Novak's face was flushed red, whether from fear or exertion she couldn't be sure. Maybe both. She could see a lone, black hair hanging from Novak's left nostril, and the lines around his eyes…

…and the white splotches of fungus growing on the shark's dorsal fin.

The creature bore down on Novak. Gail spotted its silhouette gliding beneath the surface, and realized that it wasn't one of the half-shark, half-human hybrids that they'd encountered, but instead, just a regular old run-of-the-mill shark. Tatiana would have called it old school, but Tatiana was still aboard the ship, and the ship was gone.

What the hell is wrong with me? Focus, damn it.

She stretched out her arms. "Come on, Novak. You can make it."

At the last minute, the shark turned away from Novak and seized Warren's corpse in its jaws. It shook the body and then tugged it beneath the waves. Novak reached the boat as bits of Warren floated back up to the surface and spread out on the currents. Gail tugged Novak into the boat. He collapsed onto the deck, chest heaving. When he tried to sit up, he was overcome by a bout of coughing. Gail pounded him on the back.

"I'm okay," he rasped. "Just…swallowed saltwater. Give me a…minute."

Gail turned her attention back to the sea. The shark was still there. Warren's body had bobbed back up to the surface, and the creature was ripping off chunks, swimming away, and then returning for more. Three more fins appeared in the water. Each of them rushed toward the grisly prize. They were ignoring the boat, at least for the moment. She glanced around, searching for something to use as a paddle, but there was nothing except Novak and McCann. For one second, Gail considered using the unconscious man. She saw herself dipping his arm or leg into the water and using it to propel them forward. She dug her fingernails into her palms, horrified that she could actually envision such a thing.

Novak coughed again.

"You okay?" Gail asked.

"Yeah. I needed a bath anyway."

He snickered, and then began to laugh. Gail stared at him in shock. Then she started giggling. She sat down on one of the benches and found that she couldn't stop laughing. Tears ran from her eyes. Her stomach began to cramp, but still she couldn't stop. Novak joined her on the bench. They clung to each other.

They were still laughing when McCann finally stirred. He opened his eyes, blinked, and then sat up. Frowning, he rubbed the back of his head.

"What's so funny?" he asked.

Novak and Gail fell silent. They looked at McCann and then at each other. Novak snorted and then both of them burst out laughing again. The sound echoed out over the waves.

"We're screwed, aren't we?" Gail asked, gasping for breath.

"Yeah." Novak nodded. "I think we are."

"Do you still think we should consider a group suicide pact?"

"At this point," Novak said, "does it really matter?"

They drifted for a while, too tired to speak. The only sounds were the rain and the waves. All three of them stared out into the swirling mist, watching for—and expecting—a new threat to emerge from the fog, but nothing did. They kept watch for Lynn, and called her name, but there was no sign of her.

Gail rubbed her shoulders and shivered. Her clothes and hair were soaked, and her skin had turned pale. She frowned, staring at the white marks her fingers made on her flesh when she pressed. She wondered how long they could survive under these conditions, and then tried to remember the signs of hypothermia. It was hard for her to think. She felt drunk—whether from delayed shock or simple exhaustion, she didn't know, and then realized that she didn't care. Better to die sooner than later. Gail decided she'd rather slip over the side and into the water, either drowning or getting eaten, rather than sit in this boat and die slowly. At this point, fighting to survive would be an exercise in futility. She was going to die from exposure to the elements or starvation or as a meal for one of the underwater denizens. And even if, by some miraculous turn of events, they did find shelter from the weather and food to eat, then there was still the white fuzz to contend with. They still didn't know much about it, but Gail presumed that floating in the middle of the ocean was probably a good way to catch it.

"We're gonna die out here," McCann moaned.

Neither Gail or Novak responded to him. Gail stared straight ahead, looking at nothing. She became aware of noises out there in the fog. There were occasional muffled splashes, as if something had briefly jumped out of the water. She heard birds calling from somewhere overhead. Clicking noises echoed from their starboard side, and then faded. A few times there was something like a dolphin's chatter, but it was low-pitched and harsh. And once, a deep, rumbling baritone rumbled across the sea like a blast from a horn.

"Do we stay here and wait for Lynn?" Gail asked.

"I don't think we're going to find her," Novak admitted. "Not in these conditions. As much as I hate to say it, I think we—"

The boat lurched as something bumped into it. Gail squealed. Her hands gripped the sides tightly. Novak leaned forward, his shoulders tense, and then he visibly relaxed. When he glanced back at her and McCann, he looked relieved.

"It was just a tree."

Eventually, the fog lifted. Gail assumed that she must have zoned out for a while, because she wasn't even aware that it was gone until she realized that she could see structures in the distance, sticking up above the surface. With the fog gone, their spirits seemed to lift, if only slightly. They spoke to one another again in hushed, cautious tones, mindful of what might be lurking beneath the waves, listening for them. They grieved briefly for Warren and Lynn. Novak checked McCann over and made sure he was uninjured. Then he tried to make his second-mate and Gail both as comfortable as possible—a hopeless cause, given their current situation. Still, Gail smiled at the attempt. Not for the first time, the gruff ship's captain had touched her heart.

They drifted slowly past the structures she'd seen in the distance—the upper floors of buildings that had yet to be fully submerged. None of them would offer viable shelter. The sickly white fungus clung to the exposed sides, climbing up the masonry with fuzzy tentacles. Gail stared down into the coffee-colored water and saw an entire town beneath them—office buildings, cars, housing developments, gas stations, playgrounds, shopping malls, schools, churches and fast food restaurants, all completely submerged: a town for the new denizens of the deep. She wondered if the shark people and some of the other creatures they'd encountered would move into the dwellings now that their previous inhabitants were gone.

"So what do we do now?" McCann's voice quavered.

Gail turned to look at the others. Water dripped from McCann's nose, and Novak's hair was plastered to his head. Both men were shivering. They appeared as uncomfortable and miserable as she felt.

"Well," Novak said as they glided over a sunken grocery store. "One thing is for sure. This boat is too light and too hard to navigate when shit gets choppy. We're okay now, because we're in a relatively shallow area. But once we get out over a valley or low spot again, we might have trouble. Keep an eye out for any long pieces of wood without that fucking white shit on them. We need something to help us row."

"It's too bad we can't anchor," Gail said. "Then we could stay in one spot and wait for the others to find us."

Novak shook his head. "I don't think the others are coming back."

"But Riffle wouldn't have just left us like that, boss." McCann's tone was earnest and adamant. "There's no way he'd abandon us out here."

"Maybe he thought we were dead, or maybe that monster fucking island went for them, and they had to run. I don't know the reason, but I know that they're nowhere in sight, and I don't look for them to return. We're on our own out here."

His words seemed to echo out over the water.

SIXTEEN

There was no way of telling time. The sun was a pale, muted disc hidden behind the impenetrable clouds. Eventually, the waters grew calmer. The waves died down to nothing more than ripples, and the sound of the raindrops pelting the surface grew louder. When Gail leaned over the side, she was able to see more ruins beneath them. The rooftops were closer to the surface, and much more debris floated around them.

"We must be entering higher ground," McCann said. "The water is getting shallower."

Novak nodded in agreement. "Keep an eye out."

Soon, the bottom of the boat began to scrape overtop the underwater structures. Treetops, steel girders and jagged, exposed construction timbers jutted from the water like skeletal fingers. Other than the rain, the area was completely still. There was no sound or movement. Even the seabirds had disappeared. The white fuzz wasn't as prevalent in this region as it had been in other places they'd sailed through in recent weeks. It clung to a few of the trees and girders, but most of the ruins were relatively free of it.

They passed a circular water tower and a church steeple. Both towered above the waterline, but neither structure offered shelter from the elements. The current took them close enough to the steeple that Gail could have reached out and touched it, but there was nothing to salvage other than roofing tiles. Novak made a half-hearted attempt to grab one of the gutters, announcing his intent to use it as an oar, but the gutter held fast. The boat rocked dangerously beneath them, and Gail urged him to sit back down. The boat bumped against the side of the steeple and then kept drifting.

"Look ahead." McCann pointed. "How about that? It looks secure."

Gail and Novak turned in the direction he had indicated. Ahead of them was a large, rectangular office building. The four topmost floors were above the water. An array of antennae and ductwork covered the roof. It appeared deserted, and intact. There were no broken windows, and no cracks or holes in the sides of the building.

"It looks solid," Gail said. "But the current isn't taking us anywhere near it."

Novak stood up again, more carefully this time.

"What are you doing?" Gail asked.

"Getting us there. I'm already wet, right?"

Without another word, he draped his legs over the side and then slipped into the water, nearly capsizing their boat in the process. Novak clutched the bow with one hand and blinked water from his eyes.

McCann paled. "I don't think that's such a good idea, boss-man. Look at how dirty that water is. The pollutants are a lot thicker here than they were further out to sea."

"Then I'll make sure I don't swallow any."

"Are you crazy?" Gail moved to the front of the craft. "Have you forgotten about the shark-men already?"

"We want to get away from them," Novak said, "along with all the other creepy-critters out here. That building looks like our only shot. Now sit down, Gail. If you guys want to help, paddle with your hands."

Still gripping the bow with one hand, he began to propel them through the water, grunting with the effort. McCann leaned over the side and began paddling with his hand. After a moment, Gail did the same from her side. They moved slowly, and she kept her eyes on the water, waiting for something to charge up from the depths.

Treading water, Novak pulled the boat alongside the building. The hull bumped gently against the side, scraping the wall. Novak grasped for a handhold. Foul seawater dripped from his hands and arms. Gail eyed the droplets, thinking about her suspicion that the strange fungus was possibly spread by contact with the water. She kept her misgivings to herself. After all, if that were true, they'd all be infected by now. After suffering through endless days of rain, it was impossible to stay dry. The air itself felt drenched.

Novak latched onto a windowsill and steadied the rocking craft. Small waves lapped against the concrete walls. Raindrops made circular patterns on the water's surface—no two alike. Gail turned her attention to the office building. While only the four topmost floors were above the surface, the structure seemed stable. It wasn't leaning, and there were no cracks, holes or broken windows that she could see—at least on this side. The swirling fog hid the ductwork and antennae array she'd seen on the roof earlier. There were no lights behind the windows. Gail tried peering through one, but it was fogged over.

"What do you guys think?" McCann asked.

"It's quiet," Novak said. "Sealed up. Looks stable. There's no way of knowing what kind of shape the interior is in, but I say we try to get inside."

"What if it's not deserted?"

"Then we'll ask them if they mind sharing."

Something splashed loudly far out in the mist, and the little boat rocked harder. Gail glanced behind them. There was a dark shape in the mist—something large, looming above the surface. She turned back to McCann and Novak to verify that they saw the same thing, but both men had their attention focused on the office building. She looked again, and the shadow was gone.

"Novak…"

He grunted in response.

"I think we'd better hurry," Gail whispered.

Nodding, Novak pushed and pulled at the window. It wouldn't open. He sighed, treading water, and then tried again. The window was about a foot above the surface, and the waves kept pushing Novak into the wall.

"Maybe we should check the other sides of the building," McCann said. "Might be an easier way in."

"I want to get out of this water," Novak said. "The damn *Jaws* theme keeps running through my head."

He pulled off his shirt and wrapped the wet garment

around his fist. Then, gritting his teeth, he drew back his arm and struck the window with the side of his fist. The boat rocked back and forth from the momentum. The glass remained intact. Grimacing, Novak rubbed his hand.

"Shit. That hurt."

Gail noticed that the waves were growing bigger.

"Hit it again," she urged. Something splashed softly in the gloom.

Novak struck the window three more times. A spider-web pattern of cracks appeared in the glass. He struck again. On the sixth attempt, the window shattered. He leaned forward and sniffed, testing the air.

"Smell anything?" McCann asked.

Novak shook his head. "Mildew, but it's real faint. I don't hear anything, either. I think we're okay."

Gail noticed that his speech was different. His words were clipped—tense, as if he were in pain and trying to hide it. He clung to the side of the boat with his free hand. Gail started to speak, but Novak cut her off.

"Can you guys clear the glass out of the way, so we don't cut ourselves climbing through?"

McCann stood up carefully, waited for the boat to settle, and then began picking shards of glass from the frame and dropping them into the water.

"Are you okay?" Gail asked Novak.

"No." His face was pinched and the color had drained from his face. "I think I just broke my goddamn arm. That's all we need right now, huh? When it rains, it fucking pours."

"Shit." McCann finished clearing the shards of broken glass out of the way. "Are you sure it's broken?"

Novak shook his head. "No, but it sure feels that way."

"Okay, well, I'll go inside. Make sure it's okay. Then I'll pull you up. Gail can push on your feet."

Nodding, Novak blinked water from his eyes.

McCann grabbed the windowsill and hoisted himself into the open space. His head and shoulders disappeared inside. He pulled one leg through the window, and was about to pull the other one through, when a shotgun blast filled the air, drowning out even the sound of the rain. McCann tumbled backward and splashed into the water, narrowly missing the boat. He vanished beneath the surface. Gail leaned forward but before she could cry out, an armed figure appeared in the window.

"Don't move, motherfuckers!"

The stranger's face was hidden beneath wet bandages. Only his eyes were visible, but they were covered by a pair of aviator goggles. He wore a hooded yellow poncho and his feet, legs and waist were covered by a pair of green rubber waders. His voice, guttural and angry, was a man's. Smoke still curled from the barrel of the shotgun in his hands, and water dripped from the stock.

"Get your fucking hands up," he ordered.

Gail did as commanded, but Novak refused to comply.

"That's not going to happen," he told their attacker.

The man pointed the shotgun at him. "Then you can go to hell."

"How about this instead?" Novak raised one hand as the shotgun centered on his chest.

"Both of them, motherfucker."

"I can't," Novak insisted. "I think I may have broke my other hand."

"He's not kidding," Gail said. "Please…"

Their attacker swung the weapon toward her. "Shut up. Both of you just shut the hell up."

"Look," Novak said, his voice calm and assured. "We don't have anything except the clothes we're wearing. If you want the boat, you can have it. You can take it and sail right on out of here. Just don't kill us."

The stranger didn't respond. Indeed, he gave no indication that he'd even heard Novak's offer. His yellow poncho flapped around his waist as the breeze picked up. Raindrops pattered against his green rubber waders. The wet gauze covering his face seemed to move on its own. Gail tried to see past his aviator goggles and into his eyes, but they were shadowed. The man twitched his shoulders, let the shotgun slip lower, and then cleared his throat.

"I want the boat. But that can wait. Come here, lady. And don't try anything funny."

Gail felt like she'd been kicked in the stomach. Everything seemed to stop. Even the rain. The waves became silent.

"Come on." The man gestured with the shotgun. "Get in here."

Lump in her throat, Gail moved toward the window. The boat rocked beneath her feet, nearly spilling her into the water. The man adjusted his grip on the weapon, holding it with one hand. He stretched his other arm out toward her and leaned forward.

"Take my hand."

Gail did, trying all the while to keep her own hand from shaking. Her fingers closed around his wrist. The man leaned closer, and began to help her up. As he shifted his weight, Gail suddenly yanked his arm and flung herself backward. The attacker uttered a surprised cry and then toppled forward. Gail's back struck the bottom of the boat. The man crashed down on top of her, driving the air from her lungs. The shotgun, still in his grasp, slammed against the deck with a ringing sound.

"You bitch." His breath stank, and he smelled of mildew and sweat. "Now I'm gonna—"

Roaring, Novak erupted from the water behind them, and looped his uninjured arm around the attacker's neck. The man tried to raise the shotgun, but Gail pried it from his hand. Then, Novak pulled him off Gail and into the water. The two of them slipped beneath the waves.

Stunned, Gail wiped water from her eyes and blinked. Then she leaned forward and peered into the water, gripping the sides of the boat so tightly that her knuckles turned white. Sound returned—first the rain, then the cries of the birds overhead, and then the waves.

"Novak?"

Shadows moved beneath the surface, but she couldn't identify them. Was it Novak and their attacker? McCann? A mermaid or shark-person or fuzzoid or other weird denizens of the deep? Shivering, she reached for the discarded shotgun.

Novak burst from the water, gasping and coughing. Screaming, Gail skittered backward. The boat lurched hard to one side.

"It's okay," he panted. Novak grabbed the side of the boat with his good hand and clung to it, eyes closed. "It's okay. He's dead."

Gail opened her mouth to respond, but all that came out was a low, guttural moan. She closed her mouth, took a few deep breaths through her nose, and then tried again. Her voice still trembled.

"Are you okay?"

Novak nodded.

"What about McCann? Did you see him?"

"I'm right here."

Novak's eyes snapped open. Gail turned around and looked behind them. She gasped with relief when she saw McCann paddling toward them.

"Son of a bitch," Novak said. "I thought he shot you."

McCann shook his head, spraying water droplets as he climbed into the boat. "I thought he did, too. But he didn't. When the gun went off, it startled me. I slipped and fell into the water. Where is he?"

"Sinking to the bottom," Novak replied.

"Think he had friends inside?" McCann nodded at the office building.

Novak shrugged, wincing in obvious pain. "I don't know. If so, you'd think they'd have come running when they heard us fighting."

The three of them fell silent for a moment, catching their breath. Birds continued wheeling overhead. Eventually, a few of them landed on the rooftop and studied the new arrivals with interest.

"Wonder what they're thinking?" McCann asked.

"Dinner-time," Novak said. "They look as hungry as I feel."

"Well," Gail said. "We can't just sit out here in the rain. You're injured, and McCann and I are both shaken up. I vote we go inside. If there was anybody else in there, they'd have taken a shot at us by now."

"Unless they're waiting," McCann said. "It could be a trap."

Novak grunted. "It could be, but I'm with Gail. Better to take our chances inside, where it's at least partially dry, than to sit out here and wait to get eaten."

"Those birds won't really eat us," McCann said.

"No," Novak agreed, "but there's things in the water that will."

Without another word, they guided the boat back over to the open window. McCann went inside first, muttering about getting shot at a second time. When that didn't happen, he reached out and grasped Novak's good arm, and hoisted him inside. Gail followed, after tossing up the line to McCann. Once inside, she offered the shotgun to Novak. He shook his head.

"You keep it."

The room was dark and quiet and devoid of furnishings, other than a desk, a chair and a filing cabinet—the latter of which was lying on its side and badly dented, its moldering contents scattered across the floor. The air smelled thick and musty. Gail waited for her eyes to adjust, but she could make nothing else out in the gloom.

"Wish we had a flashlight." Novak's voice echoed.

McCann tied the end of the line around the desk, and then pushed the piece of furniture, grunting with the effort. He stood up and wiped his hands on his wet clothes.

"It's pretty heavy. I don't think the boat will go anywhere."

"Let's hope not," Novak said. "Otherwise, we might be here for a while. Come on. Let's explore our new home."

"No," Gail said. "McCann and I can explore the building. You're sitting your ass down and getting some rest."

"I'm fine."

"You're not fine. Your arm might be broken, not to mention you almost drowned out there."

"It's not broken." Novak flexed his fingers, wincing even as he grinned. "It hurts like a son of a bitch, but it's not broken."

"Wiggle it."

He did as she requested, rotating his arm around and

swinging it back and forth. He hissed air through his teeth and then let the arm hang limp again.

"I still want you to rest," Gail said. "Obviously, you're in a lot of pain. You're not going to be much good to us if you don't recuperate."

Novak sat down with his back against the wall and positioned himself so that he could see out the broken window. Water dripped from his clothes, running across the floor. He sighed. "And here I thought you guys wanted me along for my sparkling personality. You just need me to help fight monsters."

Gail didn't respond. Instead, she watched the rivulets of water. Rather than pooling around Novak's feet, they made their way to the far wall, as if the office building itself was leaning in that direction. Frowning, she shifted her feet. The floor certainly felt level. She wondered if it was just exhaustion playing tricks on her mind. She'd never felt so tired in her life. All she wanted to do was lay down and sleep for a day.

"Come on," McCann said. "If we're going to do this, then let's get it over with. I'd like to sit down at some point tonight."

Nodding, Gail led the way. She hoisted the shotgun in her cold, wet hands, using it to push open the office door. It led into a dark, dank hallway. Mildew stains covered the once-white walls. The carpet squelched beneath their feet. Other than the roar of the surf, steadily beating against the walls, the building was silent. Gail and McCann went from room to room, making sure each one was clear and also looking for anything useful. Most of the offices were identical to the first, but they also found two restrooms, a lunchroom with several vending machines, and a storage closet full of cleaning supplies. On the top shelf of the storage closet was a first aid kit. It had been rummaged through—probably by the man with the goggles, Gail assumed, but there were still plenty of antiseptic wipes, bandages, an assortment of over-the-counter pills, and half a roll of medical tape. The vending machines had also been broken into. The doors were unlocked, and swung open with the slightest touch. The soda machine was about half-full of bottled water and various soft drinks, all warm. The second machine, which had once held junk food, was empty. The third vending machine had held perishable items—sandwiches, yogurt, juice, and other food that had long since gone bad. When McCann opened it, a terrible stench wafted out. Both he and Gail coughed.

"Close it," Gail gasped, her eyes watering. "That stinks!"

"I don't think we'll be eating any of that," he agreed. "Looks like our attacker left us with some water, though. At least we won't die of thirst anytime soon."

"Hooray. Instead, we can stay alive for those things in the water."

They continued onward, passing by a set of closed elevator doors and then coming to a stairwell. Gail nudged the door open and listened. It was quiet. Far below, she heard the sound of water lapping.

"Lower levels are flooded," she whispered. "Probably better to be quiet until we come out on the next floor. If something's down there, we don't want it to hear us."

McCann nodded, and she led him upward. They emerged onto the floor above, and found an identical layout to the floor they'd just left. Shutting the door behind them, they resumed their exploration.

"Do you really think something could be living down below?"

Gail shrugged. "I don't see why not. The building is submerged. Something could be swimming around down there—those flying fish or maybe the shark men."

"What do you think they all are?" McCann opened an office door and peered inside. "These creatures. I mean, if they've always existed, how come we never saw them until the rains started? And what else is there? We've seen shark-men, flying piranha, snakes made out of seaweed, starfish with faces like humans, mermaids, fuzzoids, and giant worms, crabs, lobsters and octopuses—not to mention that fucking island thing that landed us in this position."

"Octopi," Gail said.

"What?"

"You said octopuses. I think it's octopi rather than octopuses."

"I don't give a shit what they are," McCann said. "I just want to know where they came from and how the hell we can get rid of them all."

"I can help you with that," a voice called from the end of the hallway. "Provided you help me first."

The shotgun wobbled in Gail's trembling hands. She and McCann glanced at each other in surprise, and then stared into the gloom at the end of the hallway. Their eyes had adjusted to the darkness, but the shadows were thick.

"Who's there?" She hoped her voice wasn't shaking as bad as the rest of her.

"You can call me Simon. And you are?"

"Never mind that," Gail said. "Come on out with your hands up, and do it slow."

"Sadly, I can't comply with your request."

"Listen," McCann shouted. "Don't fuck with us, buddy. We've had enough of this bullshit. Keep it up and you'll get what your friend just got."

"I don't know who you mean."

"The asshole with the aviator goggles. He took a shot at us. Last thing he ever did."

The sound of chuckling drifted out of the office at the end of the hall.

"What's so funny?" Gail called.

"The man you describe," Simon said. "He was no friend of mine."

"I don't care what your relationship was. Come out slowly with your hands up."

"As I said, I'd like to, but I'm afraid it's impossible."

"Why?"

Simon's tone grew annoyed. "Because I'm chained to a desk."

Gail and McCann turned to each other again. McCann arched an eyebrow. Gail shrugged, and then nodded toward the door. She took a hesitant step forward, then another. She moved to the side, keeping her back against the wall, and crept into the shadows. McCann followed behind her.

"Hello?" Simon called. "Are you still there?"

Neither of them answered him. They paused in front of the closed office door. Gail knelt on the floor and trained the weapon on the doorway. Then she took a deep breath, and nodded at McCann. He reached out, turned the knob and flung the door open. It banged against the wall.

"Well," Simon said, "I guess that answers my question."

Gail stood up and rushed into the room, making sure to keep the shotgun extended. McCann hurried in behind her. The office was identical to the ones on the floor below, with one noticeable difference—the naked man tied spread-eagled to the desk. His wrists and ankles were bound with black rubber bungee cords of the type usually reserved for tying down furniture in the back of pick-up trucks. His pale skin was slick and covered with open sores, cuts and scratches. Both Gail and McCann winced at the stench wafting up from him. A broken fish tank lay on the floor, shards of broken glass glittering in the gloom. Atop of the tank's stand were a number of household tools—pliers, wrenches, screwdrivers, box-cutter, claw hammer and more. Judging by the dried blood crusting their edges and the captive's wounds, they'd been converted into instruments of torture. In the corner was a large coffee can half-filled with human waste.

"Jesus," McCann whispered.

Simon grinned. "Oh, I called on him, among others, to help me, but as you can see, my situation didn't improve."

"Hang on," Gail said. "We'll untie you."

"What if it's a trap?" McCann glanced back out into the hall. "What if there are more of them, waiting to rush us."

"I'm not the one you need to be worried about. Indeed, I may be the only hope you have left. All you have to do is free me."

Gail leveled the shotgun, pointing the barrel only inches from Simon's head.

"Untie him," she said to McCann. "If he so much as breathes funny, it will be the last thing he ever does."

Simon studied her calmly. "Believe me, madam. If we don't act soon, our actions here may very well be the last thing *any* of us do."

McCann approached Simon timidly, with all of the caution normally reserved for a soldier navigating a minefield. Gail kept the shotgun pressed against the bound man's head. Simon seemed unperturbed. He licked his lips and then smiled at her. McCann tugged on the bungee cords, and Simon winced—his smile vanishing.

"Sorry," McCann mumbled.

"That's okay."

The rubber cords fell to the floor. McCann stepped back and glanced at Gail. She took a deep breath and then removed the shotgun from Simon's head. She backed away, just out of arms reach and nodded.

"Thank you," Simon said. "Thank you both."

He sat up slowly, groaning slightly as he did. His head drooped and his shoulders slumped. Then his body went slack and he began to swoon. Gail and McCann rushed forward and kept him from falling to the floor.

"He passed out," Gail said.

"No, I'm still conscious." Simon's voice sounded weak. "I've just been here for a while. I sat up too quickly. Just give me a few moments."

"How long have you been tied up here?" McCann asked.

"I don't know. I've had no way of telling the passage of time in this room—not that keeping track of the days is easy anymore, even if I'd been outside. The perpetual cloud cover makes that difficult sometimes. Don't you agree?"

Gail and McCann nodded.

"It felt like an eternity." Simon wiggled his feet and hands, trying to get some circulation into them.

Gail stared at the wounds covering his naked body. The sheer number of cuts and sores were horrendous. This close to him, the stench of body odor and infection was almost overpowering.

"Find him something to wear," Gail told McCann.

"Where? The nearest Men's Wearhouse is at the bottom of the ocean."

"I don't know. Search the offices. Maybe somebody left a suit jacket or a uniform behind."

"You going to be okay here?"

"Yes," Gail said. "But be careful. There still might be more of them."

"There's not," Simon confirmed. "My captor was the only one. Thank God for that. He was quite mad."

"What did he want with you?" Gail asked.

Simon shrugged. "I honestly don't know. I was traveling with two associates. They…didn't make it. I was adrift for days. Nearly dead. Slipping in and out of consciousness. The last thing I remembered clearly was spotting this place. My captor rescued me. When I woke up again, I was strapped down. He… tortured me, but he never asked any questions. Which is a shame, really. I know the answers to many things. I might have been able to help him find what he was looking for."

"I'll be back," McCann said. "Maybe I should let Novak know what's going on, too."

Gail nodded. "Good idea. Be careful."

"I will."

After he'd left the room, Gail felt a momentary rush of panic. She was all alone with Simon now, and despite his injuries and condition, she knew nothing about the man. He spoke with a slight British accent, and was educated, judging from his vocabulary. But his story was as clouded and mysterious as the motives of the man who had shot at them.

"You mentioned that you had associates," Gail said.

"Yes. Two of them. We always travel in threes, unless special circumstances dictate otherwise."

"What happened to them?"

"One of them, Kroger, fell victim to a giant worm. The other, Mark, was seduced by a mermaid with a bad case of vampirism. We are part of an international organization. The surviving members of that organization were trying to stop what has happened. Half of our group were searching for something—convinced that it was needed to halt the rains. The other half of us were determined to stop them."

"But why would you want to stop them?"

"Because their methods are abhorrent, and uncalled for. They were convinced that a newborn infant was required to seal the gate, but my friends and I learned of another method—a ritual favored by a recently-extinct race of intelligent amphibians."

Gail frowned. "Just what kind of organization did you and your friends work for?"

"A group called Black Lodge."

McCann found Novak sitting where they'd left him, with his back up against the damp, mildewed wall. He trembled beneath his wet clothing, and when he turned at McCann's approach, the younger man noticed that his teeth were chattering.

"You okay?" McCann asked.

Novak nodded. "Just cold. Arm still hurts like a bitch, but I'll be okay. What's up?"

"We found someone. A man."

"You shoot him?"

"No." McCann shook his head. "His name is Simon. He says he was a prisoner here. I believe him. He was tied down when we found him, and he's pretty banged up. Looks like he's been tortured."

"Where is he now?"

"Upstairs with Gail."

Novak frowned. "You left her alone with this guy?"

"She's got the shotgun. And trust me, dude, this guy isn't going to be able to do much. Seriously. He's all messed up. He's weak and looks like he's probably running a fever. That fucker who attacked us did a number on him. I just came down to tell you, and to find him something to wear."

"He's naked?"

"Yeah. Why? Is that important?"

Novak shrugged. "It's better for Gail. Naked people often feel more vulnerable. He might be less likely to attack her if he's feeling that way."

"Oh." McCann's ears turned red. "I thought you were going to make a joke about leaving her alone with a naked man."

"Well, there's that, too." Grunting, Novak stumbled to his feet. "Introduce me to this Simon."

McCann turned to leave but then realized that Novak wasn't following him. Instead, he was staring out the broken window they'd entered the building through.

"What's wrong? Did you see something?"

Novak hesitated. "No…while you guys were gone, I kept hearing splashing sounds out there. Couldn't tell if it was the waves or something else. It's hard to see through the downpour and all that mist."

"Maybe one of us should stay here and stand guard."

"You think this Simon can walk down here?"

"I don't know. Maybe, if Gail and I help him."

"Let's try that. I don't like leaving this hole unguarded. We're in enough trouble as it is. See if he can make it down here. If he can't, come and get me."

"Sounds like a plan." McCann started to leave again, but then turned back and studied Novak carefully.

"You sure you're okay, boss man?"

"Yeah." Novak sighed as he sat back down again. "I'm just tired. I could sleep for a week. Too bad there's not a dry bed left anywhere in the world."

McCann studied Novak closely, noticing for the first time the dark circles beneath the older man's eyes, like smudges of soot. His skin seemed pasty and colorless, his lips thin and pale. His fingertips were wrinkled from overexposure to moisture and his posture was stooped and sullen. It was a marked contrast from the man he'd been before the rain—or even the man he'd been just a few weeks ago. That version of Novak had seemed to still have hope. This version seemed to cling to survival out of some grim sense of duty more than anything else. McCann considered everything they'd been through since leaving the ship, and decided he couldn't really blame Novak. He probably looked and felt the same way himself. He'd just been too busy to realize it yet. In fact, now that he thought about it, he felt out of sorts, as well.

"Get going," Novak said. "Naked and injured or not, I don't like the idea of Gail being alone with this guy for too long."

Without another word, McCann headed back down the

hallway. The carpet squished beneath his feet and the stairwell echoed with his footsteps. On the second floor, he passed by an office that he and Gail had missed on their first search. It was located at the rear of a reception area. He realized upon passing it that they'd checked the chairs in the waiting area and behind the switchboard but had forgotten to check the office itself. Perhaps he'd find something for Simon to wear inside the room. He listened at the closed door, but heard no sound from within. Reaching down, he turned the knob and found it unlocked.

He took one step into the dark room, pausing to let his eyes adjust to the gloom. Something moved in the shadows. Gasping, McCann stumbled backward as the sound rustled toward him.

McCann scrambled out into the reception area and glanced around for something—anything—to use as a weapon, but the space was empty, save for fragments of fallen plaster and puddles of water. At some point, the desk had surely held a computer and some type of phone switchboard, but both were now missing, as was the receptionist's chair. The skittering sound drew nearer. The shadowy form rose up and squeaked.

"What the hell?"

In the doorway, a large, brown rat stood on its hind legs and studied him cautiously. Its nose twitched at the sound of McCann's voice, but the rodent didn't run away. Instead, it dropped back down to all fours and crept closer.

"You're a brave little son of a bitch."

As if in agreement, the bold rodent darted forward and stopped at McCann's feet. It stood up on its hind legs again and squeaked once more. It showed no fear—only curiosity.

"If I didn't know better, I'd say you were tame. Is that it? Were you a pet rat? Did you belong to the guy who shot at me?"

Moving slowly, McCann knelt in the doorway. His knee joints popped and his stomach growled. Both sounded loud in the silence, but still the rat remained. He studied it closely, looking for any sign of the white fuzz, but the creature seemed free of infection. Holding his breath, McCann reached out with one finger and cautiously touched the rodent's back. When it didn't bite him or flee, he stroked its soft, damp fur. The rat arched its back, obviously enjoying the attention. McCann smiled.

"Look at you. You're a friendly little guy. What's your name, I wonder? Did he give you a name?"

He spoke in soft, cooing tones, and the rat gazed up at him with rapt attention. McCann petted it a few more times and then stood up. The rat remained at his feet.

"Well, I guess I'll have to come up with a name for you. How about 'Dinner'? You like that? Come here, Dinner."

McCann's grin vanished. He raised one booted foot and brought it down on the rat's head. Its skull crunched beneath his heel. The rodent's legs and tail twitched, and then it lay still. The thought occurred to McCann that this could have been the last rat left alive in the world, and that he'd just made their entire species extinct. Then his stomach growled again, and he dismissed the thought with a shrug.

Now that his eyes had adjusted to the gloom, McCann stepped into the small office and looked around. It was a windowless room, and had probably served as some sort of storage area at one time. Judging from the clutter, the man who'd attacked them earlier had been using it as a place to sleep. McCann nodded with begrudging approval. Unlike the other offices, the room was hidden from the ocean, and easy to defend if attacked. It was tucked away and not easily noticeable. Indeed, he and Gail had missed it during their initial search. It might be just as easily missed by anyone—or *anything*—that entered the building hunting for prey.

The floor was strewn with makeshift bedding composed mostly of dirty, damp linens, tablecloths, sofa cushions and scraps of torn clothing. The walls were lined with metal shelving, and stacked on these was a wide assortment of various odds and ends—everything from cases of bottled water to knives and other weapons. Spying a sports coat that was relatively unsoiled, McCann made a mental note to thoroughly search the room and inventory its contents later. He selected a handgun from the assortment of weapons, but couldn't find ammunition for it. He lay the pistol back down and took a butcher knife instead. Just holding it in his hand made McCann feel more secure. Then he picked up a pillowcase from the floor, placed the rat's still-bleeding corpse inside, and tied the pillowcase shut, forming a makeshift sack. He slung this over his shoulder, grabbed the sports coat, and then headed back upstairs to find Gail and Simon.

He whistled as he walked, and it wasn't until he was halfway up the stairwell to the next floor that he realized the moisture on his cheeks wasn't remnants from the rain, but fresh tears.

"So, are you going to tell me more about this group…what did you say it was called?"

"Black Lodge."

"Right." Gail nodded. "How come I've never heard of them?"

Simon smiled. "You obviously didn't spend your free time trawling the internet. There was endless speculation about us on the various conspiracy-minded forums and blogs. In truth, the internet was our undoing. We've existed for ages, but it wasn't until the advent of the internet that we became exposed."

"Centuries? So, you're not some offshoot of the CIA or FBI?"

"No, nothing like that. Tell me, are you familiar with the story of the nativity?"

"The birth of Jesus? Sure. But what does that have to do with—"

"The three wise men were also known as magi. They were representatives of our group. But we go even farther back than that."

Gail opened her mouth to respond, but before she could, they both heard footsteps coming down the hall. They turned to look as McCann walked back into the room. He carried a butcher knife, suit jacket, and a pillowcase that was leaking fresh blood. Gail watched as a suspended droplet dripped down onto the carpet.

"What's in the bag?" she asked.

McCann grinned. "Dinner."

"Are you okay? You seem…I don't know. Tired."

"I am tired," McCann said. Then he approached Simon and handed him the suit coat. "I found this for you. Hope it fits."

Simon stood up, and Gail quickly turned away, but not before catching another glimpse of his wounds. She heard the whisper of cloth over bare flesh, and then Simon cleared his throat. She turned back around. The injured man's face was red. He glanced down at his exposed lower half and blushed harder.

"I suppose it's better than nothing."

"There's more downstairs," McCann said. "I found the cubbyhole where our boy was living. Most of the clothes are torn or wet or dirty, but you can probably make do."

"I've got an idea." Smiling with his split and swollen lips, Simon took the coat off and tied it sideways around his waist, like a loincloth. Then he held his arms out to the side and slowly turned all the way around until he was facing them again. "Is that better?"

"Much better," Gail said, surprised at the flutter in her voice.

"There's other stuff downstairs, too," McCann said. "Water. Weapons. We should be able to stay here for a bit, and recuperate. Not that it matters, though. Not really."

Gail frowned. "What do you mean?"

"I figured it out," McCann replied. "None of this matters, because we're already dead. Think about what's happened. The weather doesn't act like this. It can't rain like this all over the world. It's not scientifically possible. And all those monsters—the worms and the things in the water. They can't be real. We're dead. We're dead and we're in Hell."

"I thought you didn't believe in Heaven and Hell."

McCann shrugged. "No sense not believing in something that's right there in front of your face. We're in Hell, Gail. Only difference is that Hell isn't hot. It's wet."

Simon took a faltering step forward, wincing in obvious

pain. They reached out to support him, but he waved them away. Grimacing, he took another step, and placed his hand on McCann's shoulder.

"I can assure you that we're not dead, friend. At least, not yet. But you are partially correct. Another realm of existence—not Hell, but the Great Deep—is crowing over into our own. And if we don't act soon, then we will indeed be dead."

He brushed slowly past them and walked toward the door. Gail and McCann stood staring at him. When he reached the hallways, Simon turned and beckoned.

"Come. We have much to discuss."

When they were all together, Gail suggested they move to the secure room that McCann had discovered, but Novak was against that idea. He wanted to stay where they were, pointing out that should something happen to the small boat anchored to the side of the building, they'd have no means of escape.

"I don't know," Gail said. "I think I'd almost rather take my chances in here than out there on the open water. At least in here, we can defend ourselves. We're sitting ducks outside."

"I'm not against staying here a while," Novak agreed, "but we still need the boat. We've all seen the size of some of those things out there. Some of them could smash this building with one flap of their tail. Then there's the shark-men and those flying piranha to contend with. If they attack, we may have to leave in a hurry. If something happens to the boat, our only option is going to be swimming, and that's as good as suicide."

"So we're back to that again?" Gail asked him. "You still think we should commit group assisted suicide?"

"I'm not saying that. I'd like to live long enough to track down the others and kick their collective asses for leaving us behind. But I do think it's still an option."

"They're dead already," McCann muttered. He sat huddled in the corner, gutting and skinning the rat with a knife. "So are we."

Gail shot a worried glance at Novak. Nodding, he sighed and shook his head.

"We're not dead, McCann. You need to get your shit together, shipmate. You're starting to lose it, and I need you with us and clear-headed."

Simon sat cross-legged, his back against the damp, mildewed wall, observing their conversation with the air of a stranger figuring out their group dynamic. He said nothing, and his expression remained calm, almost serene—but Gail saw a deep weariness in his eyes.

"Let's not talk about all that right now," she said. "We're all tired and banged up. Novak and Simon could both use some rest, McCann, and so could you and me. I vote we eat something and try to relax, if just for a little bit."

McCann held up the bloody, skinned carcass of the rat and arched an eyebrow. "Dinner is served, but I don't know how we're going to cook it. I found some matches in the cubbyhole, but they're wet."

"I've still got a lighter," Novak said. "But it was in my pocket when we ended up in the water. I don't know if it will work or not. Even if it did, there's nothing in here that's dry enough to burn."

Simon leaned forward. "Please, allow me. Mr. McCann, if you could gather some wood for us? Perhaps some of that office furniture?"

Grumbling, McCann lay the rat aside and did as Simon requested. He returned a short time later with the legs and drawers from a wooden desk, along with several cans of vegetables and some bottles of water from the secure room.

"How's this?" he asked, dropping the wood on the floor.

"That will be fine." Smiling, Simon arranged the wood in a pile. Then he simply sat there, staring at it. His brow furrowed as if he was concentrating on something. Gail noticed a vein standing out in his forehead.

"I still don't know how you're going to get it to burn," Novak said. "Damn moisture gets into everyth—"

The kindling burst into a bright, smokeless flame. Gail and Novak gasped. McCann scampered backward.

Gail turned to Simon. "How did you do that?"

"It was easy," he replied. "However, like any other fire, it won't last without more fuel. I suggest we cook our dinner and savor the warmth the fire brings. While it's cooking, perhaps we can gather some more wood."

"Do you have pyrokin..." Novak frowned. "Pyrokinesis?"

"That's the scientific name for it," Simon agreed. "I must admit, it is a useful ability in situations such as ours."

"Won't the floor catch on fire?" Gail asked, eyeing the flames nervously.

Simon shook his head. "It's controlled. We're perfectly safe."

It occurred to Gail that all of them, herself included, were apparently taking this all in stride. Maybe they were all suffering from Post-Traumatic Stress Disorder, or maybe they'd just been through too much weird stuff for this to really faze them. After all, when you'd been hunted by shark-men and giant worms, and ninety percent of your planet was flooded, was a magical campfire really that disconcerting?

"Gather round," Simon suggested. "Warm yourselves."

Novak grinned. "Mister, you are one spooky son-of-a-bitch, but right now, I don't care. Let's eat."

Their moods picked up as the room filled with the aroma of roasting meat. Gail felt a little queasy over the fact that it was a rat, and tried to tell herself it was chicken she was smelling. Soon, however, her hunger took over and she decided that rat would be just fine. They divided the meat into four portions. Some of it was burned and other parts were still half-raw, but all of them agreed that it was delicious. They topped it off with the vegetables and washed it all down with a bottle of water each. When they were finished, the four of them huddled around the fire. Novak licked the grease from his fingers and burped in contentment. McCann gathered some more wood and fed it into the flames. Gail warmed her hands and feet, relishing the feeling of being dry for the first time in months.

"Better?" Simon asked.

All three nodded. Novak belched again, long and heartily, earning a round of laughter.

"Well then," Simon said, staring into the dancing flames, "I suppose it's time I told you my story."

SEVENTEEN

"Our organization," Simon said, staring into the flames, "deal with the things the rest of humanity is unequipped to battle. Things like what is currently occurring outside."

"What is occurring outside?" Gail asked. "Where did the rain come from? And all these…monsters?"

"It's global warming," Novak said. "I mean, it's got to be, right?"

"No." Simon shook his head. "It's not global warming. It's magic run amok. And I would appreciate it greatly if you'd allow me to tell this story without interruption. We've delayed long enough as it is, and there is much to tell."

Gail and Novak apologized simultaneously, and Simon continued.

"There are thirteen entities—supernatural beings—neither demon nor angel, but something far older and far more powerful, whose only goal is the complete destruction of all creation and existence. They are older than our universe and they intend to be here still when our universe is gone. Are any of you familiar with string theory or alternate dimensions?"

All three nodded.

"Good. Believe me when I tell you, there are other Earths than the one we occupy. There are other Mars and Jupiters and Milky Way galaxies, as well. Everything in our own universe—every star and every atom—has myriad duplicates in other planes of existence. The Thirteen seek to destroy all of these dimensions, or levels, as my people call them. Like any other power, the Thirteen have those who worship and serve them, including here on our own Earth. A cult in Baltimore who was loyal to their cause managed to unleash two of the Thirteen—Leviathan and Behemoth. Behemoth takes the form of a monstrous worm and Leviathan takes the form of a giant, squid-headed abomination. They are the source of many of our legends—dragons, the Kraken, and the like. Loosed upon our planet, Leviathan and Behemoth have been hard at work, along with their spawn. Neither will rest until this Earth is utterly destroyed. As we speak, their minions overrun the planet. The seas are full of Leviathan's children. On what little land is left, Behemoth's worms leave behind a disease—a fungal infection that turns solid matter into water. You've probably seen signs of this."

"The white fuzz," Gail said.

"Indeed. The Book of Job tells us that 'The waters wear the stones and wash away the things which grow out of the dust of the earth, and destroy the hopes of man.' Although much of the Bible's content has been perverted, re-written, and obfuscated by mankind, that particular passage still rings true. Everything around us—this building, your boat, ourselves…all solid matter—will eventually transform into water. Thales, the pre-Socratic Greek philosopher, called this the First Principle. He proposed a cosmological doctrine—the foundational principles of existence, based upon the belief that the world had originated from water. He believed that the entire universe was nothing more than a giant ocean that he referred to as the Great Deep. Earth formed by solidifying from the water on which it floated. One day, it would return to such. Obviously, we know that the universe isn't an ocean, but when you consider what is happening outside, his theory that the planet would revert back to water isn't that far off."

Novak cleared his throat. "I'm sorry to interrupt, but I need to get this straight. You're saying that all matter on this planet is slowly turning into water?"

"Yes. Forget the supernatural aspect of what I'm saying and look at it scientifically for a moment. One of the first laws of physics is that matter cannot be created nor destroyed. It can only change form. Matter on our planet is slowly changing into water."

"But if that's true," Novak said, "then maybe the water around us isn't getting higher. Maybe the ground is actually liquefying."

Simon opened his mouth to respond, but McCann cut him off.

"That's bullshit. If the planet is turning into water, then what keeps all that water from just floating out into space?"

"The planet still has a core," Novak reminded him. "At least for now. It's still rotating on its axis, so we still have gravity. Picture a big bucket of water. If you tip it over on its side, the water spills out, but if you spin the bucket as you tip it over, the water stays inside because of the centrifugal force. So we'd be okay until the planet's core began to liquefy."

"We won't simply float off into space," Simon said. "The Earth is changing form, yes, but as that happens, the Great Deep is absorbing it. Thales was partially correct about the existence of such a place. The Great Deep does exist, but not on Earth. It is another dimension, one composed of nothing but water—a vast, supernatural sea. The Great Deep is Leviathan's home. As our planet slowly liquefies, it is being absorbed by The Great Deep. The barriers between our dimensions are weak right now. Our plane of existence is crossing over into the Great Deep. Picture two sheets of paper. One of them is the Earth. The other is the Great Deep. Now slowly place one sheet of paper atop the other, until they are lined up evenly, appearing as one sheet rather than two. That is what is happening to our planet."

"So how do we stop it?" Gail asked.

"We don't," Simon said. "We can't."

They sat in silence for a moment as the enormity of what Simon had said weighed on them. McCann sniffled and turned away. In the flickering firelight, Gail thought she saw tears shining on his cheeks. Novak simply stared into the fire. His expression was sullen. Finally, Gail cleared her throat and spoke.

"But when we first found you, Simon, you said you could help us get rid of the things outside. You said that if we didn't act soon, our actions might be the last thing any of us do."

Simon nodded. "Right before you freed me, Mr. McCann stated that he wanted to know where the creatures had originated from and how we could get rid of them. I advised you that I could answer those questions for you if you freed me, and now I have. I've told you where they came from. Sadly, at this stage, there's no way to rid the Earth of them. Our planet is finished."

"Turning into water," Novak said. "Getting sucked into this other dimension—this...What did you call it?"

"The Great Deep."

"Yeah. That. So what you're saying is that we're pretty much fucked."

"At this point, I'm afraid so. There are still individuals out there who are valiantly trying to save the planet. A biochemist named Steve Kazmirski, for example. He has a theory about how to reverse the white fuzz. He believes that if he can obtain a pure sample of a protein that is essential in the machinery that replicates the white fuzz's DNA, then he can stop it with drugs. If the DNA can't replicate, the fungus can't grow, and therefore, will stop liquefying everything it touches."

"Is he right?" Gail asked.

"I don't know. The white fuzz is supernatural in origin, but his theory is scientifically sound. Sadly, Mr. Kazmirski will never get a chance to learn if it would have worked, because it's already too late."

"At least he's trying to do something."

"My group were trying to save the planet, as well. Black Lodge defends humanity."

"You did a hell of a job," McCann muttered.

"As I explained to Gail earlier, we ended up divided. Half of Black Lodge wanted to enact an old ritual that called for the sacrifice of a human infant. Summoning Leviathan and Behemoth—opening a doorway for them to enter our world, required the sacrifice of an infant. A number of our members believed that banishing them and closing the doorway would require the same thing. They learned of several surviving infants—one in Australia, one in Illinois, and one or two elsewhere, and went in search of them. The other half of my group labored to stop them. We were convinced that there was another way to banish Behemoth and Leviathan, seal the gate, and undo the damage caused by the cultists. Regrettably, we wasted too much time in-fighting when we should have been acting together, and now it's too late. Behemoth and Leviathan have both moved on to another version of Earth—another level."

"I can't accept that," Gail said. "There has to be a way. Thousands of years of human history—all of our struggles and achievements. It can't just be over!"

Simon's smile was sad. "The planet is already destroyed. It's already being absorbed. I'm afraid there's nothing I can do."

"But you said you could save us! Were you lying, just so we'd free you?"

"No, I told the truth. I can save us. I just can't save the planet."

Gail scowled. "You're not making any sense."

"I told you before that there are other realities—other versions of Earth. The cult in Baltimore opened the doors to other dimensions and brought both Behemoth and Leviathan through. I can do the same. We can escape to another world. A version of Earth where this hasn't happened yet. But we're running out of time."

"Why?"

"Because opening a doorway into the Labyrinth isn't my forte. There were some in my organization who were quite adept at it. I was not one of them. But there are certain places on Earth—places of great power—and in those areas, my skill won't matter. In those places, on spots such as Stonehenge, the great Serpent Mound, and the area known popularly as the Bermuda Triangle, the doorways already exist. All we have to do is go through one of them."

"Are we near one?" Novak asked, looking up from the fire.

"Not near, as in, right next door. But I can guide us to one, yes."

Gail leaned forward, staring at Simon intently. "Where?"

"An area in Central Pennsylvania called LeHorn's Hollow. It is undoubtedly under water by now, but the doorway should still be there. All we have to do is reach it."

"Let me see if I've got this right." McCann's sarcastic tone was unmistakable. "We're somewhere over what we think is Kentucky right now. All we have to do is hop in our little boat, cross the ocean to Pennsylvania, avoid getting eaten by all the different monsters, and then dive down to the bottom of the sea and go through this door. Shit, what are we waiting for? Let's go. That sounds easy enough."

If Simon was offended, he gave no indication. "I didn't say it would be easy, Mr. McCann. I only said that I could do it. I can save us. But we're running out of time. We should leave soon."

"We're not going anywhere until we've slept," Gail said. "Novak's still hurt, and McCann, you ought to rest up from earlier, too. And Simon, no offense, but you don't look like you're in any condition to go anywhere. Not after how we found you."

Simon smiled. "I heal quickly. But you are correct. I think we could all do with a bit of sleep. By morning, I'll feel right as rain."

Gail, McCann and Novak all winced at the unintentional pun.

"Sorry," Simon apologized. "I suppose I could have chosen a better phrase."

"I'll take watch," Gail said. "There's no sense in all of us staying awake."

"Bullshit." Novak shifted around, trying to sit up. Doing so elicited a groan. He slumped back down again.

"You need your sleep," Gail chided him. "So does Simon. I'll stand watch."

"I can help," McCann offered. "You take the first half and I'll take the second."

Gail hesitated. She was reluctant to give McCann that much responsibility, especially considering the erratic behavior he'd been exhibiting since their encounter with the living island. It seemed strange to her that it had all happened just a short time ago—the creature, the disappearance of the ship, and everything else that had happened. Events had conspired to lead them here, to this refuge of a madman and his prisoner—a prisoner who might be their only hope. Gail had never believed much in fate or providence, but the events they'd recently experienced made her wonder.

It occurred to her how insane Simon sounded. Not his voice or tone, both of which were perfectly pleasant and rational. It was the words themselves that sounded crazy. Secret paramilitary occult organizations and doorways to alternate universes were the stuff of fiction. But then again, so were the plethora of monsters they'd encountered. If she wanted fantasy, all she had to do was look outside. Even the weather was unnatural.

She realized that McCann was staring at her, waiting for her response. She smiled.

"That's okay, really. You should get some sleep, too. You almost drowned today."

"I'm fine," he insisted. "Stop treating me like a baby."

There was an edge in McCann's voice that wasn't normally there, and Gail wondered once more what was going on inside of him.

"How about this? I'll take the first shift and you go to sleep. When I get tired, I promise that I'll wake you up. Does that sound fair?"

McCann shrugged. His expression was sullen. "I guess."

Gail checked their boat and made sure it was still secure. Then she turned to the fire, relishing the warmth.

"We should put this out, I guess." Her voice rang with regret. "No sense in attracting whatever might be lurking outside overnight."

"I concur," Simon said. "And don't fret, Gail. I can always start another come morning."

Snuffing the flames, she nodded. As the ashes hissed and smoked, Gail felt a deep sense of loss. The warmth had brought comfort and a long-missed feeling of normality. With the fire gone, the cold and dampness seemed to creep back into her joints almost instantly. She sat down wearily in front of the open door and stared out into the darkness, listening to the waves and the rain. Soon, Novak began to snore behind her. McCann soon followed. When she turned to look at Simon, she couldn't be sure if his eyes were closed or not. They seemed to be, yet there was a glint in the shadows. He sat still and his breathing was rhythmic and shallow. She turned her attention to the ocean again, and wondered how the hell they'd get across it in their rinky-dink boat with only a few weapons and supplies.

She wasn't aware that she'd fallen asleep until something cold and wet coiled around her leg and began dragging her towards the water.

Gail's eyes snapped open as she slid toward the water. In the darkness, the ocean was just a black wall. She couldn't see anything of the creature that held her. It's shapeless bulk reared up from the roiling surface, blocking most of the opening. She glanced down at the black-green tentacle coiled around her ankle. Its tapered tip flexed, burrowing beneath her pants leg even as the rest of the tendril squeezed tighter.

"Shit! Guys…help me! Somebody?"

She reached for the shotgun, but the weapon was too far away, and her hands slapped the damp, slick floor.

Simon, Novak and McCann awoke at her cries just as a second tentacle whipped into the room. It swayed back and forth, snake-like, and then darted toward Novak. Groaning, he rolled out of the way.

Gail scrabbled at the floor, trying desperately to find a handhold or purchase. Splinters of wood speared the soft flesh beneath her fingernails, but she barely felt the pain. Panicking, she grabbed the tentacle and tried to dislodge it. The appendage pulsated, squeezing tighter. Her ankle and foot went numb. She slid closer to the opening. Mist drifted over her skin, chilling her. She gasped, tasting salt and brine.

"Help me! Please, guys…It's got me!"

Simon jumped to his feet, tore the suit coat from around his waist, and darted forward—naked. At the same time, McCann charged the second tentacle. He shouted nonsensically, brandishing the butcher knife, and slashed at the intruder. The blade cut deep into the flesh. Blood the color of India ink flowed from the wound. The appendage recoiled, whipping back and forth in the air as if frenzied. Then it lashed out again, going directly for McCann. The crazed sailor attacked a second time, plunging the knife deep into the tentacle. Grinning, he twisted the blade with both hands and then yanked it free. Black fluid splashed his hands and face. The second tentacle retreated back into the rain.

Outside, the creature moaned. The sound reminded Gail of the cries whales made in the documentaries she'd seen on television. She tried to get her fingers beneath the tentacle and pry it free, but the monster was too strong. It burrowed deeper beneath her pants leg, moving up toward her knee. She noticed a small trickle of blood on her calf and wondered where it had come from. Gail slid another few feet, and found herself teetering at the edge.

"Grab my hand," Simon shouted, reaching for her.

Gail stretched her arm, and Simon's hand encircled her. His touch was immediately reassuring, and despite her immediate peril, she felt the panic leave her. Simon braced his feet and tried pulling her backward, but the monster yanked harder, engaging him in a game of tug-of-war. Gail shrieked.

"McCann," Simon yelled. "Mr. Novak. Take her!"

The two men rushed forward and grabbed Gail's arms. Grimacing, Simon pulled the suit coat over his hands and arms, and then grabbed the tentacle around her leg. He muttered something in a language that Gail didn't recognize. There was a crackling sound, and the air suddenly smelled of grilled fish. Then the tentacle uncoiled, freeing her.

"Pull her out of the way," Simon ordered.

McCann and Novak helped Gail to her feet, and the three of them retreated to the far wall, while Simon knelt and dipped his fingers in a pool of the creature's blood.

"Well done, shedding our opponent's blood, Mr. McCann. This will prove useful."

McCann nodded. "Whatever you say, Simon."

"Indeed. It's not whatever, I say, though. What I say next must be very specific."

He moved to the opening and began chanting. Again, Gail tried to identify the language, but she couldn't. As he spoke, Simon hurriedly painted symbols on the walls, using the monster's blood as ink. Outside, the creature raged. Then, with a mighty splash, it vanished beneath the waves. Panting, Simon whipped his wet bangs from his eyes, looked at them, and grinned.

"It won't bother us anymore."

"I've gotta tell you," Novak said, "that was some Gandalf-style shit, Simon. What did you do?"

"I prevented it from crossing the threshold. It can't harm us or the building. The same can't be said of its brethren, however, so I suggest that we spend the rest of the night in one of the other rooms. Agreed?"

The three of them nodded. Then they started down the hall. Gail had only taken three steps when her vision began to blur. She felt Novak grip her arm. He said something to her, but his voice was muted and she couldn't hear him.

Then the world went dark.

EIGHTEEN

When Gail awoke again, she panicked, convinced that the monster had her in its clutches once more. She sat up, gasping for breath and glancing around. Novak smiled at her.

"It's okay," he said. "You're okay. Must have been one hell of a nightmare."

"I don't remember. Was I dreaming?"

"You were talking in your sleep. I assumed you must have been dreaming."

"I thought…" Gail yawned. "Never mind. I don't want to think about it. What time is it?"

Novak shrugged. "Who knows? Your guess is as good as mine. That bothers me sometimes—not knowing. Like the dates. I wish we'd kept track of days on a calendar. I'd like to know what day it is. Hate to think we'll miss Christmas or Halloween, and never know it."

"You seem like you're feeling better."

"I am. How about you?"

"I'm okay. Hungry. I could go for some more rat." Gail paused. "God, I can't believe I just said that."

"I can," Novak replied. "That rat was fucking tasty."

She grinned. "Tastes like chicken?"

"Hell, no. It tasted like a rat. But it was better than nothing."

"Where's Simon and McCann?"

Novak pointed. "Out front. Surprisingly, the boat is still there. That thing last night didn't destroy it. But the tentacles bashed a few holes in it. McCann is patching it up now. Making sure it'll stay afloat. Simon is standing guard while he does."

"He's a handy guy to have around," Gail said. "Do you trust him?"

"After what happened when we went to the island…fish… whatever the hell it was, I don't trust anybody. They fucking abandoned us. But at this point, I don't think we have a choice but to trust Simon. He saved us last night. That's gotta count for something."

"He could have just been saving himself."

"I considered that," Novak said, "but he could have just retreated deeper into the building. He didn't. He was the first one to run forward. He was trying to pull you free before McCann and I even got moving. I think he—"

The conversation ended abruptly as Simon and McCann entered the room. Simon smiled at Gail when he saw that she was awake. He knelt beside her.

"I'd like to examine your ankle, if that's okay?"

"Sure." She nodded.

Simon gently pulled her pants leg up and stared intently at the bruises the tentacle had left behind. His expression was neutral, but Gail got the impression that he was concerned.

"Are you experiencing any dizziness?" Simon asked. "Hearing voices other than your own? Or suffering from extreme thirst?"

"No. Why? What do you think I have, Simon? What aren't you telling me? You didn't touch the monster last night. You used your suit coat. What's going on?"

He smiled again. "Nothing is going on. That's the good news. I was worried that you might have contracted the white fuzz after last night's attack, but if you had, you'd be showing signs of infection by now."

"Is that how it spreads?" Novak asked. "By touching these things?"

"I'm not sure how it is transmitted," Simon admitted. "I don't think anyone else is, either. The two biggest theories are that it was spread by the worms or by the rain. But nobody – at least nobody I've encountered – knows for certain. In any case, the good news is that Gail doesn't have it."

McCann cleared his throat. "The other good news is that the boat is seaworthy. I vote we get the hell out of here. I was all for staying. It's semi-dry and beats the hell out of floating around out there, but after last night…"

"I agree," Novak said. "Sooner we leave, the quicker we

can get to this doorway. Gail?"

Grunting, she got to her feet and nodded. "I'm ready. Let's go."

They spent the next two hours meticulously searching the rest of the building, scavenging the wreckage for whatever meager supplies they could find. Most items were water-damaged or covered with mildew and mold. Gail was relieved that the mold was of the old-fashioned black variety, rather than the white fuzz. One office closet held a janitor's uniform and a raincoat, both of which Simon donned. Novak was able to fashion some crude oars by tearing apart a set of prefabricated bookshelves. Food was scarce, except for a lone can of garbanzo beans, a few bottles of water, some energy drinks, and an unopened bag of pretzel sticks. Weapons were more plentiful, although McCann was unable to find bullets for the gun he'd discovered during his previous search. They discovered a variety of knives and other edged weaponry—letter openers, utility knives, box-cutters and even an ornamental sword that had hung on the wall inside one office. The sword's blade was dull and tarnished, but McCann brought it along anyway, telling the others even a dull sword was better than no sword at all.

When they had salvaged anything that might prove useful, they loaded up the boat and departed. McCann and Gail took the first turn at the oars, while Simon sat in the stern and Novak lounged at the bow. Gail felt her mood shift from hopeful to depressed once she was back out in the rain again. Although the office building had been damp inside, it had provided a brief reprieve from the constant feel of water droplets pelting her skin. Then again, she thought as she watched the half-submerged structure fade into the mist, the building had also almost been the death of them all. Not that the sea was any better. It wasn't. Gail knew that. She seriously doubted they'd ever make it to this gateway Simon had mentioned, if indeed such a thing even existed. They were especially vulnerable in their current craft and their physical and emotional state. It was only a matter of time before something in the water made a meal out of them.

She gritted her teeth and rowed harder, wondering then why they were bothering to continue. Why keep trying if the grim end was already foretold? She couldn't speak for the others, but Gail knew why she kept going. Because she lacked the courage for the alternative. She thought back to Novak's suggestion of…how long had it been…had it really only been a few days ago? He'd wanted the group to take a vote on whether or not they should assist each other in a mass suicide. She turned to him, studying the older man as he gazed out on the waves, and wondered if he still felt that was a viable option.

Soaked to the skin within minutes, they drifted for what felt (at least to Gail) like hours. Her arms and back muscles began to ache, and she had to keep blinking water from her eyes. Eventually, Simon and Novak traded places with her and McCann. Novak rowed slowly, favoring his arm.

"If it starts to hurt too much, let us know," Gail said. "McCann or I can take over again."

"I'll be okay," he grunted. His tone, however, indicated that he'd be anything but.

McCann was silent as they bobbed on the waves. Gail wondered if he was just tired or if the recent changes she'd noticed in his behavior were continuing to manifest. Exhausted, she closed her eyes but was unable to sleep. Every time she started to drift off, she'd jerk awake again, expecting an attack. Luckily, they continued on their way, unmolested by the denizens of the deep. Occasionally, they spotted shapes in the water. Once, a humped, elongated black form broke the surface to their starboard side, but it slipped beneath the waves before they could get a good look at what it was. Then they passed by the floating corpse of a giant crab. The decomposing carcass was easily the size of a pick-up truck. It had swollen so much from internal gasses that its shell was cracked in places. It oozed rot into the water around it, and the stench was revolting. Gail gagged as it passed them by. Several seabirds were perched on the body, picking morsels out from between the cracks. McCann wanted to try shooting one for food, but the others talked him out of it. They were too far away to retrieve the bird without going into the water, and none of them wanted to row any closer to the dead creature than was necessary.

"Plus," Simon cautioned, "we don't know what adverse effects eating that monster's flesh might have. If the birds have been eating it, and they are sick, then it's possible any such malady could be passed on to us."

"You can make fire," McCann said. "Can you summon a twelve-ounce steak out of the air, while you're at it?"

"If I could, do you think I'd be this thin?"

McCann smiled, and for a moment, he looked like his old self. But upon closer study, Gail noticed that the smile never reached his eyes.

Simon guided them as they continued on their way, occasionally changing their course. He had no compass or other navigational equipment, but the other three never questioned his directions. They saw several more sea creatures in the distance, but none of the beasts ventured close enough to the boat to be of any concern.

Gail became aware that Novak had stopped rowing. He was sitting up straight and staring intently at the horizon. She and the others followed his gaze.

"It's a ship," Gail gasped.

"That's not just any ship," Novak said. "Unless I'm mistaken, it's *our* ship."

The one hundred and twenty five foot long multi-hulled Catamaran drifted silently as the tide swept their small craft closer to it. Through the rain, it was impossible for them to see if there were any figures above deck.

McCann cupped his ear and listened. "I don't hear the engines. I had them running good when we left. The intakes were free of debris, and we had four or five days worth of fuel left. They shouldn't be having trouble."

"Yeah," Novak said, "but they don't have you onboard to tend to them, either."

"So that is your former vessel?" Simon asked.

"It was," Novak replied. "But the fuckers abandoned us."

While Novak told Simon about the living island and what

had happened to them since, Gail stared at the ship. She felt a surprising sense of homesickness. She'd hated living on the boat, hated the cramped conditions and the complete lack of privacy and having to make nice with people like Morgan, but now, it was something familiar in a literal sea of regret and heartache and terror. It felt like coming home.

"Do you think they mutinied?" Simon asked.

"They had to," Novak said. "Maybe not all of them, but Morgan certainly would have. And I'm betting he convinced some of the others. If they had enough numbers, it would have been easy for him to do it."

"Do they have weapons?"

"Yeah." Novak counted them off on his fingers. "Several rifles and handguns with plenty of ammunition. A couple of shotguns. Plus, there's machetes and spears and other weapons we fabricated with stuff we found along the way. Hell, they've even got a flamethrower."

"So do we," Gail said, nodding at Simon.

Novak's eyes widened with the realization. "That's true! Can you do that, Simon? Can you, like, shoot fire out of your hands?"

"Not quite." Simon smiled. "Pyrokinesis doesn't work that way. But I can use it as a defensive measure in close quarters."

"Great," McCann muttered. "So, we've got Simon giving them hot flashes, along with a bunch of letter openers and box-cutters and my dull-ass sword, against their guns. Sounds like a fair fight."

"We'll see," Simon said. "Perhaps there won't be a fight at all."

"That another one of your tricks? Can you tell the future?"

"No. It's merely wishful thinking on my part. It should be on your part, as well. None of us are in any shape for a protracted struggle of any kind."

"Maybe we'll get lucky," McCann replied, "and they'll just pick us off with the rifles before we get any closer."

Gail opened her mouth to respond, intent on telling McCann that she'd had enough of his surly attitude. Before she could, however, a gunshot echoed across the water. All four of them ducked down as low as they could, the makeshift oars forgotten.

Gail grasped Novak's uninjured hand and squeezed. "They're shooting at us!"

"I told you so," McCann moaned.

Another shot rang out, then a third. The falling rain muffled the blasts, but they were still loud enough that Gail twitched at the sound.

Novak gave her hand another squeeze. Then he let go and slowly peered over the side. After a moment, he glanced back down at the others.

"They're not shooting at us. They're shooting at each other!"

"What do we do?" Gail asked.

"Stay down." Novak motioned to the others as the waves pushed their boat closer to the bigger vessel. "McCann, grab an oar. Let's get alongside her."

Gail noticed a sudden change in both Novak's tone and demeanor. Gone was the hopelessness and fatigue that had seemed to surround him since his injury. He seemed to be his old self again. She could almost picture him standing up in their boat, cigar dangling from the corner of his mouth as he sprayed the Catamaran with a blast from his homemade flamethrower—if the weapon hadn't still been on the ship, of course.

"How many people are on board?" Simon asked, ducking low as yet another volley of gunshots echoed across the water.

"Well, let's see." Novak frowned, thinking. "We lost Warren and Lynn soon after we left the boat. So that leaves Riffle, Morgan, Ben, Mylon, Paris, Caterina and Tatiana."

"Seven of them," Simon said. "Those aren't such bad odds. And judging from the sounds we're hearing, a second mutiny is underway. That might benefit us even more."

They closed to within a few hundred yards of the ship. The rain parted enough that they could make out the outer decks. All of them appeared deserted.

"Gunshots must be coming from inside." Novak leaned hard into his oar. "Steady, McCann. Let's come around the aft side. There's a ladder we can use."

"We're going aboard?" Gail asked, surprised.

"Well, we can't stay out here."

"But they're shooting inside," Gail insisted. "Shouldn't we at least wait until the fight is over?"

Novak pulled alongside the bigger craft and reached for the lowest ladder rung, steadying their boat. "The longer we wait, the better the chance something comes up from below and eats us. I've kept you alive this long, right?"

Blinking rain from her eyes, Gail nodded.

Novak smiled. "Then give me a little while longer, and I'll do the same."

He swung out of the boat and hurried up the ladder. His feet slipped on the wet rungs, and the others gasped, but he managed to hold on tight. When he reached the top, he peered over the side. Then he glanced down at the others and motioned for them to follow. Simon went next, followed by Gail. McCann brought up the rear. He didn't bother securing their small boat. All of them knew that if this didn't work out to their advantage, they wouldn't need it anyway.

They huddled together in the shadows. A deck light flashed a momentary glint off of McCann's sword blade. The outer decks were deserted. Rain pounded against them in a steady drumbeat. The ship rocked slowly back and forth. Two more shots rang out from somewhere beneath their feet, followed by a woman's scream.

"Come on," Novak said, brandishing one of the knives they'd taken from the flooded office building. "Let's do this."

They crept forward in single file, moving slowly and making sure they kept a few feet of distance between one another. Gail had to reach out several times and steady herself against the bulkhead as the ship rolled and pitched from side to side. The shotgun grew slippery in her hands. When they reached a forward hatch, Novak paused. The hatch hung partially open, blocked by a body lying halfway through it.

"Is that…?" McCann covered his mouth with his hand.

"Yeah," Novak knelt beside the body. "It's Paris. At least, I think it's her."

Gail nudged her way forward and glanced down at the body. Immediately, she saw why Novak was having trouble identifying it. The corpse was partially headless. Something had sliced or bitten the top of the victim's head off, just above the bridge of the nose. The victim's brains, and everything else, were gone—not splashed onto the deck and bulkheads.

Gone.

Something slithered across the deck behind them, and a shadow fell over them all.

Gail, Novak, McCann and Simon all turned at the same time. Gail swept the shotgun up, ready to blast the attacker at point blank range. Her finger twitched on the trigger. She barely had time to stop herself from squeezing it as Caterina stumbled out of the rain. The woman was clearly distressed. Her wet clothes were torn and covered with blood, but she had no visible wounds. Her eyes were wide, her hair flattened and streaming water. She reached for them, hands flailing wildly. Novak stepped forward and took her hand. Caterina collapsed against him, sobbing. Great shudders racked her thin frame.

"It's okay," Novak soothed. "It's okay, darlin'. What happened? Are you hurt?"

"Th…they…heads like…oh God…"

Gail and McCann pressed closer, crowding around the hysterical woman. Gail noticed that Simon held back, carefully watching the perimeter.

"Caterina," Novak lowered his voice. "What happened? Where are the others?"

"M-morgan…and then…he killed Riffle. He…and then they…came, and…Paris…their heads are wrong! *Why are their heads so wrong?*"

"Calm down," Novak began, but got no further. Caterina pushed him away and glared at them all. When she spoke again, Gail had to struggle to hear her whispered warning above the sound of the storm.

"They're coming. They'll be back. The others went below but Paris and I stayed up here. That's how they…they're coming. You guys have got to hide!"

"Who's coming?" Novak reached for her, but Caterina flitted out of reach. "Who did this?"

"They did. The men with no heads."

Another volley of gunshots erupted beneath their feet, followed by a long and agonized scream.

"Fuck this shit." McCann turned back to the open hatch. "I'm heading below deck. Anybody coming with me?"

"I would recommend that we all stick together," Simon said.

More shots echoed from below. The boat rolled hard to the right as a wave crashed against the hull.

"We've got to hide," Caterina sobbed. "Please!"

Gail held up a hand and took a step forward. "Caterina. It's me. Gail. Who did this, honey? Who are these men with no heads?"

Caterina started to answer, but then her eyes grew wide. Her mouth hung open. Gail realized that the frightened woman was not staring at her, but at something over her shoulder. Before she could turn to see what had terrified Caterina so much, McCann screamed.

"I think," Simon shouted, "that we just found out."

Gail spun around, shotgun at the ready. A moment later, she forgot all about the weapon. The thing that stepped out of the open hatch door startled her so badly that she could barely breathe, let alone act.

The creature emerged onto the wet deck and rose to its full height. It towered over them all. Gail judged it to be at least eight feet tall. Its naked body was that of a well-developed human—two legs and arms, slightly longer than normal, all attached to a powerful torso. The skin was pale, and the muscular chest sported what looked like gills. Still, the overall effect was that of a human male except for two differences. Where its penis should have been, there was a tentacle, and in place of a head, the monster had a giant starfish. Its short, stumpy neck merged with the starfish, right between two of the creature's five upper stalk-like appendages. At the tip of each stalk was an eye. In the center of the creature's face (although Gail supposed it wasn't a face—it was just where she'd expected a human face to be) there was a circular, lipless mouth lined with razor sharp teeth.

The beast lunged forward, thrusting at McCann with a weapon. Gail blinked, trying to determine what it was exactly.

It looked like a piece of coral fashioned into a trident. McCann parried the blow with his sword, but the force of the creature's attack knocked him backward. He slipped on the wet, rolling deck and landed on his back, sprawled at the monster's feet. The thing raised the trident over its head and thrust at him again. McCann shrieked. The sword fell from his grasp.

Gail squeezed the trigger. The shotgun roared, drowning out the thunder overhead. Gail staggered backward across the wet deck. The blast hit the monster in the chest, punching through the pale skin and spraying reddish-pink pulp all over the bulkhead behind it. The creature dropped the trident and stumbled forward, squealing in pain. The sound reminded Gail of a boiling tea kettle.

"Hit it again," Novak shouted. "McCann, get the hell out of the way!"

McCann skittered away from the staggering beast. Gail braced her feet shoulder-width apart and fired again. The monster toppled over, convulsing on the deck. Blood and rainwater swirled around it. The stalks on its head waved weakly, and then went still. All five eyes stared sightlessly.

"Well, we know a chest shot works on them," Novak said.

While he helped McCann to his feet, Gail inched forward. Keeping the monster covered with the shotgun, she prodded the corpse with her toe. The beast didn't move.

"Nicely done," Simon said.

Gail nodded, unable to speak. Her chest hurt. The shotgun's kick had been worse than she'd imagined. She was certain that if she lifted up her shirt, she'd find a bruise.

"Caterina," Novak asked, "how many more of these things are there?"

The frightened woman shrugged. Gail noticed that her color was returning and her eyes no longer seemed dazed. Perhaps the shock was passing. When she spoke, she no longer stammered and her tone seemed more confident.

"At least seven. Maybe more. I'm not sure. It all happened so fast and things got confusing."

"How many of us are left? We've found Paris. Is there anybody else alive?"

Caterina nodded. "Morgan, Ben, Mylon and Tatiana."

"What about Riffle?" McCann asked.

"Morgan tossed him overboard when you guys left."

"Fuck these starfish men," Novak growled. "I want Morgan."

Caterina looked at each of them. "Where are Warren and Lynn?"

"They didn't make it," Novak said. "But this is Simon. We picked him up along the way. Simon, meet Caterina."

Simon smiled. "A pleasure."

"Simon's a wizard," McCann said, "but so far, the only thing we've seen him do is start a fire."

"I have other talents," Simon said.

"Then why didn't you do something just now?" McCann bent over and retrieved his sword. "Why didn't you wave a hand and turn this thing into a crab or something?"

Simon sighed. "It doesn't work like that—at least, not with me. This creature is natural, rather than supernatural. It comes from the Great Deep, but it is not supernaturally produced. An exorcism wouldn't work on it. There are spells that would have aided us, but by the time I would have finished preparing them, you'd have all been dead. And besides—the last thing you'd want me to turn that creature into is a crab. Obviously, you've never seen a Clicker."

McCann frowned. "A what?"

"Never mind," Simon replied. "Wrong level."

"Let's go," Novak said. "We've got people to help, a ship to regain, and Morgan to kill."

Simon picked up the fallen trident and tested its weight. "Lead on, Mr. Novak."

Novak turned to Gail, and held up his knife. "Want to trade weapons?"

"No."

"Then you've got point."

"Shit." Swallowing hard, Gail stepped through the hatch. Novak followed her, then Simon, McCann and Caterina.

"Morgan," Novak whispered. "You'd better hope these things kill you before I do."

NINETEEN

As they crept down the passageway, Gail tried to remember if she'd racked another shotgun shell. She'd shot the starfish man twice, but had she readied the weapon after the second shot? It wouldn't do to come across another of those creatures and not be ready. That split second could make all the difference between life and death. She was reluctant to pump the shotgun now, because the noise could give away their location if one of the beasts was lurking around the next corner.

Indeed, that was the problem. The multi-hulled, one-hundred and twenty five foot long Catamaran was a labyrinth of passageways, hatches and ladders. Most of them had only the red emergency lights for illumination. Some didn't even have that. She moved as quietly as possible, but that meant going slowly. Occasionally, when she slowed her pace too much, Novak bumped into her from behind.

They reached a ladder leading down to the lower level. Pausing, Gail glanced back at the others.

"What now?" she whispered.

"We go down," Novak said.

Gail glanced at the others for confirmation, and noticed that Simon was admiring the trident he'd taken from the dead creature. "Everything okay?"

He didn't answer. The others turned to look at him, as well. McCann tapped him on the shoulder and Simon finally stirred.

"Hmm? Oh, my apologies. I was transfixed by this relic. If I'm not mistaken, it dates back to before the Great Flood. These markings are distinctly Atlantean."

"That's impossible," Novak said. "It looks brand new!"

"Craftsmen in Atlantis knew how to make things last. That's why the city itself is still mostly intact, albeit at the bottom of the ocean." Simon smiled sadly, and then added,

"How ironic is that, given our current situation?"

"Atlantis," Caterina said. "Are you serious?"

"Oh, he's full of surprises like that," Novak said, and then nodded at Gail and the open hatch. "Let's go."

Gail descended the ladder to the lower deck, followed by Novak, Simon, McCann and then Caterina. When they reached the bottom, Novak pointed aft. Holding her weapon at the ready, Gail led them forward. They'd gone through two compartments when they found what was left of Ben. Like Paris, the top of his head was missing, and his gray matter had been sucked out. The corpse of a starfish creature lay across him, and lumps of Ben's half-devoured brain leaked from its gaping mouth. A fire ax jutted from the monster's back. The head of the weapon had been buried so deeply into the beast's flesh, that the only part visible was the axe handle.

"Somebody took this one out," McCann said.

"Yeah," Novak whispered. "Too bad they didn't kill it in time to save Ben."

"Don't feel too bad for him" Caterina said. "He was in on the mutiny with Morgan."

"Fuck him, then. Good riddance."

"My thought exactly," said a voice from behind them. It was punctuated by the sound of a shotgun being racked.

"Shit," Gail said.

"Didn't expect to see you guys again," Morgan said. "Now drop your weapons…nice and slow."

"You must be Mr. Morgan," Simon said.

Ignoring him, Morgan motioned with the shotgun. "Go on. You heard me. Drop your weapons now. I don't have time to fuck around. There's still one more of those things loose on the ship."

"If there are more of those things," Gail said, "then maybe we should put aside our differences and work together."

"Teamwork?" Morgan snorted. "You mean like Novak's talk of a suicide pact? Yeah, that would have been a group effort alright?"

Novak winced. "Morgan, I—"

"Shut up! I'm in charge here, and no, I won't be working

with you guys. You didn't want to work with me, Novak. Oh, no. You threatened to toss me over the fucking side! Or have you forgotten that already?"

"You left us to fucking die," Novak countered. "Or have *you* forgotten *that*?"

"Maybe so," Morgan said, "but you started this shit."

None of them responded. The only sound was a small whimper from Caterina. Gail cursed herself once more for not knowing if her weapon was readied or not, and weighed the possibility of taking a chance. But if she was wrong, and a shell wasn't chambered, she doubted that Morgan would give her time to try again.

"Now," Morgan continued. "I don't know how in the hell you survived, or how you got back on board the ship, but I won't ask again. Drop your fucking weapons."

"As you wish." Simon knelt slowly, keeping his gaze focused on Morgan, and laid the trident on the deck.

Novak and Gail glanced at each other. Sighing, Novak dropped his knife. It clanged against the bulkhead. Gail was about to put down her shotgun when McCann shouted. He charged toward Morgan, bellowing with rage, the sword raised over his head with both hands.

Gail yelled, "McCann—"

The blast from Morgan's shotgun drowned her out. McCann stumbled backward as his skull parted. His brains splattered against the bulkhead with a wet smack. His blood painted Gail, Simon and Caterina's faces. McCann tumbled forward at Morgan's feet, leaking onto the gunman's shoes.

Gail swung her shotgun up and squeezed the trigger. The sound of the hammer was very loud, audible despite the echoing kill shot, but it was the only sound. The weapon didn't kick. She'd been right all along. She had forgotten to rack it. Morgan had no such problem. He'd already done so after shooting McCann. She watched the barrel of his weapon swing toward her, and time seemed to slow. She closed her eyes…

…and opened them a moment later when Morgan screamed. Caterina and Novak shrieked along with him.

When Gail saw why, she cried out, too.

The starfish creature had snuck up behind him, probably attracted by the sounds of the struggle. Now it towered over Morgan, its broad hands on his shoulders, its tentacle wrapped around his waist, and lowered its mouth over the top of his head. As they watched, it bit through his skull, neatly slicing off the top of his head. Morgan's screams reached a feverish pitch as the monster slurped his brains out. He whimpered twice, and then went limp.

Before the beast could drop the corpse, Simon swept forward, snatched up the trident, and plunged it through Morgan's chest. He threw all his weight behind it, pushing the weapon through the dead man and into the creature, impaling them both. The monster screeched, flailing both its human arms and its starfish appendages. Blood gushed down the shaft of the trident, slathering Simon's hands.

"Novak," he grunted, shoving harder. "Gail…help me!"

Gail dropped the shotgun. The two of them rushed to his aid, adding their weight to the trident. Together, they drove the thrashing creature against the bulkhead. It slapped at them with its hands, but they held firm.

"Push," Novak yelled.

The monster's claws raked across Gail's forearm. She flinched, gritting her teeth against the pain. Then she shoved harder.

They kept it pinned there until it was dead. Then Simon yanked the trident free. Both Morgan and the starfish creature slumped to the deck. Simon gasped for breath as he turned back to face the others.

"Holy shit," Novak said. "You're in pretty good shape for a guy who was almost dead yesterday."

"I heal quickly."

Gail knelt over McCann. She had the urge to check his pulse and see if he was alive, even though he was clearly dead. She closed her eyes. The smell of blood and gunpowder hung thick in the air. She sensed movement next to her, and when she opened her eyes again, Novak was kneeling beside her. His cheeks were wet with tears.

"Why did he do that?" Novak whispered. "Why charge Morgan like that? He must have known it would be suicide."

"He's been acting weird for a while now. Ever since the island…monster…whatever it was. Maybe he finally snapped."

Novak opened his mouth to reply, but sobbed instead.

"I'm sorry about Mr. McCann," Simon replied. Then he pointed at Caterina. "You said there were two more people on this vessel?"

She nodded. "Mylon and Tatiana."

"Well, then. I suggest you, me, and Gail find them, and make sure they are okay. And I recommend we do so carefully, just in case Mr. Morgan was wrong about the number of creatures left on board. And while we conduct our search, Mr. Novak can prepare to set sail."

"We've got engines," Novak said, standing up and wiping his eyes.

Simon smiled. "Then check the engines, Captain."

Sniffling, Novak grinned back at him. "Can I find my flamethrower first?"

Simon laughed. After a moment, Gail and Novak did the same. Gail had a fleeting thought that perhaps it was wrong, laughing this way with McCann barely five minutes dead. But it felt good. She felt…alive.

"I'm still confused," Caterina said. "Where are we going, again?"

"That's easy," Simon told her. "We're going to the edge of the world."

PART THREE

THE EDGE OF THE WORLD

TWENTY

As she did every morning since she'd killed him, Sarah went to the large windows and looked for Kevin's ghost. It had been two weeks since Henry's arrival and Kevin's death, and Sarah was pretty sure that she wasn't coping with it in a healthy manner. She'd felt grief and guilt and sadness in the first few days, but they'd quickly been replaced with an emotional malaise—a numbness that seemed to coat her very soul. She didn't feel anything anymore. She didn't eat enough, not that it mattered. Henry ate enough for them both. She'd had to remind him several times about rationing their food. She slept too much, but there was no release even then, because every time she closed her eyes she dreamed of Baltimore and the cultists, or Teddy and Carl.

Or Kevin.

If she could see his ghost, if she could see a Kevin-shaped apparition standing at the base of the tower and waving up at her, it would be proof that he wasn't really gone. Proof that the sum total of his existence hadn't ended with a bullet and then melted away into a puddle of water. Because if he didn't exist anymore, if there wasn't some part of him, some part of his consciousness, some part of his essence that didn't survive beyond this, then what hope was there for any of them? What was the point of going on? She thought back to her conversation with Henry when he'd first arrived at the ranger station. She'd asked him if he was ready to kill himself, and he'd said he wasn't. She hadn't been either.

But now…?

Sarah wiped condensation from the window and peered outside. Kevin's ghost wasn't there to greet her, but Earl and the others were. If the thing outside was really even Earl anymore. The creature was man-shaped, having a head, two arms and two legs, and stood about Earl's height, but its mass was nothing more than white fuzz. Its clothing, skin and hair had all been covered by the fungus. It certainly didn't look like Earl. Sarah could only take Henry's word for it that it was. Henry's word…and the fact that the creature seemed to grow agitated when it saw her, as if it recognized her, remembered her from before. And if it was Earl, then what had happened to Teddy and Carl? Could they have been transformed into one of these things, as well? The thought of those two sweet old men stumbling around as one of these fungal-zombies filled her with remorse.

Henry stirred behind her. Sarah turned, smiling sadly as he stretched and yawned.

"They still out there?" he asked.

Sarah nodded. "They haven't moved. Still in the same spot they were in yesterday. But there's more of them now."

"Wonder how they know we're up here? I mean, how is it that more and more of them keep showing up? It's like Earl called for reinforcements. You reckon they can communicate in some way?"

"They must," Sarah said. "Or maybe they're just converging on the last piece of dry land."

She turned back to the window and stared at the horizon. The forest was gone, submerged now beneath the waves. A few treetops still jutted from the water, but with each passing day less of them were visible. The rain kept falling and the waters kept rising, and their mountaintop refuge was now nothing more than a very small island in a very big ocean. Sarah figured that they had about another week before the waters reached the tower itself. After that, it would only be a matter of time before the ranger station sank beneath the surface, as well. That was unless the white fuzz got them first. She and Henry had managed to stymie Earl's attacks by barricading the door and booby-trapping the stairs, but that didn't impede the strands of fungus that were slowly growing up the sides of the tower, encasing the steel girders like vines. Sometimes at night, Henry told her he could feel the tower swaying back and forth as the supports weakened, but Sarah insisted it was just his imagination.

"What next?" Henry muttered, running a hand through his dirty hair and crawling out of bed.

"That's just what I was wondering," Sarah whispered. She looked again for Kevin, but only saw more rain.

The hours crawled on. Neither Sarah or Henry owned a watch. Both had used their cell phones to tell time. The forest ranger station only had one clock, and it was broken and as useless as their phones. There was no way for them to truly mark the passage of time. Even day and night was becoming muddled as time wore on. There was no moon or sun to go by. Both were blotted out by the cloud cover now. Still, there was light—a murky, gray haze that allowed for visibility. Sarah supposed that would have to pass for daylight.

Neither of their sleeping or eating routines approximated any semblance of normalcy anymore. They slept when they were tired and ate when they were hungry. Gone was the pretense of three square meals a day or catching a solid seven or eight hours of sleep. The only schedule they were adamant about was making sure that one of them was awake at all times to keep an eye on Earl and his friends.

When Henry had first arrived, Sarah had been grateful. He was someone new, someone alive, a fellow survivor. A fellow human being. They had talked non-stop the first few days. Henry had told her all about his parents and friends and Moxey, and about what it was like to grow up in West Virginia. Sarah had been delighted to learn that the boy had known Teddy and Carl, but was crushed by his news of what he'd seen at Teddy's former home. She'd told him about her former life, her family and her ex-girlfriends, and what she missed about them. They'd also shared survivor's stories. Henry related his experiences at the top of the grain silo, and Sarah commiserated with tales from the top of the Marriott in Baltimore. But after the first week, their conversation dwindled. Now, they struggled to find topics to discuss. It wasn't like they could turn to pop culture or the news anymore. There were no current events, other than the rain. And talking of news from the past served only to deepen their mutual depression.

Occasionally, they still got broadcasts from Sylva, the guy

with the pirate radio station in Boston. But his signal grew weaker and his messages had become heartbreakingly insane. The man was obviously infected with the white fuzz. Still, his was a human voice, and those were in short supply.

The situation had impacted their hygiene, as well. Sarah tried to keep her clothes clean, but there was only so much she could do when there was no water to wash them with. She didn't dare use the rainwater. There was no telling what it would do to the fabric—or to herself. She brushed her teeth every day, regardless of whether she'd eaten or not. In an effort to further conserve their drinking water, she didn't rinse, and the toothpaste often left her tongue feeling gritty and dry. She still used deodorant, although sparingly. She secretly wished Henry would, too. The teenager reeked of underarms—a musty, dank smell not at all dissimilar to that of the worms.

Sarah thought about the worms a lot. She wondered what had become of them. They hadn't seen one in quite some time, and the sudden disappearance of the creatures left her unsettled, although she didn't know why. It reminded her of rats deserting a sinking ship. Was the mountain going down soon? Was that why the worms had vanished? And where had they gone to, if not here? From everything she knew about them, Sarah seriously doubted that the worms could swim. She was ruminating over it again when Henry spoke.

"We could build a boat."

"Hmmm?"

"I reckon we could build a boat and float on out of here. There's got to be other folks who are still alive somewhere out there."

"And run into one of those shark men you mentioned? No thanks. Besides, where are we going to find the lumber to build a boat?"

Henry shrugged. "I don't know. The tree, or maybe that shed out yonder."

"The trees, the shed, and everything else outside is covered with the white fuzz now, Henry. It's even growing on the tower. If we go out any farther than the top of the stairs, we risk becoming infected. We're better off staying put."

"Maybe you're right."

"What prompted this?"

"I'm just bored, I guess. Just trying to make conversation."

Sulking, he turned back to the observation window. Sarah was about to apologize to him when Henry suddenly gasped.

"Oh, shit…"

"What's wrong?" she asked.

"Earl and them are gone!"

Sarah jumped to her feet. "That means they're going to try for another assault. Come on."

Henry put his ear to the door and listened.

"Anything?" Sarah asked.

The boy shook his head.

"Okay," she whispered. "Get back."

Henry removed the barricade and Sarah rushed out into the rain. She clutched a hefty axe that she'd retrieved from the utility shed before Kevin's death. Henry hurried out behind her, carrying a large pickaxe. They hovered on the top landing, peering down into the gloom below, where seven shadowy figures were laboriously making their way up the wet and slippery metal stairs. Five of the figures were roughly-human shaped, each possessing two arms, two legs and a head. Another of the creatures had once been either a dog or a coyote—or possibly a wolf, though Sarah wasn't sure if West Virginia had wolves or not. The seventh's original form was unrecognizable. Whatever it had once been, it was now nothing more than a shambling mound of pallid fungus. As they watched from above, the thing burst apart on the second landing, turning to liquid and spilling back down the stairs. Its companions, including the thing that had once been Earl Harper, ignored its demise.

"There's a gasoline can in the far corner, over next to the radio," Sarah said. "Grab it, and that box of wooden matches. I've got an idea."

Henry frowned. "You're not thinking of going down there, are you?"

Far below, the creatures moaned and gurgled, attracted by their voices.

"Just do it, Henry. Please? And hurry."

Nodding, he ducked back inside.

"Soft..." Earl cried, his voice phlegmatic and inhuman.

"Yeah," Sarah called, "we've been through that already, Earl. You sound like a broken record!"

"Soft...SOFT!"

Beginning at the fourth landing, Sarah and Henry had erected a series of crude but so-far effective barricades and booby-traps, using materials they'd recovered from the utility shed and the ranger station. When the monsters reached that level, they were confronted with a maze of lumber, fencing rolls, and other debris. Sarah and Henry had been mindful to avoid using anything that Kevin might have touched while inside the shed, but that didn't seem to matter now. Most of the blockade had white fuzz growing on it. Much of the fungus had appeared in only the last few days. Already, Sarah noticed, several lengths of two-by-four were missing. She assumed that they'd already liquefied. How long before the same thing happened to the rest of the barricade? How long before it happened to the ranger station, as well?

Henry returned with the gasoline can. Sarah took it from him and unscrewed the cap. The liquid sloshed inside and the pungent fumes made her wince. She walked to the railing and lifted the can over the side.

"Hey, Earl!"

Below, six mold-covered faces peered up at her, toothless mouths agape.

"Heads up." Sarah laughed as she poured the gasoline. The liquid seemed to fall faster than the rain, splashing on the creatures. Immediately, they recoiled, shrieking in either pain or fright. Sarah couldn't be sure of which, nor did she care. "Quick, Henry. Give me the matches."

He handed them over and Sarah fumbled one from the box and tried to light it. When she had no luck, she ducked into the open doorway and tried with a second one. A third and fourth also refused to light.

"Shit! Shit, shit, shit..."

"It don't matter none," Henry called, looking over the rail.

"They're running away. And parts of them are coming off. Look!"

Sarah moved to the railing and watched the attackers retreat. Sure enough, their hides had turned black where the gasoline had splashed on them. A few were now missing appendages, and the stumps were black, as well.

"Maybe gasoline kills it?" she mused.

"At the very least, they don't like it," Henry agreed.

Sarah grinned. "Henry, I've got an idea."

"What's your idea?"

Ignoring him, Sarah pushed past the teen and ran back into the ranger station. Her wet shoes squeaked on the floor. She clutched the empty gas can with one hand. Henry trailed after her, frowning in confusion. Water dripped from them both, pooling at their feet. A blast of thunder rumbled overhead.

"It will work," Sarah yelled, her tone excited and frantic. "I know it will! This is our way out, Henry. We don't have to die."

"What is? I don't understand."

Again, she acted as if she hadn't heard him. Henry's frown deepened. He stood watching as Sarah rushed from corner to corner, obviously looking for something.

"It's here somewhere, damn it. Did you grab it all?"

"Did I use all of what? The gasoline? I did just like you said, Sarah. I got that can in the corner next to the radio. Is it empty?"

She turned to look at him and rolled her eyes. Then she held up the can and jiggled it. "Does it sound full to you?"

Henry lowered his head. "Well, I reckon that's because you just dumped it all on Earl and his friends."

"Right. So we've got to get more. That's all. We just get a bunch more gasoline and fight our way out of here. You saw what it does to them!"

"But, Sarah..." Henry paused. "There is no more gasoline. That's all there is. I mean, maybe there's some in the storage shed down below, but that thing is covered in white fuzz. It's already starting to melt. We can't get in there."

"You're lying."

Sarah moaned—a mournful, terrible sound that scared Henry worse than their attackers had. Her wet eyes seemed black, and her lips turned pale as she grimaced.

"Sarah," Henry said softly. "Are you okay? What's wrong with—"

"You're lying, Henry! You're wrong. You have to be. There's more gas here. We just have to look. That's all. We just need to find some more gasoline. Then we can go home. Don't you want to go home? D-don't y-you…you…want… don't you w-w-wan…"

She backed into the wall and slid slowly to the floor. Her speech dissolved into sobs. When Henry approached her, Sarah began to scream. Her cries were so loud that he almost didn't notice the second round of thunder until the tower began to tremble.

That's not thunder, he thought. *That's us! The damn building is shaking...*

Henry grabbed the edge of the desk as the floor bucked and trembled beneath his feet. A deep, sonorous groan echoed from outside, followed by the sound of screeching metal. The tower shook harder, dislodging gear and hardware from the shelves. Items crashed to the tiles and rolled toward him. Henry cried out, terrified, but Sarah's reaction was quite different. Her screams abruptly turned into laughter.

She's snapped, he thought, as the ranger station shook harder. The sound of breaking glass came from somewhere over his head, but Henry squeezed his eyes shut, too afraid to look. *Sarah's gone crazy. That must be it. But so fast! What the hell am I gonna do now?*

Then, just as suddenly as they'd started, the tremors stopped. Henry didn't loosen his grip on the desk. He feared it would start all over again if he did. The only sound, other than his breathing, was Sarah giggling. And the rain.

Always the rain.

"Do it again, Henry," she said. "Make it go again!"

"It wasn't me, Sarah. I reckon it's the mold. We've seen how it turns everything into water. Figure it's doing the same thing to the station. We can't stay here."

"We'll be okay," she said. Her voice was clear and confident. Gone was any trace of insanity. "Kevin will be here soon."

"Kevin? Sarah…Kevin's dead. You know that. You told me that you shot him yourself, because he was turning into one of them."

"He'll be here," she insisted. "He's in the helicopter, with Salty. They'll be along any minute."

Henry took a deep breath. Letting go of the desk, he stepped toward her. "Sarah, we're alone here. Well, except for Earl and them others. Don't you remember?"

And then someone spoke behind Henry, making a liar out of him. Henry yelped in surprise. Spinning around, he saw that the station was empty, except for him and Sarah.

"Who's there? Come on out, god damn you!"

"My name is Steven Kazmirski. I'm here with my wife, Nahed Shahabi, and our Himalayan cat, Burman."

"The radio," Henry yelled, feeling foolish. "It's the radio."

He wondered for a moment what had become of the previous broadcaster, Sylva. The man had been infected. Had he finally succumbed? Henry glanced back at Sarah. She seemed calm now, though her eyes had a glazed look. She too was listening. Henry turned his attention back to the speaker.

"…left the John Hancock Tower and rowed over here in the darkness. We didn't want to use the boat's motor or spotlight, because we didn't want to attract predators. There were a lot of corpses in the water. They…bumped into…"

The signal faded. Henry cursed, tensing, until it came back again after a short burst of static.

"…have stayed in California. Hindsight is always twenty-twenty, though. But we moved cross the country to Newton. We liked it there, especially with Nahed being pregnant. But then the rain…major pharmaceutical company in Cambridge, just across the Charles River. I solve protein structures with potential drug compounds… Nahed attended…"

There was a particularly long burst of static. Frantic, Henry ran over to the ham radio set, staring at the controls and wondering which one to use. Then the speaker returned. The signal seemed weaker.

"…the Prudential Building…Sylva's last communication was twelve hours ago. We came…dead. I had to shoot him three times. His last…for his son, Alex, whom I believe he mentioned several times during his broadcasts. I only wish our boat had washed up on our tower sooner, so I could have helped Sylva and his friends before the disease…am sure…my biochemistry and drug development background. If I can learn more about how it spreads…if the white fuzz is fungal, alien, or bacterial, but it's certainly alive, and therefore contains different proteins...obtain a pure sample of a protein that's essential in the machinery that replicates the white fuzz's DNA, then I could stop it with drugs. If the DNA can't replicate…can't grow, so I'll collect fungus samples and extract the protein…using gravity…chromatography columns. Then…add the drug… either a small chemical molecule or a bio-molecule that's been purified...once …the drug complex to crystallize, I could have a potential cure within a week."

"You hear this, Sarah? It's gonna be okay. This fella on the radio says he can stop the fungus!"

"I want to know," Sarah sang, "who'll stop the rain?"

"One thing at a time, I reckon," Henry muttered.

"…need an X-ray generator…university, pharmaceutical company, or government lab that's not underwater. I've heard that the Havenbrook facility in Pennsylvania is still functioning…try for that. I'll also need power to run…for the math and structure viewing. If Havenbrook doesn't have electricity, I can always rig up some gas generators…with a baby on the way…I'm doing everything possible to ensure my family's protect…but I'm itchy and my skin feels funny… the cat has been hissing at me…"

"He's got it," Henry whispered, feeling his heart sink. "This poor guy has it, too."

Sarah began to sing louder, punctuating the chorus with sobs and laughter. Henry felt like doing the same.

Henry switched off the radio and stood there, shoulders slumped, head down, arms hanging limp. He felt drained, both physically and emotionally. His ears felt hot and were filled with a droning buzz. He swayed back and forth, unsure if the tower was shaking again or if he was just about to pass out. The heat spread to his cheeks and forehead. His vision began to blur.

"No," he mumbled. "Ain't got time to pass out. Earl and them others will be back. Got to barricade the door again."

He turned unsteadily. Sarah still sat on the floor, her back against the wall. She'd stopped singing, but her shoulders still shook with laughter. Her cheeks glistened with tears. More streamed from her red-rimmed eyes.

"Do it, Henry," she moaned. "Let's just get it over with."

Ignoring her, Henry made his way to the door. It was more difficult than he'd expected. His legs were wobbly, and he kept bumping into things. His mind kept returning to what Steven Kazmirski, the man on the radio, had said. Here was a guy who had a cure, who had a means for saving the world, or at the very least, stopping the white fuzz. But he'd never be able to do it. Henry hadn't understood all the scientific jargon the man had spouted, but even if he did make it all the way from Boston to that Havenbrook Research Center, he was still infected. He'd be dead before he ever finished the cure.

They all would be, Henry realized. Even if the man on the radio had been able to stop the fungus, he couldn't stop the rain. The weather was merciless and unchanging. The rain would not stop. It would still be there long after they were dead. Henry stopped halfway to the door and glanced out the tower's large window. Where once had been a tree-lined horizon, there was now an ocean. Debris floated atop the churning surface—halves of buildings and uprooted trees, cars and trucks, corpses, and even an apparently unmoored ship. The ranger station stood at the very top of the mountain, anchored deep into the rocks, yet black water now lapped at the cliffs just a few hundred yards beneath the tower's base. In another week, maybe two, it would reach them. But did they even have that long? The steel was weakening, turning to liquid, and those mold monsters were determined to get in.

"Oh, Ma," Henry whispered. "I miss you and Pa and Moxey. I can see the end of the world from here."

He stared down at the waves. Two weeks at most, unless the tower collapsed beneath their feet or Earl and the other creatures got inside before then. As if on cue, Henry heard a familiar shuffling gait on the stairs outside. Then a muffled voice rasped.

"Soft..."

"Shit! Here they come."

"Do it, Henry."

"Do what?" he snapped, hurrying by Sarah. As he did, he realized that her voice had changed again. She sounded sane once more. He glanced at her. Sarah's expression was calm.

"Get the pistol. The one the forest rangers left behind."

"That won't do shit against them."

"Not for them. For me! Kill me. I don't deserve to live. Not after what I did to Kevin. Not after everything that's happened? What's the point? To end up like Earl? Or worse? Kill me, okay? I don't want to die like that. Please? And if you're smart, you'll kill yourself, too."

Fists hammered at the door, slowly at first, but growing more insistent. The door rattled in its frame. Henry glanced at the door and then back to Sarah.

"Do it, Henry. Please? I'm so tired. I'm just so fucking tired…"

The pounding grew louder and more violent. Tendrils of fungus slipped through the crack at the bottom of the door, wriggling across the floor like tentative feelers.

"Soft," Earl called. *"Soft..."*

Swallowing, Henry picked up the .357 and stood looking down at Sarah.

"Is it loaded?" she asked. "It holds five bullets. I don't remember if I loaded it after…the last time I used it."

He checked it and then nodded. "It's fine."

"Good."

"You sure about this?"

"I am. Just don't miss. Okay?"

Henry tried to speak but found that he couldn't. His tongue felt dry and swollen. Sarah closed her eyes and lowered her head. She folded her hands in her lap, waiting. Henry put the gun to her head.

And that was when the world outside exploded.

TWENTY-ONE

There was no sound to accompany the explosion, but Henry assumed that was what must have happened. How else to explain the blinding flash of light outside the ranger station's observation windows? One moment, there had been only gray, dreary bleakness. The next, everything was illuminated in starkly vivid shades of orange and red.

Blinded by the flash, Henry staggered backward, flailing for something to hold on to as the tower swayed yet again. The gun, almost forgotten, nearly slipped from his hand. He grasped at it, sucking in breath and hoping the weapon wouldn't accidentally discharge. The irony was not lost on him. Only seconds before, he'd been planning to kill Sarah and then himself, thus fulfilling their mutual suicide pact. Now, seconds later, everything had changed.

I've seen the light, Henry thought. *Boy, have I!*

Spots floated in his field of vision. Blinking, he readjusted both his balance and his grip on the handgun. Then he made his way to the window.

"What's happening?" Sarah asked.

Henry's reply was cut short by another burst of light. Unlike the first time, this flash was accompanied by a strange sound. Henry cocked his head, listening. After a moment, he realized the sound was that of Earl and the others screaming. He looked out on the scene below, and was shocked to see two men—at least, he thought they were men—making their way toward the tower. The two figures walked single file. Both were covered head to toe with some kind of bizarre makeshift body armor consisting of hardhats, welder's facemasks, dust respirators, boots, the type of pants and coats worn by firefighters, and lots of duct tape. The one in the rear carried a rifle, but Henry barely noticed this. His attention was focused on the weapon the first figure wielded—a homemade flamethrower. The man swept it back and forth in front of him, clearing a path for him and his partner to walk that was devoid of any white fuzz. As Henry watched, a horde of fungus-infested creatures swarmed toward them.

"Look out!" He pounded his fist against the glass.

Behind him, Sarah groaned, rising to her feet.

Henry doubted his warning had been heard, let alone heeded, but it didn't really matter. The man with the flamethrower met the attackers head on. Fire spewed from the nozzle, engulfing the creatures and once again lighting up the horizon. Several of the fungal zombies were incinerated on the spot. Others fled, burning as they ran.

The pounding on the door recommenced, but it had taken on a different, more urgent tone.

"Soft..." Earl called. His voice sounded almost plaintive.

"Hear that?" Sarah grinned, running to the door. "The fucker is scared!"

"Don't open it," Henry said.

"I'm not. I just want to listen."

Henry looked outside again. The two figures were out of sight, which meant that they were most likely on the stairs. That would certainly explain Earl's reaction. He glanced toward the horizon. The ship he'd seen earlier, the one he'd thought was a derelict, was still there amidst the other debris, but now he noticed something else. Parked on their shore and tied to the top of a mostly-submerged oak tree was a small rowboat. When he turned back to Sarah, she had her ear to the door.

"Get away from there!"

"I told you what Earl did to my friends and me. Whatever has him spooked, I want to hear him get what's coming."

"Mr. Garnett and Mr. Seaton were my friends, too," Henry reminded her. "As for what's outside, it's two fellas. One of them has a flamethrower."

"Could it be the Army?"

"I don't reckon so. They're wearing some kind of—"

He was cut off by a scream from right outside the door, followed by the pounding of boots on the metal stairs. Earl shrieked again—a terrible, high-pitched squeal that faded away into a sizzling sound. Sarah backed away from the door. She and Henry exchanged a frightened glance. He put his finger to his lips and motioned for her to come to him.

"We should hide," he whispered.

"Where?"

Before he could answer, there was another knock at the door. Unlike Earl's, this knocking was quick and self-assured. Five raps, a pause, and then two more.

"Shave and a haircut?" Henry frowned.

The melody was repeated, and before Henry could stop her, Sarah—still in the grip of whatever emotional breakdown she'd suffered—ran to the door and flung it open.

"Shit!"

Henry brought the handgun up, pointing it at the two figures as they stormed into the room. Both of the new arrivals had their weapons ready, as well.

"Are either of you infected?" It was the figure with the flamethrower who spoke. A man's voice, muffled slightly through the welding shield and respirator. "Are there any more of those things here?"

Slowly, Henry shook his head.

"How about you drop that pistol, kid?" This time, the voice belonged to the one with the rifle. Henry was surprised to learn she was female.

"Are you here to kill us?" Sarah asked. Her tone was almost pleading.

"No," the man said. "My name's Novak. This is Gail. We're here to rescue you."

"R-rescue…?" Sarah's voice had a disbelieving, dreamlike tone.

"Yeah," Novak said, "unless you'd rather hang out here. Your call. But you should know we risked our asses coming here like we did, so the very least you could do is let us haul you out of here."

"Yeah!" Henry nodded, tears running down his face. "Hell, yeah! Take us with you. But how did you get here? How did you—?"

"We've got a ship anchored out there. We were able to spy

you with our binoculars. These observatory windows don't give you much privacy. Anyway, we saw that there were two of you, and that you had lots of supplies. We could use them."

"What if we'd been infected?" Henry asked.

Gail shrugged. "Then we would have killed you the same way we killed those things outside, and then taken the supplies."

"Fair enough," Henry muttered. "I reckon I'd do the same."

"Look," Novak said, "we don't have time to stand around talking. I'm sure you two have been through a lot. We have, too. Why don't we start by lowering that pistol?"

Nodding, Henry lay the weapon on the radio console.

"Good," Novak said. "Now the two of you strip out of those forest ranger uniforms and let us check you out."

Sarah made a squawking noise.

"It's okay," Gail soothed. "We just need to make sure you aren't infected with the fungus before we take you back to the ship. We won't touch you."

"Come on, Sarah," Henry said. "It'll be okay."

Slowly, he and Sarah stripped. Henry felt his ears turn red as he exposed himself to the two strangers. They stepped forward, had the two of them raise their arms and stand with their legs apart. Then they did a quick but thorough examination. When they were done, Novak stepped back and removed his mask.

"Good. You're both clear. Go ahead and get dressed. Then you can help us load this stuff into the lifeboat and we'll get you back to the ship."

Henry and Sarah got back into their uniforms. Excited, Henry was full of questions, but he decided they could wait. It occurred to him as he buttoned his shirt that perhaps he was trusting the new arrivals a little too quickly. But then he decided that he didn't care. He had no choice. He could go with them, and hope their intentions were true, or he could stay here and die.

The station shook again. All four of them grabbed on to supports until the trembling stopped. Then Henry and Sarah finished getting dressed.

"Is there anybody else here?" Novak asked.

"Nope," Henry said. "Just us. There was a little mouse running around, but we haven't seen it in a few days."

"Okay. Gail will stand guard in case any more of your friends show up."

Sarah moaned, and then collapsed. Her head struck the floor with a loud whack. Henry rushed to her side.

"Is she okay?" Gail asked.

"I reckon. Her head's not bleeding or anything. I think she just passed out."

"Is she sick?"

"No…at least, not physically. She's had a rough patch. Couple of weeks ago, she had to kill her best friend. He was turning into one of them things. It's been eating at her ever since."

Novak stepped forward and put his hand on Henry's shoulder. "What's your name, kid?"

"Henry, sir."

"Well, Henry. Help us get this stuff loaded up, and then we'll introduce you and her to a bunch of new friends."

Henry swallowed. "That would be nice."

Sarah regained consciousness while Henry helped Novak and Gail pack the supplies. She moaned, and her eyes fluttered. She sat up, her expression confused and alarmed. Henry rushed to her side.

"You're okay," he said. "You just passed out."

"Who…?" She pointed at the new arrivals, unable to finish the sentence.

"Don't you remember? They're here to rescue us."

Frowning, Sarah shook her head. "Everything… everything is messed up. I can't think straight. What's wrong with me, Henry?"

"Stress? You're tired. I don't know. But we're safe, Sarah. Once we get onboard their ship, you can get lots of rest. And I'll watch over you."

Smiling, Sarah touched his cheek. "You remind me of… Kevin. He would have liked you."

Henry opened his mouth to respond, but a shadow fell over

them. He glanced up, and Gail stood there, holding several black garbage bags.

"Put these on," she said. "You'll have to tape or tie them around you."

"What for?" Henry asked.

"To keep yourself from getting infected. You're both clean now. We need to keep you that way until we get to the ship."

"Make no mistake," Novak added. "If either one of you comes into contact with the fungus between here and there, we'll have to leave you behind. I don't like saying that, but you deserve to know it before you go outside."

The tower trembled and groaned again, silencing further debate. It listed to the side, and this time, it didn't right itself.

"Jesus…" Gail whistled. "We need to go. This thing won't hold much longer."

"You two prep," Novak said. "Gail and I will finish with the supplies. You guys will carry them, while we take the front and the rear. We'll take care of anything that crosses our path. You think you're up to hefting supplies, Sarah?"

She nodded. "I'm better. I promise."

He studied her carefully, and finally said, "Okay."

While Novak and Gail finished packing, Henry and Sarah covered themselves in plastic. They taped the bags around their ankles, wrists, waists and necks. Then added smaller bags to cover their hands. Then they fashioned ponchos out of more trash bags, covering their heads. When they were finished, only their eyes and noses were exposed. Novak and Gail helped them shoulder the packs.

"We appreciate what ya'll are doing," Henry said. "But I've got to tell you, it don't feel right going outside without a weapon."

"That's understandable," Gail said, "but can either of you manage a weapon and the supplies?"

"I've got a Taurus," Sarah replied. "It's a snub nose, and I can holster it over the plastic."

"How about you?" Gail nodded at Henry.

"Just a hatchet," he said, "and this here knife. It belonged to our friend, Mr. Garnett. I reckon I can tape the knife to my hip and carry the hatchet."

"Okay," Gail agreed. "But understand—if those things are close enough to fight off with a hatchet, then chances are you're going to get infected. And we won't hesitate to fire."

Henry nodded. "Fair enough."

He and Sarah quickly armed themselves.

"Ready?" Novak asked.

They nodded.

"Then let's do this. I'll take point. Gail will bring up the rear. Stick close. If we get spread apart out there, they'll be on us in seconds. Just let me clear a path with the flamethrower, and then follow right behind me."

He opened the door and stepped out onto the stairwell. Swallowing hard, Henry followed. He heard Sarah rustling along behind him, and then the light disappeared as Gail shut the door.

"Soft..." a chorus of voices rasped from below. *"Soft..."*

Henry said, "Oh shit."

The rain fell like nails and sheets of mist curled up from the ground far below. It was hard for Henry to see anything on the landing, but he assumed that one or more of the creatures must have made it back up the stairwell, because Novak unleashed a gout of flame and shouted at him and the women to fall back. The liquid fire lit up the dark, and something inhuman shrieked.

"Back inside," Novak yelled.

"We can't," Gail hollered. "I shut the door already. We fall back now and they'll have us trapped. We've got to push through!"

"God damn it..."

More fire erupted from the nozzle of the weapon, and was followed by a second shriek. Henry closed his eyes against the sudden flare of brilliance. The heat from the blast brushed against him. He smelled something like burning hair, and hoped it wasn't his. When he opened his eyes again, there were spots in his vision.

"Okay," Novak said. "Stick close."

The tower buckled and swayed as they made their way down the stairs. Henry gasped when he saw the extent of the damage to the steel beams and girders that held the structure aloft. They were overgrown with white fuzz, and twisted and bent in places where the metal had grown soft and started to liquefy.

"Jesus," Sarah gasped behind him. "If we had stayed here any longer…"

She didn't finish the sentence. She didn't have to. Henry felt the same way. The imagery in his head was of the World Trade Center towers collapsing on 9/11. He'd been younger then—elementary school—and while he hadn't understood all the implications of that fateful day, he remembered being awestruck that the support beams in the skyscrapers had melted and liquefied. The same thing was happening now, only at a much slower pace.

"Soft..." The voices echoed from below.

"I'll turn you soft, motherfuckers!" Novak released another gout of flame, bathing the landing below them. More creatures howled.

"Careful," Gail said.

Henry turned around and saw that she'd been cautioning Sarah, who had almost brushed against the hand railing, which was covered with the sickly-pale fungus.

"Thanks," Sarah said, shrinking away.

Henry smiled. She still seemed cowed and unsteady, but at least she wasn't freaking out anymore. Maybe they'd get through this after all.

His hope and bravado faltered when at last they reached the ground—because he wasn't sure it qualified as ground anymore. The mold grew thick, covering the rocks and trees and soil. Tendrils of it hung from the underside of the ranger station, swaying in the rain like vines. He sidestepped, avoiding one particularly low-hanging bit, and then froze as one of the fungal zombies crawled toward him on its hands and knees. It paused, reaching for him, and then melted before Henry's eyes, quickly transforming into a watery pool of muck. The liquid trickled toward them.

"Don't get it on you," Gail warned. "Novak?"

Nodding, he complied by training the flamethrower on the remnants. They evaporated within seconds.

"How do we get to your boat?" Henry asked. "That stuff is everywhere."

"I made a path on the way in," Novak said. "But you can see how quickly it grew back."

Frowning, he strode forward, sweeping the weapon back and forth, and burning a pathway for them. Swallowing, Henry trotted along behind him, hurrying to keep up. Sarah and Gail followed. A moment later, Gail's rifle boomed.

"They're coming in behind us."

"I've got them up front, too," Novak yelled. "Henry, Sarah? How's the sides?"

Henry glanced to the left and saw shadowy figures lurching through the mist.

"I reckon they're trying to flank us," he said.

Sarah screamed. Henry turned to the right and saw that the creatures were closer on that side, almost within arms reach. Their bodies and faces were completely covered with the fungus. Even their mouths and noses were obscured. Their eyes were sunken pinpricks of dull grey. Many of them had root-like appendages sprouting from their arms and feet.

"Stand and fight," Novak ordered. "Backs together. Form a circle!"

They did as he commanded. Henry and Sarah dropped the supplies they held in their arms. The items splashed on the wet ground, sinking into the mud. Henry shrugged his shoulders, readjusting his backpack's weight. Then the creatures were upon them. Gail and Sarah squeezed off shot after shot, and Novak swept the flamethrower in a wide arc, spraying burst after burst. Henry gripped his hatchet, feeling worthless.

One of the things made it through the gauntlet and reached for his head. Moaning, Henry swung at it with his hatchet. The blade bit through the monster's wrist like soft butter. The appendage burst, and Henry was reminded of the water balloon battles he'd had with friends when he was younger. The creature reached for him again. The fungus on its face split open, revealing a toothless maw. Henry buried the hatchet in its mouth. The creature exploded. The stench was nauseating—musky and damp. Henry closed his eyes and turned away. He felt something splatter against him, but he didn't know if it was the creature or merely the ever-present rain.

The battle continued. Henry acted as a spotter, calling the other's attention to the creatures as they attacked. More and more of the things emerged from the mist—both humans and animals. All of them were covered with the same disgusting mold.

"We've got an opening," Novak screamed. "Let's go. Gail, you take point."

Sarah bent over, reaching for the supplies they'd dropped, but Gail rebuked her.

"Leave them."

"But we need them," Sarah said.

"We do," Gail agreed, "but they're infected now. Leave them."

Gail charged forward with Henry and Sarah hot on her heels. Novak brought up the rear, blasting the hordes with sheets of flame. They reached the rowboat and piled inside. Behind them, the darkness returned as the flames flickered and died. Novak dropped the flamethrower on the ground and climbed into the boat.

"What are you doing?" Gail frowned, her expression perplexed.

"I got mold on the barrel. No sense bringing it back to the ship. Hate to leave it behind." He turned to Sarah. "Can I borrow your handgun, please?"

Nodding, Sarah handed the weapon to him. Novak waited until they had rowed away from the steadily shrinking shore. Then he fired three shots. The third bullet hit the flamethrower, and it exploded, creating a fleeting false dawn. The monsters screamed and moaned as the flames engulfed them.

"Very pretty," Gail said, "but it still seems like a waste to me."

"It ain't like we'll need it again," Novak said. "Where we're going, it's all ocean now. These things won't be there."

"Where are we going?" Henry asked.

"Pennsylvania," Gail said as they rowed into the fog. "We're going to drop anchor above a place called LeHorn's Hollow."

Henry shook his head. "Where? I don't understand."

Gail sighed. "The end of the world, kid. We're going to the end of the world…"

Behind them, there was a loud, echoing splash as the tower finally collapsed.

"Can't believe we went through all of that just to come away empty-handed," Novak said as they rowed toward the ship. "Such a waste."

Henry wanted to take issue with the comment, and point out that they had managed to save him and Sarah, not to mention the backpack of meager supplies he had strapped over his shoulders, but he was too terrified to speak. The water was silent, save for the raindrops pelting its surface and the small waves lapping at the sides of the boat. The black depths below were thick with an almost palpable menace. He sat still, muscles tensed, jaw clenched, remembering his escape from the grain silo to land and waiting for one of the shark men to attack.

Instead, he just got wet. Henry shivered as the rain managed to creep beneath his makeshift armor. When he glanced around the boat, he saw that the others were equally miserable.

"How you holding up?" he asked Sarah.

She shrugged. "We're still alive. I didn't think we would be. I guess that counts for something."

"I reckon so, given what we were thinking about doing."

"What was that?" Gail asked, slipping an oar through the water.

Henry blushed. "We…we were thinking about…killing ourselves. Maybe it sounds stupid, but we really thought…"

"Don't sweat it, Kid," Novak said. "We'd been discussing the same thing not too long ago."

"Really? What made you change your minds?"

Novak turned away. "A mutiny."

The ship loomed out of the mist and they pulled alongside. Henry noticed four other shadowy figures looming around the rail, but the fog concealed their features. Once he and Sarah had removed the plastic from their shoes and were safely aboard, the rest of the crew stepped forward, and Novak made introductions.

"Henry and Sarah, meet Simon, Caterina, Mylon and Tatiana."

"Howdy." Henry stuck out his hand, but the others recoiled.

"No offense, Mr. Garrett," Simon said, smiling, "but you'll need to be detoxified before we shake. We can't risk the chance of infection. I'm sure you both understand."

"How do you know my last name?" Henry asked.

"Simon does parlor tricks," Novak said. "You think that's something, ask him to light your cigarette."

Mylon cleared his throat. "Speaking of which, where's the flamethrower?"

"We had to leave it behind," Novak said. "It was contaminated."

"Was that the explosion we heard?"

"You guys didn't see the flash?" Gail asked.

"Nope," Mylon said. "Too foggy."

"We had to leave the supplies, too," Novak said. "Except for the few things Henry has in his pack."

Mylon shook his head. "Well, this whole thing has been one big cluster-fuck."

"That's no way to talk to our guests," Simon scolded. "I suggest we get out of the rain, raise anchor, get underway, and allow Mylon and Caterina to continue their shift at watch. I'm sure our new arrivals would like some dry clothes and something to eat."

Nodding, Henry said, "That would be great. Me and Sarah—"

A loud splash echoed off the portside. Whatever had caused the disturbance, it was enough to increase the size of the waves. The ship rocked beneath their feet.

Simon tensed. "How soon can we be underway, Mr. Novak?"

"Ten minutes."

"Make it five. It's no longer safe to stay here."

"Not for nothing, Simon, but the same could be said of the rest of the world."

"That's what I meant, Mr. Novak," Simon replied. "That's exactly what I meant."

TWENTY-TWO

Sarah and Henry both slept for most of a day, and when they awoke, both were momentarily confused as to their surroundings. Sarah found herself tearing up when she looked at Henry, overwhelmed with affection and gratitude for everything he'd done. During their time together in the forest ranger station, she'd begun to think of him as a little brother. Since Kevin's death, he'd been the only other voice she heard, with the exception of Sylva's last few increasingly crazed broadcasts.

She kissed him on the forehead. "Thanks."

"What for?" Henry's ears turned scarlet. A moment later, his cheeks followed suit.

"For helping. For not giving up on me. I really lost it back there, Henry. I can only imagine what it was like, dealing with me. I'm not a person who likes to lose control—of anything, but least of all myself. Thanks for being there for me when I couldn't be."

"No problem. You've been there for me, too."

"You miss your family?"

He nodded. "Still. I keep thinking it's been long enough, and so much has happened, that I just ought to be numb by now, but I ain't."

"Neither am I. I think that's why I…got like I was. I miss Kevin and Teddy and Carl, but I miss the people before this. Before the rain started. My Mom and my girlfriend."

"Perhaps you will find them again," said a voice behind them.

Sarah and Henry glanced up to find Simon standing in the hatchway to the berthing area.

"What do you mean?" Sarah asked.

"What do either of you know about string theory? Alternate

realities and universes?"

"I used to watch Star Trek," Sarah replied.

"Well, I'm sure you are both hungry. Come up to the galley. Let's get you something to eat. And while you do, I'll explain our plan. You might feel incredulous at first, but I assure you it is the truth."

He beckoned for them to follow. After a moment's hesitation, they did.

"Perhaps you'd like a quick tour of the vessel on our way to the galley?" Simon suggested.

Sarah shrugged. "Why not? I guess this is our home for now."

"Merely temporary," Simon said. "So don't get too comfortable."

He led them topside. The wind and rain pelted them the moment they stepped out onto the deck, and Sarah shivered. For the brief period she'd been asleep below, she'd felt warm and dry, and hadn't realized how much she'd missed both sensations until that moment. She glanced down at the churning water below.

"Where are we?" she asked.

"Mr. Novak says we are somewhere over the border between West Virginia and Virginia, on a northeast course."

Sarah frowned. "Well, then where are the mountains? There should be mountain peaks sticking up above the surface."

Simon shook his head. "Not anymore, I'm afraid. Bald Knob was the last, and soon, it will vanish beneath the waves, as well. It is fortuitous we came across the two of you when we did."

"There ain't as much junk floating in the water, either," Henry said. "I mean, I reckon them things in the water have eaten all the dead folks by now, but where's all the trees and cars and other stuff that's been floating around?"

"It's liquefied," Simon said, opening a hatch and stepping back inside the ship. "The debris. The mountains. Everything is liquefying."

Sarah shut the hatch behind them and latched it. She wiped rain from her eyes. "The white fuzz?"

"Indeed," Simon said. "All matter on this planet is being

turned into water. The planet still has a core, and is still rotating on its axis, so gravity still exists. Sooner or later though, even the planet's core will begin to liquefy. As all this occurs, the Earth is being absorbed into another dimension—one composed entirely of water—called the Great Deep. I'll explain in detail while we eat."

Sarah wasn't sure what to think as Simon led them into the galley. She glanced at Henry. The boy's expression seemed to mirror her own confusion.

Caterina and Mylon, who were just coming off watch, were also eating in the galley. Gail was present, as well. Sarah, Henry and Simon took seats next to them. Sarah thanked Gail again for rescuing them. The ship rolled slowly back and forth beneath their feet.

"I trust the night passed uneventfully?" Simon asked Mylon.

"Heard some big splashes out there in the dark," Mylon said. "And at one point, Caterina thought she heard singing. But other than that, no."

Sarah had been eating a dry Saltine cracker. When Mylon mentioned the singing, she choked on it, startled and remembering what had happened in Baltimore. It seemed so long ago, now, but the fear was still very real. Henry clapped her on the back and handed her a small juice box. Sarah sipped from the straw and then gasped.

"You okay?" Henry asked.

She nodded, but before she could reply, Caterina spoke up.

"It sounded like a woman. I'm sure I must have imagined it, though."

Simon frowned. "I'll have to ask Mr. Novak to go faster. And we need to start doubling the watches."

"Why's that?" Mylon asked.

"Because we are being followed."

"By who?"

"An entity known as Leviathan."

Sarah choked on her juice.

Henry pounded Sarah on the back, and the others looked at her in concern, except for Simon, who merely arched an eyebrow and stared at her intently. She bent over and coughed some more, before sitting up straight again.

"Are you okay?" Henry asked.

Sarah nodded. "Yeah. Sorry. I just choked on my drink."

"You know the name Leviathan." Simon's tone indicated a statement rather than a question.

"I do."

"May I ask how?"

Sarah closed her eyes and shuddered. Suddenly, she was back in Baltimore again, fleeing through the hallways as the giant, squid-headed monstrosity demolished the hotel, their last safe place of refuge and one of only two buildings not submerged. She could smell the mold and the mildew, hear the sound the creature's massive tentacles and smaller tendrils made as they lashed through the air, see those huge, baleful eyes looming out of the rain and staring down at them, and hear the sounds her friends made as they died. Only she, Kevin, and Salty had escaped alive. Now she was the only one left. The weight of it suddenly seemed to press down on her, and Sarah's thoughts turned once again to Kevin.

"I'll tell you," she whispered, opening her eyes again, "but I only want to talk about it once. So how about you get Novak and everyone else down here?"

Simon reached out and gently patted her hand. His palm was warm and dry—a sensation she hadn't believed could actually exist anymore in this world.

"Of course," Simon said. "Mylon, would you be so kind as to summon the others? We'll hear Sarah's encounter with our foe, and then we'll talk about what we can do when we face him."

"Do you really think he's coming?" Sarah asked.

"Oh, yes. I feel him, even now, getting closer. I am aware of him as he is of us. You see, I'm the one he wants."

Once they were all gathered together in the galley, Simon thanked the group for their attention.

"We have to make this quick," Novak warned him. "I dropped anchor because I don't trust letting us drift. Not with all the debris out there. But we don't have a guard posted on the decks, and I like that even less."

"I'll try to be as succinct as I can," Simon promised. "Although Sarah has some things to share, as well."

She nodded.

"I suppose we'll start at the beginning," Simon continued. "In the beginning, God created—"

"I don't believe in God," Caterina interrupted.

"Yeah," Novak said. "I've got to be honest, Simon. If this is going to be nothing more than a Sunday School meeting, then I think we should get back to work right now. While we're down here talking, there's no telling what could be creeping up on us out there."

"You may call it God," Simon said, ignoring them. "Others know it as Yahweh, Allah, etcetera. All the name refers to is the power behind the creation of the universe. Regardless of your individual beliefs, there are certain universal truths, and one of them is that the Creator, whose true name is known only to a handful of people, created the heavens and the Earth and everything between them. In order to create this new universe, the Creator needed a lot of energy. So the Creator destroyed the universe that existed before ours, down to the very last atom, and utilized the harvested energies as building blocks. The old universe ceased to exist."

Gail frowned. "So God is Galactus?"

"Pardon?"

She grinned. "Never mind. Benefits of reading comics when I was a kid. I'm sorry for interrupting."

"Thirteen denizens of that previous universe escaped the destruction. These beings are collectively known to my organization and other occultists as the Thirteen. They are not gods or demons, and are not susceptible to the same magic and supernatural laws that govern, banish or bind demons, angels, and other entities. Very specific methods must be used when confronting them. They are one of the reasons Black Lodge was created. The Thirteen have one single-minded goal—the total obliteration of everything the Creator has made, meaning our Earth and all of the other Earths, as well as the rest of our universe."

"Other Earths?" Henry asked.

"Yes. The universe is composed of alternate realities. In my organization, we referred to these alternate planes of existence as levels. Just as there are different planets in the sky, there are also different versions of those planets, existing simultaneously on a different level of the universe. The Thirteen wish to destroy them all."

"And Leviathan is one of the Thirteen?" Gail asked.

"Exactly. Our Earth recently came under attack by both Leviathan and Behemoth—two members of the Thirteen. I no longer sense Behemoth's presence, which means his physical form may have been destroyed."

"Is Behemoth a giant worm?" Sarah asked. "I mean, bigger than the rest of them?"

"Yes. Don't tell me you've encountered him, as well?"

"I think maybe I have."

"Then you do indeed have a story to tell. Nevertheless, Leviathan is still present. He is aware of me just as I am aware of him. Black Lodge operatives have stopped him on other levels. As the last of my kind on this Earth, he will seek me out and destroy me. That's what he is doing right now."

"But what is he?" Henry asked.

"I had a friend that called him Cthulhu," Sarah said.

Simon nodded. "That is one name for him, yes. As is Kraken, Tlaloc, Dagon, He of One Thousand Tentacles, and the Lord of the Great Deep. His true size and measurements are unknown. Suffice to say, he is massive. He has a squid-like head, a beard of tentacles, webbed hands and feet, a long tail, and wings."

"Sounds like Godzilla," Mylon mumbled.

"That's a remarkably apt comparison," Simon said.

Novak groaned. "And now he's coming for us?"

"I'm afraid so."

"Well, fuck that. Short of tossing you over the side so he leaves us alone, how do we get rid of him?"

"I'm hoping Sarah can tell us," Simon said, turning to her. "After all, if she's escaped him once before, perhaps she knows a way we can do so again. If not, then I'm afraid all might be lost."

They sat in silence for a moment, pondering the ramifications of Simon's dire pronouncement. Then, one by one, they turned to look at Sarah.

"Well," Gail asked, "how do we defeat this thing?"

"I don't know," Sarah said. "I honestly don't. When it attacked us in Baltimore, the creature eventually just left."

She recounted her encounter with Leviathan, beginning with the cult on the nearby rooftop, the arrival of the vampire-like mermaid, the ill-fated rescue mission that Kevin and the others had launched in an attempt to disrupt the cult's sacrificial ceremony, how that – and the murder of the mermaid – had led to Leviathan's emergence, the creature's subsequent attack on their building, and how she, Salty, and Kevin had escaped.

"And it just left?" Novak asked. "That doesn't make any sense."

The others all began to talk at once, but Simon held up his hand, signaling silence.

"It makes perfect sense," he said. "The girl, Lori, was a sacrifice. Leviathan held Kevin responsible for killing one of its brides—the mermaid. In retaliation, it took Kevin's female. Sated, it then departed."

Caterina frowned. "But why wouldn't it kill the rest of them?"

"I've always wondered that myself," Sarah muttered.

"It's because we are insignificant to Leviathan," Simon said. "Normally, humanity is beneath his attention, other than as bothersome insects who must be destroyed. But we as individuals? Leviathan couldn't care less. When we come across a nest of wasps, do we have a stronger loathing for one particular wasp from the hive more so than the others? No. All we know is that we want to destroy the entire nest. That's how Leviathan views us. He didn't bother with Sarah and her two friends because he figured they'd die anyway, sooner or later, once his ultimate goal was achieved."

"Then why is he after you?" Novak leaned back in his chair and propped his feet up on the table. "If we're nothing more than gnats to this thing, why is he now focused on you?"

"Because I am a particularly bothersome wasp," Simon said. "Leviathan senses my presence…and my power. He knows that I have abilities not shared by most of humanity. He thinks I have it in me to halt his destruction and reverse what has happened."

"Do you?" Henry asked.

Simon shook his head. "No. As I said, all I can do at this point is save our lives. I can't save our planet. But Leviathan doesn't know that."

Novak dropped his feet to the floor with a loud thud. His chair squeaked across the floor as he stood abruptly. "Then what the hell do we do, Simon?"

"Hope that we reach LeHorn's Hollow before Leviathan reaches us."

Novak opened his mouth to respond, but suddenly, the hull clanged like a bell, the sound deep and hollow and reverberating throughout the entire ship. The vessel lurched violently to one side, spilling the crew's gear and belongings onto the deck. Screaming, they held on tight as the ship rocked again.

"I reckon maybe it's too late," Henry said.

"Did we hit something?" Gail asked.

"No," said Novak, his face ashen. "Something hit us…"

With Novak and Simon in the lead, they raced up the ladder, weapons at the ready, and ran out onto the deck. The wind had picked up again, and Sarah squinted against the cold rain as it stung her face. She glanced around in panic, expecting to see giant tentacles with teeth-lined sucker-mouths, or a bulbous elephantine head sticking up out of the water and peering at them with baleful yellow eyes, but there was nothing. Fog rolled in over the ocean, obscuring their view.

The boat listed to the side again, spilling them onto the deck. The vessel groaned, as if under great stress.

"Grab on to something," Novak yelled, struggling to his feet. "Be ready for—"

A clacking sound interrupted him.

"The hell is that?" Mylon scrambled backward. "Sounds like a big pair of maracas."

The boat tilted more, and waves splashed over the side, drenching them. Then something else came over the side, as well.

At first, they only saw the eyes—two basketball-sized black dots attached to stalks that waved back and forth like wheat. Then a massive, serrated claw latched on to the railing, snapping it in half. A second claw appeared, and seized a length of metal ductwork. The steel bent as the claw squeezed. Then the claw's owner heaved itself over the side and onto the deck. The deck shook beneath them.

It was a giant crab. Sarah gaped at its size. It was big enough that the eight of them could have used its hollowed-out shell as a lifeboat. The eye-stalks wiggled as the creature surveyed them. It waved its arms in the air, clacking its claws together. Then it scuttled forward, its segmented legs clacking across the wet deck. Tatiana screamed as the beast bore down on her. Sarah saw Simon and Novak trying to reach her, but both men slipped as the ship rolled even further to the side.

Tatiana jabbed at the crab with her makeshift spear, but the creature grasped it, snapping the weapon in half. She shrieked as it pinned her down with two of its smaller legs, the tips piercing her chest and thigh. Then it seized her head in its other claw and squeezed, slicing the top off. Tatiana's brains slipped from her open skull and slid across the deck, leaving a grayish-pink trail behind.

Novak and Gail opened fire, pelting the crab with shot after shot. Most of the rounds were ineffectual, unable to penetrate the hardened shell, but they succeeded in blasting off one of the creature's eyes. Hissing, it stomped on the deck, writhing with agony.

"Aim for the other eye," Gail yelled, reloading.

She and Novak unleashed another volley, driving the enraged crab back to the rail. The ship rolled again, and Novak's shots went wild. The others ducked, except for Henry, who crouched next to Sarah, gaping. She grabbed his pants leg and pulled him down.

"Hold on to me," she shouted, wrapping her arms around a cable. "Don't let go!"

Nodding, Henry closed his eyes and shuddered.

Novak and Gail continued firing, forcing the crab back into the water. It paused on the railing, claws waving in frustration, lone-remaining eye glaring at them. Then it dove. As it did, the boat rocked hard. Tatiana's lifeless body slipped over the railing after it. The others screamed, hanging on for dear life. Then the boat splashed back down again, and rocked back and forth.

"Everyone back inside," Novak ordered.

"This was just the first," Simon said. "There will be others like it. Leviathan will send more denizens of the Great Deep after us. I suggest you make haste, Mr. Novak."

"I don't think we have enough fuel, Simon. I gun it, we're going to run out that much faster."

"If you don't, then we'll die here."

"Lift anchor, and pedal to the metal, then," Novak said. "Next stop, Pennsylvania. If we can find it, that is."

"Pray we do," Simon answered. "All of you pray that we do in time."

TWENTY-THREE

Hours later, Sarah, Henry, and Mylon were sitting in the galley, hastily grabbing a meal of granola bars, canned fruit, and bottled water before heading topside for a turn on watch. Mylon was sullen and sat apart from them, quietly sipping the juice from the can.

"Penny for your thoughts," Henry said.

At first, Sarah didn't think the older man had heard him. But then Mylon slowly raised his head and looked at them with red-rimmed eyes.

"Uh," Henry stuttered. "I'm sorry. I didn't realize you were…crying."

Mylon shrugged. "It's okay. I reckon you didn't mean any harm."

"Do you want to talk about it?" Sarah asked.

"Just thinking about my family. My wife and two daughters."

"Are they…did they?" Sarah wasn't sure how to phrase the question.

"They died," Mylon said. "No need to tiptoe around it. They died early on, before the flooding got bad. Remember when the super-storms first started, and those really bad winds were tearing down whole cities?"

Sarah and Henry both nodded.

"Well," Mylon continued, "one of those gusts hit our house. We were hunkered down in the basement, hiding from the worms, but it sheared our home right off the foundation. My wife and one of my daughters were killed by the debris. The worms took my other daughter soon after."

"I'm sorry," Sarah said.

"It's okay. Like I said, I've had time to deal with it. What I'm struggling with is that…I…well, I can't remember what they looked like anymore. I mean, I have a recollection, but it's not complete."

"Do you have a picture of them?" Henry asked.

"No. They got me one of those smart phones last Christmas, before all of this. I stopped carrying my wallet, and had all my pictures on the phone. Once the electricity and phone service went out, I didn't see the point in lugging it around anymore. Not to mention all this dampness in the air probably gummed it up anyway. Only pictures I have of them are in my mind, and some days, my mind feels like it's starting to fade."

"That's normal," Sarah said. "I've certainly felt that way. We're scared all the time, half-starved, cold, wet, and exhausted. It's natural for us to feel a little cloudy."

"That's not what I mean," Mylon said. "It's like earlier today, when that crab crawled over the side. It's terrible what happened to Tatiana, but afterward, I got to thinking that she was the lucky one. She doesn't have to deal with this shit anymore. We do."

"Not for much longer." Henry gulped the rest of his water. "If Simon can do what he says, then we'll be okay. You can even see your family again!"

"And run into another world's version of myself? No thanks. I reckon I'll just—"

A burst of static squawked out of the intercom, startling them. Sarah took a deep breath, expecting Novak to announce that yet another monster was pursuing them. Since the crab's attack, the crew had spotted various dark, humped forms in the water, but Novak had maintained maximum speed, and so far, they'd been able to shake the pursuit. What he announced instead was the last thing Sarah expected.

"Folks, this is your captain speaking." Novak sounded surprisingly cheerful. "I just thought you might like to know that we've just made radio contact with another vessel. We're talking to them right now, if anybody would like to come up to the cabin and listen in. The man in charge says his name is Kevin Locke. It sounds like he's got a pretty big group with him."

"Holy shit," Henry gasped. "We're not the only ones left alive!"

"Let's go," Sarah said, standing up. "I want to hear this."

Mylon joined them, and the three made their way to the bridge, where they found Novak and Gail gathered around the radio, while Simon stood to one side, listening. Through the fogged windows, Sarah caught a glimpse of Caterina, standing watch outside in a yellow raincoat.

"You guys can listen in," Novak said, muting the microphone, "but don't say anything. We think he might be a little crazy."

Sarah, Henry, and Mylon nodded. Then Novak keyed the microphone.

"Go ahead, Mr. Locke. Sorry about that."

"No problem," the man on the other ship said. "Like I was saying, God told me to build the ark before the rains started. My wife, Taya, thought it was just a dream I'd had, but I knew better. My neighbors thought I was crazy."

"Who could blame them?" Gail whispered.

"What's that?" Locke asked.

"Nothing." Novak shot her an angry look. "Please continue, Mr. Locke."

"Anyway, we lived in Lafayette, Indiana. I started building it right in my backyard. Eventually, I got Taya, and our neighbor Rudy to help me. Once the rains started, a bunch of other folks pitched in, too. As Lafayette began to flood, our ship just floated up off its moorings. By that time, it was only me, Taya, and Harley onboard. Harley is our dog—a little Yorkie. I don't know what happened to Rudy or his wife or our other neighbors. But we were safe and dry, and when the water levels reached the rooftops, we floated right out of our neighborhood. Since then, we've just been picking up survivors—plucking them off roofs and mountaintops. There's about thirty of us onboard. Dashiell is the youngest. He's a toddler. Cute little kid. A Korean lady is our oldest. We don't know how old, exactly. She doesn't speak English."

"And there are thirty of you?" Novak grinned as he asked it.

"Yes."

"That's amazing! Where are you guys now?"

"As near as I can figure, somewhere over Illinois."

Novak's grin turned to a frown. He muted the microphone again.

"What's wrong?" Gail asked.

"They'd never make it to Pennsylvania in time."

"Give them the coordinates, anyway," Simon said.

"Is there a way you can stall?" Novak asked. "I thought time was crucial?"

"It is, Mr. Novak. And as you said, there is no way they can reach LeHorn's Hollow before I open the gate into the Labyrinth. But I want you to give them the coordinates anyway."

"But why?" Novak asked. "It doesn't make any sense. Unless you…"

One by one, they stared at Simon as the truth dawned on them.

"A sacrifice," Gail gasped. "You want to use them as a sacrifice? As bait!"

Nodding, Simon stared at his feet, unable to look them in the eyes.

Gail stormed across the rolling deck. "How is that any different than what your captor did to you, Simon?"

"Because," he said, still not looking up, "this is to save our lives. Leviathan's monsters are converging on LeHorn's Hollow, and any other point in this region where we might effect an escape. Leviathan himself can sense my presence. His intelligence is far vaster than our own, but the same can't be said of his children. Some, like the mermaids or the starfish-men, are quite smart, in their own fashion. But most of them are mere predators, driven by hunger and a need to destroy, than by anything resembling real craft or cunning. Their master has driven them forward. They understand they're supposed to be hunting a large group of humans in a boat. But they have no way of determining which boat. Mr. Locke's ark will serve as a distraction."

"It doesn't bother you that there are children on board?" Mylon asked.

"Of course it bothers me." Simon glanced up. "I feel for everyone on that vessel. But I cannot save them. None of us can. Soon, what remains of this Earth will be completely absorbed into the Great Deep. That includes anyone left alive. They will never reach us in time, and I cannot open a door at their location. I can't save them, but I can save us."

The group fell silent. A burst of static came from the speakers.

"Novak?" Locke's voice sounded faint and distorted. "You still there?"

Frowning, Novak keyed the microphone. "I'm still here. Sorry. Just spotted something starboard. Give me a minute." He released the microphone again and stared sullenly at the others. "I'm tired of being in charge. Hell, I'm just tired in general."

"We all are," Gail said. "We've been—"

Novak held up a finger, interrupting her. "I'm tired of everything depending on my decision. I can't make this one by myself. What do you guys think?"

"It ain't right," Henry insisted. "What if it was us out there? How would y'all feel then? Them folks ain't done nothing wrong. They don't deserve this."

"And we don't deserve to die, kid," Caterina said. She stood in the hatchway. Water dripped from her yellow raincoat. They'd been so intent on the discussion that they hadn't heard her come in. "I vote to go with Simon's plan."

"We should at least tell them the risks," Gail said. "Rather than just sending them to their fucking doom!"

"If we did," Sarah said, "then the people on that ship would turn right around. I vote yes."

Henry glanced at her, his expression wounded.

"You're a hard one, aren't you?" Gail's tone thick with contempt.

"Let me tell you something." Sarah's voice was low and dangerous. "I killed my best friend to survive. He was infected with the fuzz, so I shot him. I've done a lot of other things, too, since the rain started. I'm not proud of them, but I'm alive. Do not judge me, and do not cast dispersions at me. From where I stand, you were pretty worried about your own fucking skin when you and Novak first met me and Henry in the tower."

"That's not true!"

"Isn't it?" Sarah balled her hands into fists. "Want me to refresh your memory?"

"Enough." Simon didn't raise his voice. He merely gestured. "This bickering is pointless. The matter isn't up for a vote. If you want to live, then do as I say."

Gail glanced around the bridge, studying each of the crew members. All of them refused to meet her gaze.

"Mylon? You're okay with this, too?"

He shrugged, shifting his weight from foot to foot. "I don't want to die, Gail."

"I shouldn't be surprised, I guess. You sold us out easy enough during the mutiny."

"No, I didn't."

"That's not how it looked to Novak and me."

"Gail…" Novak held up a hand. "Stop. What's done is done."

"The hell with the monsters out in the water. The real monsters are in here."

She strode out of the cabin. The steel hatch clanged shut behind her. After a moment, Henry followed. The rest of them turned to Simon, who nodded at Novak.

"Go ahead."

"God forgive me," Novak whispered. Then he keyed the microphone. "Hey, Kevin. Sorry about the delay. Everything's cool, now. Listen, how fast can you go in that thing?"

"A good eighty knots when we've got a strong wind. And we've had a lot of those since the rain started."

"Okay," Novak said. "I'm gonna give you some coordinates and I want you to head there fast as you can. We've found a safe place."

Watching the tears stream down Novak's cheeks as he spoke, Sarah wondered if Locke could hear that he was crying.

They sailed on, and over the next few days, the mood of everyone aboard the ship became even tenser and more paranoid. On the first night, only a few hours after Simon and Novak lured the crew of Locke's ark into a trap, Henry snuck onto the bridge and tried to radio the vessel while Novak and Simon were asleep. Mylon stopped him before he could warn the survivors. In the ensuing scuffle, the radio was smashed beyond repair, as were the older man's two front teeth.

After that, Henry and Gail began spending most of their waking hours apart from the others. Novak insisted they not stand guard together, suspecting that the two of them might try to attempt further mischief if given the chance. Gail was assigned a shift with Novak. Henry stood watch with Caterina. When Sarah tried to talk to the teen and explain her reasoning, Henry rebuffed her. He grew sullen, and began spending most of his time sleeping in his rack, when not on watch.

The rest of the crew pulled away from each other, as well. Sarah noticed that the decision had effected Gail and Novak's friendship in much the same manner as it had impacted her and Henry's. They seemed to avoid each other whenever possible. Caterina and Mylon stood their watches without talking to each other, or anyone else. What few meals the group ate together were uncomfortable and silent. Even small talk seemed forced and futile.

Simon kept entirely to himself, explaining that he needed to fast and meditate before arriving at their destination. He sequestered himself in the ship's aft section, demanding absolute privacy. He took no meals, and as far as Sarah could tell, didn't even emerge for water or a bathroom break.

And all along, the rain continued to fall.

Standing watch the third day, Sarah noticed how most of the debris had disappeared from the water's surface. She'd grown used to seeing cars, trees, corpses, and even entire buildings floating in the grayish-black surf. It had been especially bad in Baltimore. Now, all of that was gone, melted away by the white fuzz. She wondered if it was growing on the ship's hull, and if so, how long they had before the boat dissolved, as well.

Before the radio had been destroyed during Mylon and Henry's altercation, they had received a faint signal from Drammen, Norway. The broadcaster's English had been good enough for them to understand that he was reporting a series of earthquakes. He had insisted the mountains in his region were melting. The crew hadn't discussed it much, other than the fact that if an earthquake triggered a tsunami in their region, there was no way Novak's boat would survive it.

Sarah thought about that radio call now as she stared out at the sea. They were sailing right over the Appalachian mountains. There should have been peaks sticking out of the water—lonely, scarred mountaintops, perhaps hosting survivors as Bald Knob had hosted her, Kevin, and Henry. Instead, there was nothing.

Her thoughts were interrupted by the sound of someone clearing his throat behind her. Sarah turned to find Novak. Rain dripped from the hood of his jacket.

"We're here."

"We are?"

He nodded. "At the coordinates Simon gave me. Although I've gotta be honest. It doesn't look much like Pennsylvania to me."

It took her a moment to realize that he was making a joke. When she did, Sarah smiled.

"I'm going to let Simon know. I've sent Mylon to wake the others. You okay on watch by yourself for a minute?"

Sarah was about to respond when a hatch squeaked open and banged against the bulkhead. A raincoated figure stepped through the door.

"I already know," Simon said, throwing back his hood. "I sensed our impending arrival a little while ago. You can be sure that others have, as well."

"What kind of others?" Novak asked.

Before Simon could answer, all three of them heard voices carrying across the waves. Female voices. Singing.

Novak frowned. *"The hell is that?"*

Six female figures broke the surface, surrounding the ship as they bobbed up and down in time with the waves. Sultry, full-lipped and full-bodied, their naked breasts seeming to float just above the water. Their blond, brunette, and red hair was plastered to their shoulders and backs, dripping seaweed. Although they were only visible from the waist up, Sarah caught a shadowed glimpse of their fish tails thrashing beneath the water. Their mouths were open in song.

"Sirens," Simon shouted. "The brides of Leviathan! Mister Novak, find something to stuff in your ears and block them right now. Have the crew muster inside the bridge. We'll need them armed with every weapon you have onboard this vessel. We have a fight on our hands."

Novak nodded slowly, but didn't speak. His eyes remained fix on the churning ocean. His expression went slack. Sarah recognized the signs. She'd seen them before, during the siege in Baltimore. Even as the thought crossed her mind, she felt the familiar stirrings. Unable to help herself, Sarah turned toward the sea. The feminine voice and melody were beautiful. She didn't understand the words, but she felt them deep down inside. The song was calming and hypnotic. As she listened, Sarah forgot all about Kevin and Teddy and Carl. Her grief was washed away in the rain. She tried to fight it, but the melody was too strong. From the corner of her eye, she saw Novak shuffling toward the rail, arms outstretched, as if greeting the new arrivals. Sarah tried to resist, but the song overwhelmed her, promising an end to sadness and exhaustion.

"Simon," Sarah grunted. "You...have to...get us both... inside."

"It's so beautiful," Novak said. "Listen. It's the most beautiful thing I've ever heard."

Simon swept forward, rushing to the rail. The ship tilted and he almost went over the side. Clinging to the rail, he chanted in a strong, loud voice, overpowering the siren song. "Cleote! Innammanna vishnatu. Ia, Cthonical. Ia, Pshtari."

The song continued, growing louder. Novak stopped at the rail next to Simon. Sarah approached from behind. Even as she saw Novak turn to look at the Black Lodge operative, she had the sudden, uncontrollable urge to push Simon into the water. She raised her hands and crept toward him.

"Ut nemo in sense tenant," Simon yelled. "Descendere nemo. At precedenti spectator mantica tergo."

As one, the sirens fell silent. Then they began to shriek as they slipped back beneath the waves. Sarah jerked as the spell was broken. Spasms jolted through her arms and legs. She saw that Novak was jittering, too.

"Inside," Simon said, turning to them. "Hurry! I wasn't able to banish them. The spell only bound them temporarily. They'll be back with reinforcements."

"What kind of reinforcements?" Sarah asked. "The worms?"

"No. That's the one thing we won't have to deal with any longer. The worms have left this planet."

"Then what?"

"Everything. Every denizen of the Great Deep. Every spawn of Leviathan. The sirens. The shark-men and starfish-men. The giant crabs. The flying piranha-like fish. And a host of others. Every terror we've been exposed to since the rain started is now descending on our location. Not to mention Leviathan himself is coming, and the hull of our vessel is weakened by the white fuzz growing on it."

"Sounds like one hell of a party," Novak muttered.

They lurched into the bridge. Panting, Novak stumbled over to the intercom and grabbed the microphone. He took a deep breath and then keyed the microphone. When he spoke, his voice was stern and powerful, barking commands with authority.

"This is not a drill. This is not a drill. General quarters. General quarters. All hands arm yourselves and muster in the bridge on the double! I repeat, this is not a drill."

He hung the microphone back up and his shoulders sagged. Obviously exhausted, he turned to Sarah and Simon, and grinned.

"So, what now?"

"We are directly over LeHorn's Hollow," Simon said. "Keep us anchored here."

"But won't that make it easier for them to attack us?" Novak asked.

Simon nodded. "Yes. It will. But I have to open the door into the Labyrinth. I'll be focusing all of my concentration on that task."

"What about us?" Sarah asked. "What do we do while you're opening the door?"

"You fight. You defend us. You hold them off long enough for me to do it."

"But that's impossible!"

"You'd better hope not," Simon said, lowering his voice. "For all of our sakes. This is the final battle."

Caterina, Mylon, Henry, and Gail rushed onto the bridge. Water dripped from their clothes, pooling on the floor. Each of them was armed with more than one weapon. Caterina had a knife from the galley and a broken broom handle that she'd turned into a makeshift spear. Mylon carried a shotgun, and had a pistol and a knife holstered at his waist. Henry clutched a rifle, and had a small hatchet dangling from his belt loop. Gail was armed with a spear gun, and wore a backpack slung over her shoulders.

"What's in the bag?" Novak asked.

"Roach killer. We're all out of napalm."

"Will that work?"

She smiled. "I guess we'll find out."

Novak returned the grin. Sarah watched the silent interplay between the two, glad that the disagreement from earlier had apparently been put aside. She turned her gaze to Henry, caught his eye, and winked. After a moment, he winked back at her.

"We okay?" Sarah whispered.

Henry shrugged and then nodded.

Simon and Novak quickly brought the others up to speed, informing them of the situation and what to expect. Before they'd even finished, the hull thrummed as the ship lurched sharply to port, knocking them all off balance.

"It's starting," Novak said. "Simon, how long will it take you to open the doorway?"

"Provided all goes according to plan, approximately ten minutes. You'll have to keep them off me. If I'm interrupted, the spell will be ineffective."

Sarah grabbed a damp, musty roll of paper towels from atop the navigation equipment. She tore off sheets and handed them out to the group.

"Stuff your ears," she told them. "It's the only way to protect against the sirens."

She held one out to Mylon, but he stared over her shoulder, his eyes wide and alarmed. Slowly, he raised his hand and pointed.

"That might protect against the sirens," Mylon said, his voice trembling. "But what's gonna protect us against *them*?"

Sarah turned. Through the window, a dozen shark-men and starfish-men were climbing over the rail. A sudden swell caused the bow to rise, spilling two of them back into the water, but the others clambered onto the slippery deck and plodded forward.

"Okay," Novak said, his voice low and hoarse. "Let's go, people."

He snatched his rifle from the corner, opened the hatch, and charged outside. Gail charged after him, followed by Caterina and Mylon. As he ran through the door, Mylon repeated a litany of "Oh shit, oh shit, oh shit." Henry and Sarah glanced at each other.

"We'll be okay," she said.

Nodding, Henry thumbed the safety off on his rifle and ran after the others. Sarah followed behind him. Rain pelted her face, and the wind zipped through her short hair. As she closed the hatch, she glanced back at Simon.

"Good luck."

"And to you, as well, Sarah. I'll see you on the other side."

Out on the deck, the others started screaming. Thunder exploded overhead, drowning them out.

TWENTY-FOUR

The ship rolled violently as Sarah raced out onto the slippery deck. Losing her balance, she slid, shrieking, toward the rail, but managed to steady herself before falling overboard. The falling rain and ocean spray stung her eyes, blurring her vision. Blinking water from her eyes, she turned, trying to make sense of the chaotic battle unfolding around her. The paper towels stuffed in her ears made everything seem muffled.

Caterina faced off against one of the half-man, half-shark creatures. The beast loomed over her, standing easily ten feet high. It swung at her with one massive fist, but the lithe woman managed to dodge the blow and dart underneath it, jabbing the creature's white, slab-like belly with her spear. Sarah was dismayed to see that the broken broom handle barely scratched the monster's hide. Roaring, the shark man swung at her again. Caterina dodged a second time, thrusting her weapon at the prominent dorsal fin on its back. The thing spun, lashing out with its tail, and knocked Caterina off her feet. She landed hard, losing her grip on both the broom handle and the knife. Blood dribbled from her nose, turning the wet deck pink. Laughing, the shark man placed one foot on her chest and lowered its head. Foam dripped from its slavering jaws, splattering Caterina's face. The girl thrashed beneath its weight, kicking and punching to no avail.

Mylon appeared at her side. With one quick motion, he shoved the barrel of his shotgun against the creature's snout and pulled the trigger, spraying both Caterina and himself with crimson. Grimacing, Mylon wiped the blood away with one hand, while clutching the shotgun in the other. As he reached out a hand to help Caterina to her feet, one of the starfish men charged them from behind. Both Caterina and Sarah shouted a warning, but it was too late. The monster rammed its trident into Mylon's back, lifting him from the deck. He fumbled with the shotgun, but it slipped from his grasp. Sarah gasped.

"Put him down, you fucker!"

She ran toward them, realizing a moment too late that she was unarmed. Sarah could barely believe it herself—to have survived for this long in a world gone mad, only to charge into battle now without a weapon. She leaped for the shotgun, but it slid farther away. Mylon's attacker turned toward her. Its eye-tipped limbs seemed to leer.

And then one of the eyes exploded. Squealing, the creature lowered its trident. Mylon slipped from the prongs, collapsing on top of Caterina. The starfish man's remaining appendages flailed as it collapsed to its knees, writhing in agony. Seconds later, another one of its eyeballs vanished in a spray of pulp. This time, Sarah heard the gunshot. She glanced up and spotted Novak, rifle stock nestled firmly in his shoulder, sitting atop the bridge. With a nod of acknowledgement, he trained the rifle's scope on another attacker.

The beast was still alive. Its screams were inhuman. Sarah snatched up Caterina's makeshift spear and rammed it into the monster's gaping maw. The thing trembled, and then went slack. Sarah pulled the broom handle from its mouth. Slime dripped from the broken tip.

"He's alive," Caterina shouted, cradling Mylon's head in her lap.

"He won't be for much longer if you don't stand up and fight. Give him the shotgun and lets go!"

"I don't need it," Mylon gasped. "You take it. I've still got my pistol."

Nodding, Caterina retrieved the shotgun and then waded back into the battle, standing side-by-side with Sarah. Sarah glanced back long enough to see Mylon propping himself up against the rails. His face was pale and his expression was pained. Blood trickled from his open mouth. Despite his injuries, he managed to free his pistol from its holster and blast another attacker.

Sarah was alarmed to see more creatures climbing onto the deck. Novak picked off several of them before they could clamber over the rails, but for each one that he dropped back into the ocean, two more took its place.

She heard Henry call out, and turned to see him being menaced by three of the shark men. The creatures had backed him into a corner, and were too close for him to use his rifle. Indeed, as Sarah fought her way toward him, one of the beasts snatched the weapon from the teen's hands and flung it over the side. The shark-man lowered its head, coming in for the kill. In his panic, Henry yanked the hatchet free from his belt loop and swung wildly. The blade sank into the closest shark's nose. Roaring, the monster flailed backward onto the deck, taking Henry's weapon—which was still lodged in its snout—with it.

Screaming, Sarah and Caterina both charged toward the group. The sharks turned, and Caterina pulled the trigger. Nothing happened. She slid to a halt, inches from Henry's attackers, her eyes wide with fear.

"Oh, sh—"

One of the shark men ripped the shotgun from her hands. The other opened its jaws and attacked, engulfing her head and body, right above her breasts. Despite the stuffing in her ears, Sarah still heard the sounds its teeth made as they snapped shut, slicing through flesh and crushing bone. Its eyes rolled up in its head with frenzied, savage delight as it shook her still-kicking form.

Shrieking, Sarah shoved the spear into its right eye. Both Caterina and her killer fell to the deck. The other monster bared its teeth at Sarah, but seconds later, a metal spear sprouted from its chest. Glancing around in confusion, Sarah spotted Gail reloading her spear gun. The creature toppled over the side as the ship rolled again. Meanwhile, Henry managed to retrieve his hatchet.

"How did you kill it like that?" Sarah asked.

Henry wiped the hatchet blade on his raincoat. "I fought one when Moxey and me left the silo. If you hit them on the nose, it really hurts them. I reckon doing so with a hatchet was more than it could stand."

Despite her fear, Sarah grinned. "Good to know."

The battle continued. Sarah, Henry, and Gail ended up back to back as the various deep sea denizens tried to encircle them. Novak continued sniping them from above, but the ship was rocking so severely now that many of his shots went astray. Mylon continued fighting, picking off the creatures as they clambered over the railing. When he ran out of ammunition, he fumbled with the weapon, his fingers slick with rainwater and blood.

"We should do something for him," Gail yelled, nodding at the injured man.

"There's nothing we can do right now," Sarah shouted. "Keep fighting. We've got to buy Simon enough time."

More through desperation and scared savagery than skill, they managed to overcome their attackers. Soon, they outnumbered the creatures left onboard.

"Now," Sarah ordered, "before reinforcements arrive—"

She paused, distracted. A few hundred yards beyond the ship's bow, the sea began to churn. A bright, dazzling light appeared beneath the surface. Slowly, a whirlpool began to form.

"What's that?" Henry asked.

At first, Sarah thought he was referring to the whirlpool, but then she realized he and Gail were staring aft. She turned, looking in the direction Henry was pointing. There, far off on the murky horizon, a shadow loomed, so large in size that its shape was difficult to comprehend. But Sarah recognized it. She knew it all too well. The bulbous head like a misshapen hot air balloon. The hulking, rubbery body. The impossibly long arms, tipped with claw-like hands big enough to tear down whole buildings. And most of all, the tentacles—both the ones dangling from its face and the slimmer, longer ones erupting from the water like a horde of snakes.

Sarah began to weep.

"What the hell is that?" Henry asked again.

Novak and Mylon started shooting as a second wave of creatures tried to board the vessel.

"That," Sarah cried, "is Leviathan…"

"Oh Hell," Henry muttered.

"Yes," Sarah said, nodding.

Leviathan trudged toward them. Sarah could only imagine the skyscraper-sized legs plodding along beneath the surface. Each step sent huge waves surging outward from the beast. The thing shook its massive, misshapen head, flapping its tentacles, and its roar echoed across the ocean, drowning out all other sound.

The group paused, stunned, as each step brought the monstrosity closer. Sarah trembled with dread, tears streaming down her already wet cheeks as memories of her encounter with Leviathan in Baltimore overwhelmed her. At her side, both Henry and Gail gaped, staring in disbelief as Leviathan raged.

Leviathan's roar faded, and Mylon cried out in anguish. Sarah turned to see him clutching his wound with one hand and trying to steady his pistol with the other, as two more starfish men slipped over the side onto the deck. Before they could reach him, Novak shot them both from his perch. Sarah watched as Novak patted his pockets. Then, he gestured at her, shouting something. The wind snatched his words away.

"What?" Sarah shouted.

"I'm out of ammo!"

Ahead of the rocking ship, the whirlpool grew larger, spinning faster as the light in its center continued to expand. Sarah couldn't be sure, because the rain obscured her vision, but for a moment, she thought she saw blue sky and clouds in the center of the light.

That can't be right, she thought.

It is, Simon's voice said inside her head. *But I need another moment to stabilize the doorway.*

Startled, she glanced at Gail and Henry to see if they'd heard the telepathic message as well, but if so, neither of them gave any indication. Instead, they'd turned back to the battle. Above them, Novak was clambering down to the deck.

The song of the sirens began anew, as the feminine forms surfaced once more. The pain on Mylon's face disappeared as the song grew louder. He lay the gun on the deck beside him and struggled to rise, leaving a bloody smear on the bulkhead behind him.

"His ears aren't stuffed," Sarah hollered at Henry. "Stop him!"

Henry, Gail, and Sarah battled their way toward the injured man. Sarah was dimly aware of Novak doing the same behind them. Leviathan roared again, and the ship lurched sharply, sending both the crew and their attackers careening. Mylon clutched the railing, steadying himself, and peered out over the side. His expression was peaceful.

"Mylon," Gail yelled. "Don't listen to them!"

"So beautiful." Smiling, he climbed over the rail. "They say they can stop the pain. All I have to do is go to them."

A starfish creature squealed as Henry buried his hatchet in its chest. Sarah leaped over the thrashing creature and slid across the wet deck, trying to reach Mylon before he leaped, but she was too late. Still smiling, the wounded man let go of the rail and plummeted into the ocean. When Sarah reached the railing and peered over the side, she saw the mermaids swarming over him, biting his throat and wrists and feasting on his blood. Mylon squirmed as if in ecstasy. A wave crashed over them all, and when it receded, both Mylon and the mermaids were gone.

You can't help him, Sarah. Focus.

"Simon…" Sarah paused, and then thought it instead. *Simon?*

I'm here, came the response.

If you were telepathic, Sarah thought, *then why didn't you use it before?*

Because when I do so, it can potentially attract the attention of other entities, such as Shtar. I'm only doing it now because I have no choice—and because in a few moments, it won't matter.

Novak reached Gail and Henry. The three turned to Sarah. Novak made a sweeping motion with his hand. Sarah glanced around the vessel and realized that all of the creatures were dead.

"I think," he panted, "we won."

Sarah shook her head. "We're going to need more than guns and broom handles to deal with Leviathan."

Novak opened his mouth to reply, but before he could, something small and silver jumped from the water and soared toward them—a shimmering school of flying fish, more teeth than body, tiny black eyes full of malevolence and hunger. The creatures swerved in mid-flight, targeting Henry. The teen stumbled backward, screaming, but Gail stepped in front of him, clutching a can of roach killer in each hand.

"I've got this." She unleashed a spray directly onto the fish, who wheeled away, plunging back into the water.

The ship rolled again as it got caught in the whirlpool's current. Sarah, Novak, Gail, and Henry grabbed on to each other to keep from falling.

Listen to me, all of you, came Simon's voice in their heads. *You need to leave this vessel immediately, before Leviathan arrives. Swim toward the center of the whirlpool. Don't fight it. Just let it take you through the door.*

How will we know when we've reached the other world? Gail asked.

Sarah was surprised that she could hear the question. Judging by Novak and Henry's expressions, they heard, as well.

You'll know, Simon said. *The important thing is that you not fight the current. Let it sweep you along. If you fight, you could end up somewhere else. The Lost Level, or a different realm than the one I'm sending you to. Or simply wandering the Labyrinth.*

What about you? Sarah thought. *You're coming, too, right?*

No, I cannot. This ritual requires a sacrifice. That sacrifice is me. Consider it a karmic debt for what we did to the people aboard Locke's ark. Had we not sacrificed them, we would not have made it this far. And now, to ensure that the rest of you make it through the door, a further sacrifice is required.

Fuck that, Novak protested. *Can't you use one of these shark-men? Hell, we could catch one of those mermaids or something. Use one of them instead.*

I'm afraid it doesn't work that way, Mr. Novak. And besides, somebody has to remain behind to stop Leviathan and his spawn from following you through the doorway.

I'm the Captain, Novak said. *If anybody is going down with the ship, it's me.*

Leviathan roared again. They glanced up, startled to see how much closer he was. He loomed over the boat now, blotting out the sky.

There is no time for bravado, Mr. Novak. Now go! All of you.

Novak stumbled as something pushed him toward the rail. Sarah felt it, too—as if a giant, invisible hand had shoved her. Gail and Henry struggled against the unseen force, as well. Above them, one of Leviathan's tentacles curled around the antenna mast, snapping it off. Novak's resolve dissipated. He turned around and jumped into the water. Gail, Henry, and Sarah followed. Even as she slipped beneath the dark, foul water, Sarah could still hear Leviathan thundering overhead.

Something brushed against Sarah's leg. She opened her mouth to scream, forgetting that she was below the surface. Cold, black water rushed down her throat. Gagging, Sarah reflexively tried to breathe, and more water flooded into her. She glanced around, frantic, but couldn't see anything. She might as well have been swimming in ink. She shuddered, choking, as the unseen form pressed against her leg again. Then, something else seized her flailing arm and jerked her upward.

Sarah broke the surface, coughing and gagging. Waves crashed over her head, threatening to plunge her below again, but the grip on her arm remained. She lashed out blindly, raking her fingernails across her attacker's face.

"Stop it," Novak yelled. "Sarah, it's me. It's okay. I've got you."

She blinked water from her eyes and saw Henry and Gail struggling to swim toward them. Both were caught in the whirlpool's current, and their efforts proved useless.

"Help!" Henry reached for her.

"Don't fight…" Sarah coughed, hacking up more filthy water. Then she took a deep breath and tried again. "Don't fight it, Henry. Simon says to go with the whirlpool!"

Nodding, the boy surrendered to the swift current, fighting to stay afloat. His eyes were wide and panicked. Gail dog-paddled next to him, her horrified expression illuminated by the light pouring from the center of the vortex.

A telephone pole floated by, spinning clockwise and trailing wires and cables like tendrils. Sarah reached for it, but Novak tugged her arm, pulling her back.

"Don't," he grunted. "It's infected. There's white fuzz all over the side."

The pole zipped past them. Henry and Gail did their best to avoid it.

"You can let go of my arm now," Sarah gasped. "I'm fine."

"Okay," Novak said. "I'm sorry. Just wanted to make sure you—"

His grip tightened and his muscles tensed. Sarah was about to ask him what was wrong when Novak screamed. Suddenly, he was jerked up out of the water. Sarah went with him, dangling by her arm, until his wet grip slipped. She plummeted back into the water and surfaced again in time to hear Henry and Gail shrieking.

Novak thrashed hundreds of feet above them, punching and kicking, caught in the grip of one of Leviathan's tentacles. Even as she began to swim toward him, Sarah knew it was pointless. Already his struggles grew weaker as the teeth-lined suckers sliced through his clothing and feasted on his flesh. She paddled in place and watched, transfixed, as droplets of his blood fell with the rain. Novak gave one last strangled cry, and then went limp.

Three more tentacles snaked toward her, parting the water like eels. Leviathan loomed over the ship, dwarfing it with his towering mass. When the creature roared again, Sarah's ears popped. She turned and kicked as the tentacles raced across the surface. Behind her, she heard the sirens screech. Henry and Gail's expressions grew even more terrified.

"Don't turn around," Henry yelled. "Holy shit, just swim! Swim toward us!"

Even as he said it, Henry began paddling away. When Gail did the same, Sarah glanced over her shoulder. A dozen dorsal fins cleaved the water, pursuing her, as were a host of sirens, starfish creatures, and other denizens of the Great Deep. In their midst were Leviathan's tentacles, leading the chase. But then, where Novak's blood had spilled just seconds before, something strange began to happen. A red line appeared in the water, quickly growing in size and length until it encompassed the whirlpool. The first of Leviathan's tendrils crossed the line and exploded. Seconds later, one of the shark-men and something that looked like a cross between a seahorse and a centipede both leaped from the water, intent on overtaking Sarah. Both disintegrated in a shower of gore as they crossed the line.

It's Simon, Sarah thought. *He's doing this.*

Indeed, his voice echoed in her head. It sounded strained and weak. *But the barrier won't hold long. Hurry, Sarah. And good luck...*

Weeping, Sarah turned back to Gail and Henry, and swam toward them. When she'd reached them, the three held on to one another, arms around their shoulders, and kicked to stay afloat. The churning current grew stronger, sweeping them toward the center of the vortex.

"My God," Gail sobbed, staring at the ship. "I just...my God."

Leviathan had focused all of his rage on the vessel. As they watched, his tentacles encircled it, lifting the ship from the water. He flung it as a child might toss a bath toy, and the ship crashed back into the water, lying on its port side. Unable to cross the mystical barrier, the other creatures swarmed toward it.

"Look!" Henry pointed at the whirlpool.

Sarah and Gail turned back to the vortex. There, in the center of the light, they saw a beautiful blue sky with white, cotton-ball clouds. Below the clouds was a line of green treetops. It was then that Sarah realized what the source of the light was.

"It's the sun," she said, squeezing Gail and Henry's shoulders. "That light...it's been so long since we've seen it. I'd forgotten..."

The current swept them forward faster and faster, making them dizzy. Sarah considered closing her eyes to ward off the vertigo, but instead, she continued staring into the sun. Behind them, Leviathan raised both massive fists and brought them down, smashing the ship into splinters. Leviathan roared again, and Sarah felt the pressure not only in her ears, but on her eyeballs and against her lungs, as well. Lightning split the sky, striking the ocean's roiling surface in a dozen locations. The whirlpool increased.

"Hang on," Gail yelled. "Oh God…the current!"

"We're going to be okay." Sarah did her best to reassure them. "Just stick together and don't let go."

The vortex swept them toward its center. Leviathan, the creatures, and even the rain seemed to fade into the background. Henry stared, blinking as the sun grew nearer and brighter.

"What happens next?" he asked.

"We start over," Sarah said. "We get to start over in a world that's still alive—a world where our loved ones are still alive."

She smiled, thinking of Kevin and Teddy and Carl and all of the others she'd lost along the way. She imagined finding them in this new reality. How would they react and what would they say? Would they even know her? Sarah decided that it didn't matter. All that mattered was that she'd see them again. When she looked up at Henry, the teen was smiling, too. So was Gail, as the sun in the center of the ocean dried the tears on her face.

Together, they sailed over the edge of the world.

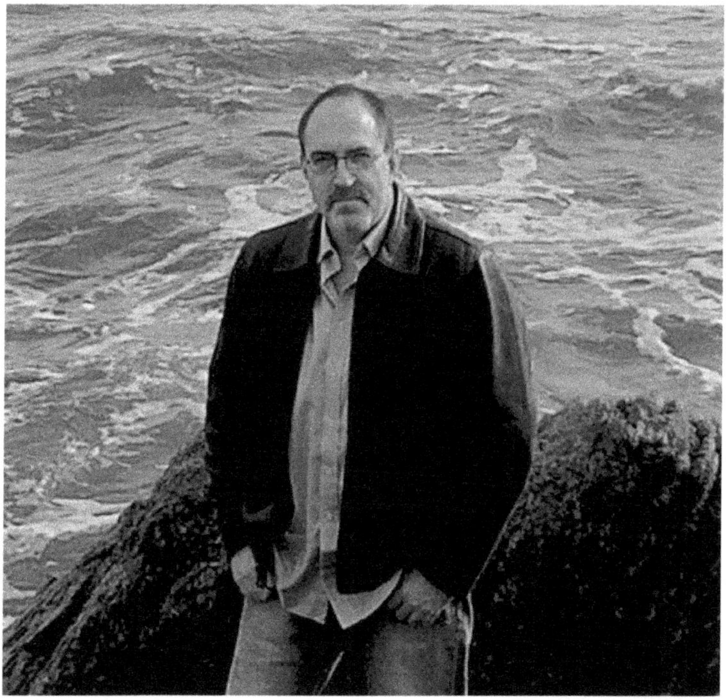

BRIAN KEENE is the author of over thirty books, including *Darkness on the Edge of Town, Take The Long Way Home, Urban Gothic, Castaways*, *Dark Hollow*, *Dead Sea,* and *The Rising*. He also writes comic books such as *The Last Zombie*. His work has been translated into German, Spanish, Polish, Italian, French and Taiwanese. Several of his novels and stories have been developed for film, including *Ghoul*, *The Ties That Bind*, and *Fast Zombies Suck*. In addition to writing, Keene also oversees Maelstrom, his own small press publishing imprint specializing in collectible limited editions, via Thunderstorm Books. Keene's work has been praised in such diverse places as *The New York Times*, The History Channel, The Howard Stern Show, CNN.com, *Publisher's Weekly,* Media Bistro, *Fangoria Magazine*, and *Rue Morgue Magazine*. Keene lives in Pennsylvania. You can communicate with him online at www.briankeene.com or on Twitter at @BrianKeene.

"Urban Gothic" Brian Keene - When their car broke down in a dangerous inner-city neighborhood, Kerri and her friends thought they would find shelter inside an old, dark row home. They thought they would be safe there until help arrived. They were wrong. The residents who live down in the cellar and the tunnels beneath the city are far more dangerous than the streets outside, and they have a very special way of dealing with trespassers. Trapped in a world of darkness, populated by obscene abominations, they will have to fight back if they ever want to see the sun again.

"Ghoul" Brian Keene - There is something in the local cemetery that comes out at night. Something that is unearthing corpses and killing people. It's the summer of 1984 and Timmy and his friends are looking forward to no school, comic books, and adventure. But instead they will be fighting for their lives. The ghoul has smelled their blood and it is after them. But that's not the only monster they will face this summer . . . From award-winning horror master Brian Keene comes a novel of monsters, murder, and the loss of innocence.

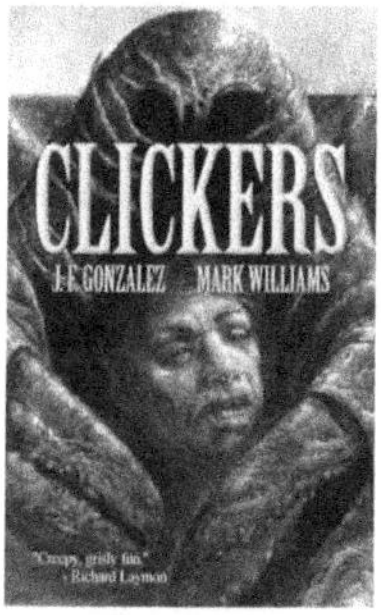

"Clickers" J. F. Gonzalez and Mark Williams- They are the Clickers, giant venomous blood-thirsty crabs from the depths of the sea. The only warning to their rampage of dismemberment and death is the terrible clicking of their claws. But these monsters aren't merely here to ravage and pillage. They are being driven onto land by fear. Something is hunting the Clickers. Something ancient and without mercy. *Clickers* is J. F. Gonzalez and Mark Williams' gore-soaked cult classic tribute to the giant monster B-movies of yesteryear.

"Clickers II" J. F. Gonzalez and Brian Keene- Thousands of Clickers swarm across the entire nation and march inland, slaughtering anyone and anything they come across. But this time the Clickers aren't blindly rushing onto land - they are being led by an intelligence older than civilization itself. A force that wants to take dry land away from the mammals. Those left alive soon realize that they must do everything and anything they can to protect humanity – no matter the cost. *This isn't war, this is extermination.*

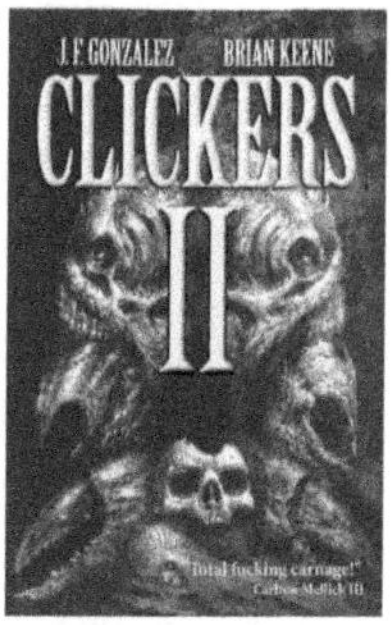

AVAILABLE FROM AMAZON.COM

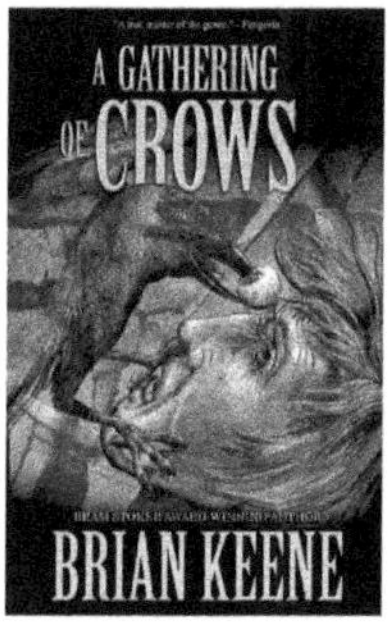

"A Gathering of Crows" Brian Keene - Five mysterious figures are about to pay a visit to Brinkley Springs. They have existed for centuries, emerging from the shadows only to destroy. To kill. To feed. They bring terror and carnage, and leave blood and death in their wake. The only person that can prevent their rampage is ex-Amish magus Levi Stoltzfus. As the night wears on, Brinkley Springs will be quiet no longer. Screams will break the silence. But when the sun rises again, will there be anyone left alive to hear?

"Take the Long Way Home" Brian Keene - All across the world, people suddenly vanish in the blink of an eye. Gone. Steve, Charlie and Frank were just trying to get home when it happened. Trapped in the ultimate traffic jam, they watch as civilization collapses, claiming the souls of those around them. God has called his faithful home, but the invitations for Steve, Charlie and Frank got lost. Now they must set off on foot through a nightmarish post-apocalyptic landscape in search of answers. In search of God. In search of their loved ones. And in search of home.

"Darkness on the Edge of Town" Brian Keene - One morning the residents of Walden, Virginia, woke up to find the rest of the world gone. Surrounding their town was a wall of inky darkness, plummeting Walden into permanent night. Nothing can get in - not light, not people, not even electricity, radio, TV, internet, food, or water. And nothing can get out. No one who dared to penetrate the mysterious barrier has ever been seen again. But for some, the darkness is not the worst of their fears.

"Tequila's Sunrise" Brian Keene - Discover the secret origins of the "drink of the gods" in this dark fantasy fable by best-selling author Brian Keene. Chalco, a young Aztec boy, feels helpless as conquering Spanish forces near his village. But when a messenger of the gods hands him a key to unlock the doors of human perception and visit unseen worlds, Chalco journeys into the mystical Labyrinth, searching for a way to defeat the invaders. He will face gods, devils, and things that are neither. But he will also learn that some doorways should never be opened and not all entrances have exits... Tequila's Sunrise.

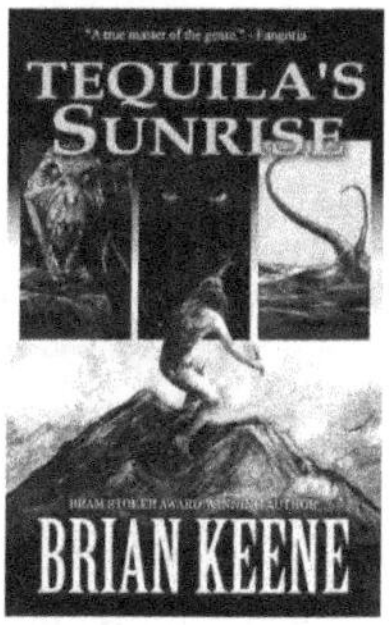

THE VERY BEST IN CULT HORROR

deadite press

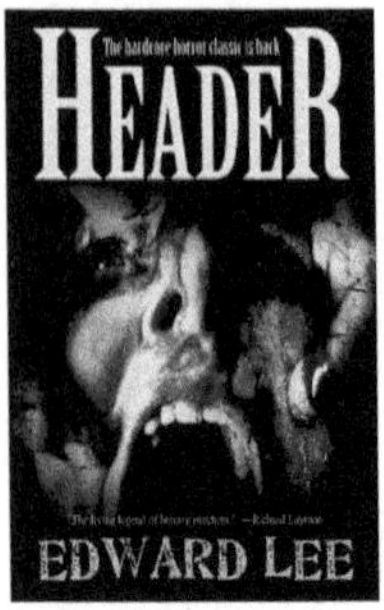

"Header" Edward Lee - In the dark backwoods, where law enforcement doesn't dare tread, there exists a special type of revenge. Something so awful that it is only whispered about. Something so terrible that few believe it is real. Stewart Cummings is a government agent whose life is going to Hell. His wife is ill and to pay for her medication he turns to bootlegging. But things will get much worse when bodies begin showing up in his sleepy small town. Victims of an act known only as "a Header."

"Red Sky" Nate Southard - When a bank job goes horrifically wrong, career criminal Danny Black leads his crew from El Paso into the deserts of New Mexico in a desperate bid for escape. Danny soon finds himself with no choice but to hole up in an abandoned factory, the former home of Red Sky Manufacturing. Danny and his crew aren't the only living things in Red Sky, though. Something waits in the abandoned factory's shadows, something horrible and violent. Something hungry. And when the sun drops, it will feast.

"Zombies and Shit" Carlton Mellick III - Twenty people wake to find themselves in a boarded-up building in the middle of the zombie wasteland. They soon discover they have been chosen as contestants on a popular reality show called Zombie Survival. Each contestant is given a backpack of supplies and a unique weapon. Their goal: be the first to make it through the zombie-plagued city to the pick-up zone alive. But because there's only one seat available on the helicopter, the contestants not only have to fight against the hordes of the living dead, they must also fight each other.

"Muerte Con Carne" Shane McKenzie - Human flesh tacos, hardcore wrestling, and angry cannibal Mexicans, Welcome to the Border! Felix and Marta came to Mexico to film a documentary on illegal immigration. When Marta suddenly goes missing, Felix must find his lost love in the small border town. A dangerous place housing corrupt cops, borderline maniacs, and something much more worse than drug gangs, something to do with a strange Mexican food cart…

"Like Porno for Psychos" Wrath James White - From a world-ending orgy to home liposuction. From the hidden desires of politicians to a woman with a fetish for lions. This is a place where necrophilia, self-mutilation, and murder are all roads to love. Like Porno for Psychos collects the most extreme erotic horror from the celebrated hardcore horror master. Wrath James White is your guide through sex, death, and the darkest desires of the heart.

"Bigfoot Crank Stomp" Erik Williams - Bigfoot is real and he's addicted to meth! It should have been so easy. Get in, kill everyone, and take all the money and drugs. That was Russell and Mickey's plan. But the drug den they were raiding in the middle of the woods holds a dark secret chained up in the basement. A beast filled with rage and methamphetamine and tonight it will break loose. Nothing can stop Bigfoot's drug-fueled rampage and before the sun rises there is going to be a lot of dead cops and junkies.

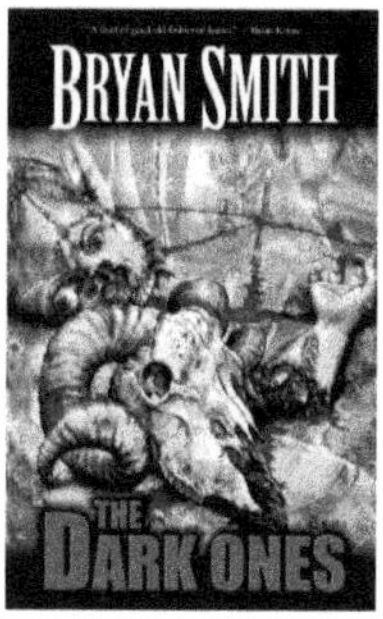

"The Dark Ones" Bryan Smith - They are The Dark Ones. The name began as a self-deprecating joke, but it stuck and now it's a source of pride. They're the one who don't fit in. The misfits who drink and smoke too much and stay out all hours of the night. Everyone knows they're trouble. On the outskirts of Ransom, TN is an abandoned, boarded-up house. Something evil happened there long ago. The evil has been contained there ever since, locked down tight in the basement—until the night The Dark Ones set it free . . .

"Genital Grinder" Ryan Harding - "*Think you're hardcore? Think again. If you've handled everything Edward Lee, Wrath James White, and Bryan Smith have thrown at you, then put on your rubber parka, spread some plastic across the floor, and get ready for Ryan Harding, the unsung master of hardcore horror. Abandon all hope, ye who enter here. Harding's work is like an acid bath, and pain has never been so sweet.*"
- Brian Keene

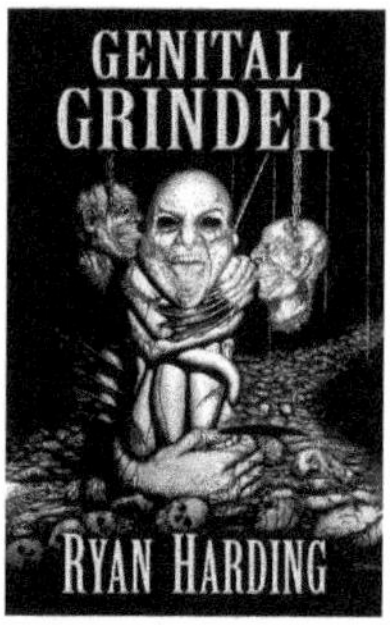

AVAILABLE FROM AMAZON.COM

Lightning Source UK Ltd.
Milton Keynes UK
UKHW020640061119
353000UK00010B/908/P

9 781621 050841